SAVING YESTERDAY

SAVING YESTERDAY

TimeShifters Series

JESS EVANDER

Saving Yesterday (TimeShifters, Book One)

March 2015 Edition

Cover by Steven Novak
www.NovakIlliustration.com

Edited by Charity Tinnin and Amanda G. Stevens
www.CharityTinnin.com
www.twitter.com/amandagstevens

Interior Design by D. Robert Pease
www.WalkingStickBooks.com

Summary
Seventeen year-old Gabby Creed discovers that she's a Shifter—a time traveler entrusted with saving human history and guarding people from creatures called Shades. But Gabby's not so sure that she wants to be a Shifter if it means following strict rules and obeying the Elders.

–For my dad and my brother–

Looks like all those hours you forced me to watch Star Trek and your sci-fi shows paid off.

"Surprises belong in YouTube videos and April Fool's Day pranks. Not my life. But I made the dangerous wish to be more than I am. So maybe I'm to blame. Because being special sucks." —Gabby Creed

CHAPTER ONE

"Gabby!" Dad's holler booms up the steps. He's waiting. Probably in some rumpled shirt and dirty jeans. Making me pancakes. It's tradition on my birthday. Even if he doesn't say the words, it's his way of letting me know he remembers.

I finish braiding my long black hair, tucking awkward bangs behind my ear. No make-up today. I've got my Mom's dusky skin, so I hardly ever wear the stuff. A splash of apple-cinnamon body mist because Porter once told me he liked it. Not that I care what Porter thinks. I don't.

In the hallway, I pass a collection of photos, captured moments from Mom and Dad's life. They grew up as next-door neighbors, so pictures of them together from grade-school days grace our walls. I guess that's why everyone gives me knowing looks when I talk about Porter, but they don't understand.

I pound down the stairs and into our odd-shaped kitchen. It's not big enough for two small children to stand together in, let alone two adults. The smell of alcohol rolls off Dad in waves and I grind my molars as my stomach revolts. Really, I should be used to it by now, but today the potency flips a switch in my mind. Who says he gets to check out on life?

He drops a kiss on my cheek. His mustache scratches me. "Hey, baby doll."

I hold my breath, hugging him back as I rein in my anger.

It's not his fault—the self-medicating. How many times have I caught him holding a photo of my mom, begging the image to come back home? Endless bottles of whiskey are better than heart-wrenching tears. A teetering drunk I can deal with. Shove him an Advil, pour water down his hatch, and tiptoe around the house. Easy.

But talk sense to a sobbing man? Make him come to terms with his loss? Yank him out of an endless depression?

Impossible.

In those moments, when I catch him with the pictures, I dig my nails into my fisted palms, and hold back the words: *She's not coming back*. Once someone's smashed in an airplane collision they can't come back.

Dad never acknowledges my birthday. Not ever. Maybe he doesn't want a reminder of the years he's missed with his one true love. Maybe as I get older, I look more like my mother—so his pain intensifies. Maybe he just can't remember how old I am. Who knows?

Maybe can't solve anything.

Whoever said time heals pain lied. Time's incapable of helping anyone. Lies, on the other hand, they go far in the healing department.

"So, what's on the agenda today?" Dad plops a plate with three slightly burnt pancakes onto the table.

I drop into a faded blue chair and use the side of a fork to slice a piece of pancake and pop it into my mouth. More char than taste. I swallow. A generous amount of syrup might help. I snatch the bottle from the table and cover my plate.

I shrug. "Not sure."

"Care to go to the cemetery?" He leans against the counter.

I take a deep breath, pushing a chunk of pancake around and around through the syrup puddle on my plate. "Not really what I want to do on my—"

"Don't." Dad covers his face. Shoulders hunched, flannel shirt missing a button.

I shoot out a long stream of breath. It roughs my bangs.

It would be so easy to snap, but I'm not capable of being rude to him. Not to the only family I have. After pounding back the rest of my orange juice, I smile at him. "I was thinking. What if we go to Molly's for lunch? And maybe we can rent a boat and go fishing on the lake."

Mind you, I'm terrified of fish. I won't even go into a lake because—what if they brush up against me? Irrational fear, but I own it. Dad, however, thinks fishing is the be-all, end-all of activities, and for my birthday it would be nice to see a smile light his face. For once.

He grunts. "Thought you didn't like Molly's Diner? Called it a grease pit last time we were there."

It is a grease pit. Complete with the splotched yellowing walls, ripped vinyl booths, and stained Formica counters. Every waitress is old enough to be my grandmother, if I had a living one, that is.

A look around our kitchen shows the same disrepair. The last few weeks I've been immersed in taking finals and addressing graduation invitations. During my absence, the normal few dirty plates have spawned into mountains. No matter.

I might not be able to fix my dad, but I can fix the mess on the counter.

I grab my dish, shuffle over to the sink, and start rinsing. "Oh, I'm not backing down on my theory. I still believe the cooks at Molly's use raccoon meat in their patty melt. But who cares? Cheese covers a multitude of sins."

One by one, I stack the mess into the dishwasher until it's full. I squeeze the last of the dish soap into the compartment and make a mental note to run to the store for more tomorrow.

My late-model cell phone vibrates and skitters across the counter. I snatch it and glance at the screen. A text from Emma.

The Park. Twenty minutes?

I wipe my wet hands on a dishtowel that should have been washed a week ago. Add laundry to my growing to-do list. I flip the phone open and text Emma back.

Sure.

It's hard to be eloquent when you lack a keyboard.

Dad lifts his eyebrows. "Is it that boy?"

"No, it's Emma." I slip the phone into my back pocket. "What's your problem with Porter, anyway? Why do you suddenly not like him?"

He scrubs his hand over his grizzled jaw. "I don't like the thought of you with boys. Not at this age."

Okay, side note: I might be graduating high school next week but I've never had a steady boyfriend. A few group dates and a pity-induced yes for prom doesn't count. Besides, Porter's just ... *Porter*. That's it. His mom used to babysit me, so we've known each other since diaper days. We're friends in an I-know-all-your-secrets-and-have-embarrassing-pictures-of-you way.

"Well, not to worry where Porter's concerned." I slip my bag onto my shoulder. "I'm meeting Emma at the park. I'll see you at the diner around noon, okay?"

Dad pulls me into a hug. "I love you, baby doll. You know that, don't you?"

"Love you too, Dad." And I mean it.

He snags my shoulders before I can leave. "Be careful out there."

We live in the quiet suburbs outside of Chicago. Not dangerous—at all. Unsure of his meaning, I start to pull away, but there's a look in his deep brown eyes that scares me.

To ease the mood I throw my hand into a salute. "Scout's honor. I'll look both ways before crossing the street and everything."

He gives me a gentle shake. "I'm serous, Gabriella. I have a mind to lock you in the house today." His eyes roam back and forth, like he's thinking a million things at once. "If I didn't know that you'd crawl out the second-story window and go see your friends anyway, I would."

A tremor goes down my back.

Tense lines form around his mouth. His fingers are now digging into my skin. "It'd be so much better ... safer if you stayed with me today. I can watch you. Make sure nothing happens."

I swallow hard. He's been delusional before, but usually not this early in the day. My vision darts to the window. A perfect amount of buttery sun paints across the room, announcing a cloudless day. The florescent pink leaves on our burning bush plant sway in a light breeze. Our neighborhood doesn't even have coyote sightings.

"Dad"—I shrug out of his hold—"you're hurting me."

"Sometimes a little pain keeps us safe."

Enough. I'll spend the rest of my birthday eating at the indigestion-inducing diner he loves and trying not to gag as he tosses suffocating fish into a cooler on the boat. This next hour is mine. He can't steal it.

"I'll see you. At noon." I tap my watch and force a smile. "Maybe I'll even be early."

Without waiting for a response, I back onto our rotting porch and then turn and hoof it across our yard. All the while praying he doesn't burst outside and make a scene.

I duck under the clothes flapping on the neighbors' laundry line. The crisp, clean scent mixes with sweet honeysuckle in the wind. I hop a fence. Someone must have just finished mowing, because the smell of freshly cut grass makes me stop and close my eyes. With five months a year spent under snow piles, we Chicagoans know how to appreciate the small joys of summer.

Even the distant sound of a jackhammer breaking apart a sidewalk sounds like music, albeit not the best-selling sort.

Grover's Park comes into view. A playground that looks like a spaceship takes up most of the area. Stay-at-home moms huddle around a park bench as their children shoot down the slides. One small kid near the swings is eating sand.

"Gabby!" Porter's deep voice makes my stomach drop. I thought only Emma would be here. Not that Porter doesn't have every right to be. But after my dad's strange behavior, I'm suddenly on edge.

Porter stands up and waves from the picnic table near the small sledding hill. I make my way over to him. The summer sun has already begun to bleach his hair blond. He greets me with his easy smile, his green eyes dancing. Most of the girls consider him handsome, and I can't argue with their assessment. His years playing forward on the soccer field have kept him in top shape and assured him a full ride for college. But when I look at him, he's just the kid who buried a time capsule with me. The one I used to race on dirt bikes.

I drop my bag onto the splintering wood of the picnic table. "Why are you here?"

He crosses his arms and makes a *tsk-tsk* sound with his tongue. "What? Not happy to see me?"

I shrug. "Emma told me to meet her here."

"Because I told Emma to tell you to meet us both here. She'll be another ten minutes or so." Porter laughs. "Who am I kidding? Knowing Emma, we have another half hour before she gets here."

"At least she's predictable. Unlike you, might I add." I break into a grin. It's hard not to smile around Porter.

Fingers looped in his front pockets, he takes a step toward me. "But it works out well, because I wanted some time just for us."

I back against the table, and the wooden bench nettles into my legs. "For us, huh?"

"You don't have to pretend with me, Gabs. Tell me, how are you doing? Really?"

Right. Not only is Porter attractive, but he has a second superhero trait. He sees straight through a sham and calls it like it is. A characteristic I often hate about him.

"I'm fine." Suddenly the button on the bottom of my shirt has become the most interesting thing in the world.

He tucks my bangs behind my ear. "Are you thinking about your mom? It's probably hard, on days like today."

I brush his hand away, casually, so I don't offend him. "What's to miss? I didn't even know her. My dad on the other hand—he acts like the accident happened yesterday."

"It's okay to wish she was here." He squeezes my elbow.

"I honestly miss my dad more than her. Is that terrible?" I search Porter's eyes for understanding. "It's like I lost them both that day." I scoot so I'm sitting on the tabletop.

"He tries."

"I know."

Porter takes a seat on the table next to me, and our knees and shoulders touch. "Okay, enough of that. I don't want to bring you down. It's not every day you turn seventeen. Got big plans today?"

"Just doing stuff with Dad." My phone in my back pocket is uncomfortable, so I pull it out and lay the thing next to my purse.

"Can you ditch him and spend the day with Emma and me instead?"

I knock my knee into his. "I really want to, but you know how he is. I couldn't do that to him."

"Well, anyway." He jabs his elbow into my ribs. "I have something for you."

"You didn't have to."

But Porter's already pulling a little wrapped present from his cargo pocket. He slips it into my hands. "It's not much, Gabs, but happy birthday."

The moment the words *happy birthday* escape Porter's lips, chills race over my arm. Goose bumps erupt on my flesh.

A metal bracelet materializes on my right wrist. Out of nowhere, it just ... appears. It bites into my soft skin, much too tight.

I shake my wrist. "Get it off!"

Porter tries to stand, to help me, but it's like something has him immobilized.

The ends of the bracelet merge and fuse, and the metal starts to heat. I jump to the ground and paw at the thing. But then there's a flash of light like an electrical zap.

The gift clatters out of my hand, onto the concrete.

At the same moment I feel like my feet are yanked out from under me. The air seems to press in from every angle, as if space has become too small to fit my body. Wind rushes past my ears.

Horror etches itself into the lines around Porter's gaping mouth. He's finally able to reach for me, but it's as if I'm not there. His hand grabs at air.

"You're fading! What's—?"

I can tell he's yelling. Even though we're only a few feet from each other, he sounds like he's calling from half a mile away.

Porter disappears.

The park too.

I'm falling, but I'm not moving. I hear something whisk by my head, but there is only darkness. I try to scream, to move, but my muscles freeze.

Then—the sensation stops.

I land on my hands and knees in a mud puddle. Sputtering, I hunch back and a wave of nausea rocks through me, the same panicky feeling that surges through you at the precipice of a roller coaster. I swallow the acidic tide rushing up my throat and blink to clear my vision. With a deep breath, I push my braid onto my back. My body starts to shake.

The air is still. I squint, trying to identify the buildings in the distance. A small town? This sure doesn't look like my neighborhood. Where *am* I?

Darkness closes in on me. Coldness from the dirt beneath my palms seeps into my bones. A distant sound that can only be horses jingling in their harnesses makes me look up. The sky bursts with an eerie amount of stars.

I stare at the sky. Where did all those the stars come from? I've never *seen* so many—

And that's when it hits me.

This is not home.

CHAPTER TWO

A man, quick as a spider, crouches down next to me. I didn't notice him standing behind me when I first landed. Before I can react, he clamps his hand over my wrist.

"Cover your bracelet. You'll freak people out if they see the metal when it's like that." His voice has a kind, lyrical quality.

I jerk my arm away and put space between us. "Don't touch me." I burn him with my best glare. "Who are you?"

My eyes lock with his chocolate brown ones and I realize he's younger than I first thought. Close to my age, maybe a little older, but not much.

When he reaches for me again, I bring my right arm up to make an instinctive shield. I freeze. My gaze fastens to my bracelet. "This. Thing. Is. Glowing. Why is it glowing?" I drop my arm and claw at it again. My heart pounds a staccato rhythm against my rib cage.

At first, I thought this whole stunt might be an elaborate birthday hoax. Porter and Emma are always up to some sort of mischief. But block out the sun? Change the landscape? Even a master prankster can't pull that off.

The guy shakes his head, a mixture of amusement and pity crossing his face, like he's watching a puppy trip over its paws.

Then he slips his hand over mine to cover the bracelet again. "It'll go back to normal soon. I promise."

I push him away, but cup my hand over the cooling metal.

He cocks his head to the side, eyes narrowing. "Don't tell me you haven't done this before?"

I clench my fist. "Done what? What's going on?"

A groan escapes his lips. "Wow. Seriously? They sent a newbie? Not what I needed on this mission."

Mission? I scoot back. Hopefully he won't notice. A casual glance shows an open field and, about two hundred yards away, a small wooded area. If I dart to my feet, I might be able to outrun him. Then what? I harbor no desire to be this guy's next murder victim, but what's to say there isn't something worse lurking in those trees? I need to bide my time, gain my bearings before bolting. I probably only have one chance.

He scans the road, tilting his head to the side. Like a hunter, his ears seem to be listening for something. A silvery wash of moonlight bathes his pale skin, and a shadow forms off his nose. A strong jaw, understanding eyes, mocha hair in disarray, full cheeks, curious quirk of his eyebrow—his features are boyish. As he bends forward, I sense power despite his lean build. He's handsome, in a unique way. Not overtly, like Porter.

He turns his head a little more and whispers. "Listen. They're coming. Follow me."

My mind races through all I learned in the self-defense classes Dad forced me to attend. Make a peace sign and plunge fingers into both eyes? That would be sick. Not to mention a shame, since he does have nice eyes. Palm to the nose? No. That maneuver might kill him. I don't want to harm him. Just get him to stop touching me and then point me toward the closest one-way bus out of this nightmare.

Besides, I'm not a fighter. Avoidance always seems the best and easier route.

Before all the money spent on self-defense can come in handy, he drags me to my feet, then shoves at my back, propelling me forward. I stumble over ruts in the pebble-strewn dirt road. But the stranger wraps his arm around me, catching me each time I falter.

Add strong-arming me to his list of offenses.

To my left, a bird of prey releases a foreboding cry as something scuttles through the long grass. A mess of bats circle near the tree-lined area. Country-sweet air surges through my lips as I let out an agitated huff.

I turn and land a firm kick to my captor's shin. "I'm *not* kidding. Let me go!"

In less than a heartbeat, he covers my mouth. His hand smells like sweat and gardening. He growls in a don't-mess-with-me tone as his lips brush against my ear. "Unless you want to get us killed more than a hundred years before either of us are even born, I'd be quiet."

What sort of messed-up nightmare is this? I shiver. For a second he pulls me closer against his chest, which, to my horror, is surprisingly solid. I arch my body, trying to wiggle away. Unsuccessful. He's stronger than I thought. My heart plummets. Scratch any escape plan. His gaze trains back on the road. Then, as if he's forgotten about me, he releases his hold.

I swipe at my mouth to banish the taste of him, glowering in his general direction. "A hundred years? Before I'm born? Are you on drugs or something?"

A snap of a boot crushing a twig not far off brings my unwanted companion to a crouch. He grabs my arm and hauls me down beside him. "Listen. The men coming are dangerous. I know you're more confused than a blind dog in a new home, but you need to trust me. If you draw attention to us, it's not just our lives you jeopardize. Everything that's happening right now is so much bigger than your fear."

As he talks, I don't even look his way. Probably all lies anyway.

We hunker in the long, itchy grass at the edge of the road.

Scooting closer, he drops his voice to a whisper. "I know it sounds crazy. Believe me. I had a hard time at first, too. And I was prepared. If you promise to be silent when these men pass in a second, I'll answer your questions. Deal?"

I gauge the distance to the trees. Can I make it there quick enough? And once I get there, then what do I do? Shimmy up a tree? For all I know, he's a skilled climber. That, or he has an arsenal of axes stashed somewhere and will have no qualms about chopping a tree down to get me.

When I don't answer, he drapes his arm over my back. I'm sure he means the gesture to feel casual, but the pressure he's adding holds a threat: *Do not get up or else.*

"I don't really have much of a choice, do I? I'm stuck here with you." I speak out of the side of my mouth. He doesn't deserve eye contact.

We lie there, waiting. My abdomen pinches against a large rock on the ground. As if I need additional discomfort in the midst of this whole mess.

How many minutes have passed since I left? Poor Porter, he probably called the cops and has them sweeping the park for clues. Soon, Dad will be at Molly's Diner, crunching his baseball hat in his hands as he waits for me. Like a string of ants, terror skitters down my spine. Not for myself, but for Dad. He won't be able to handle life if I go missing. What will he do when I don't arrive? Who will buy dish soap for him tomorrow? I have to get back home, wherever it is from here—for him. To make it out of this situation intact, I must weigh my options. Do nothing rash.

My captor removes his hand from my back, and then he presses a finger to his lips. Footfalls on the road announce proximity. He leans closer to me. "I'm Michael, by the way. Michael Pace."

A group of four men approaches. I don't have the best vision to begin with, so I squint. At least I've been here long enough for my eyes to adjust to the dark. The first three men wear matching gray uniforms. They look familiar, like I've seen the outfit in a book or museum before. Through the dim of night, I can make out that their coats almost reach their knees and they are wearing funny matching hats. Not quite fashionable, but hey, to each his own. Their tall boots are well polished, catching glints of moonbeams. Even the double rows of buttons down their chests glint despite the darkness.

The fourth man is dressed differently, in a drab, single-colored suit and funny tight hat. It resembles a hat I saw once in an old Charlie Chaplin movie one of my teachers forced the class to watch.

Now might be my chance. If I scream, the men will hear me. Even if Michael tries to drag me away, at least there will be witnesses. I swallow, getting ready. But Michael must sense my thoughts, because in a swift move he covers my mouth and his other arm yanks me snug against his side.

His head is right next to mine. "Sorry. I don't trust the look on your face."

I attempt to shove him. I pinch his hand, and his other arm snakes up and secures both my wrists. It's no use.

His sighs. "Seriously. Stop moving."

The group meanders toward the candlelit windows of the small town up ahead. A drunken laugh punctuates the silence.

Great. Just great. They won't be able to help me in that condition anyway. I might as well face the fact that I'm on my own. As usual.

One man sways, and his toe catches along the ground. He lurches forward, grabbing hold of the one man not in uniform.

"Whoa, there, Captain." The shortest man stumbles a few steps.

Yes, they will be no help at all.

"Whad you say your name was again, man?" The Captain's words come out long and in a garble.

The man in the plain suit chuckles as he straightens his hat. He's supporting the weight of the most inebriated soldier on his shoulder. "E. J. Allen, and gentlemen, I am at your service. How fortunate I came upon you tonight."

Michael's arm twitches beside me. The movement draws my vision from the passing men for a moment. I turn in the grass just a fraction to catch Michael's look—like a boy watching the first snowfall of the year.

"I knew it," he whispers.

A less drunk officer with long hair trails the group on the road. "Where do you hail from, Mr. Allen?"

Every fiber of my being wants to lean over and whisper, "*Knew what?*" Instead, I follow Michael's example as he grows still as a sleeping cat. I can't help it. I'm suddenly drawn in by the excitement in his expression. His hold loosens.

The men are only ten feet away from us now. E. J. Allen shifts, his impressive beard breaking to show a smile. "From Baltimore originally, but now anyplace in the South is home because, my dear men, I believe in the right to live as I please without some government member nosing into my business."

"If the Yanks could simply see reason like that for one minute, this protracted war could be done with and I'd be back home with my sweetheart." One man stops walking for a moment.

A second slings his arm around the first. "Imagine never having to be on another battlefield."

The long-haired man catches up with the others. "Why do you think I volunteered our group to transport the medical supplies?"

Tapping his hat, Allen says, "War's a grisly affair at best. How wonderful that you men were allowed a small respite. It does sound like you've earned one. Now, lead on, men. Hunt House with a warm fire awaits us yet." E. J. steers his inebriated companions onward toward the small town.

When the group of men mosey out of ear shot, Michael explodes to his feet. He performs a noiseless fit pump in the air. "I can't believe this. Allen Pinkerton. It's too good to be true. Do you know how long I've hoped to be pulled here?"

Then it hits me. I'm clearly stupid. Even if those men were beyond drunk, the one called Allen seemed with it enough. They disappear into the town along with my only chance for salvation. My mind whirls. First order of the evening is to distract Michael until I find a chance to break away from him.

I stretch my arms. *Think, think, think.* "Remember when you said you'd tell me everything if I stayed silent? Well, making good on that promise should happen right about now." I rub my wrists. He didn't hurt them, but he doesn't need to know that. His guilt could be my most effective ally.

"Sorry. Just excited." Michael flashes a charming smile and shrugs an apology. "You're right though. I always keep my promises. Even if you only stayed silent with my—let's just call it reinforcement." He stills and tilts his head to the side. Michael seems to be measuring me. "You really have no clue what's going on, do you?"

I smack my forehead. "Thank you, Captain Obvious. Should I?"

"It's just unusual. I've never heard of it before." He massages the back of his neck. "Most Shifters go straight to Keleusma on their first shift. But you? You didn't. On top of that, you seem clueless."

"*Shifters*? You are speaking English, right?"

"I'm floored. Your parents never told you?"

"Parent. Singular. And, clearly, no." I scan the distance to the trees versus the distance to the town. I can run fast. I started in track all through high school. If only I knew his abilities.

"Singular, right. That's all of us." Michael combs his fingers through his mocha hair. He hisses out a long breath before continuing. "Okay. Where do I start? Well, you, Miss ... Miss?"

"I don't consider us on a first-name basis yet."

"Fine then." Michael glances back toward the town. "You and I are something called Shifters. Simply put, we shift through time to wherever we're most needed and take care of whatever needs doing. We have no control over where we end up, but what we do in that moment affects the world's future."

Time travel? That's it. This guy is certifiably insane and probably contemplating how to make me into a fine stew a la Sweeny Todd. Pressing my palms into the ground, I push to my feet. I have to figure out how to get home and Mr. Michael Timeshifter isn't helping.

But that doesn't stop him from rocketing after me.

He moves too quickly, snatching my elbow. "I know it sounds crazy. Like I'm high even, but I can prove it to you."

I spin on my heels to face him and end up smacking against his chest. Michael grabs my shoulders, righting me. I shove away. "So prove it."

"Today is your birthday, right? A bracelet—this bracelet," he taps the metal, "just appeared on your wrist and started to glow. One minute you were in your time and after some truly uncomfortable time travel, you're now in 1861. Yup, I said it. Feel free to have your mind blown for a second."

"You don't have to be rude."

"Why not? I did nothing but save your life back there and all I'm getting from you are snarls and snide comments."

A creeping sensation races up my spine. "We're all dead, aren't we?"

That makes him laugh. "No. Very much alive."

"There has to be another explanation ... I'm dreaming."

"Of course, and your mind has conjured me up as some sort of hero." A humorless laugh escapes from his mouth. "Believe me. That should be the first indication that what I'm saying is true. I'm no one's hero." After a short pause, his lips tug into a soft smile. "Those guys were Confederate soldiers and Allen is a Union spy. His methods are the precursor for the Secret Service. With our help, he'll turn the tide of the Civil War. Without it, the world you grew up in might not exist to return to."

I want to run until my breath leaves me. Doing that always chases my stress away. But if I start running, where will I end up? What Michael says, well, is complete lunacy—but his words somehow click in my mind. A rush of *rightness* courses through my body. It makes me feel warm despite the chill in the air.

But I've watched enough shows on cable to know that criminals and killers are excellent at warping the brains of their victims. Self-defense class floods back into the forefront of my mind.

No time like the present.

Before Michael can react, I land a punch to his jaw. He yelps and gets ahold of me, but I drive the butt of my heel onto his foot. When he stumbles, I send a high kick to his stomach. He falls backwards. I have minutes on him, maybe.

I've never actually hurt another person before, and the moan that leaves his lips as I take off bites at my conscience. Branches nick my bare legs as I hurtle into the woods. I run another few minutes and then stop. I spin in two clumsy circles, trying to gain a bearing for time and place. An owl hoots, branches sway above me, and the song of frogs finds me from a distance. My eyes dart in a frenzy, examining the trees. I search for a nook or a crop of rocks to hide in.

The sound of someone lumbering through the forest throws me into despair. My knees shake. Is this how it feels right before you die?

Suddenly, people draped in shadows converge into the small clearing where I am. They move slowly, like zombies. Their faces are human, but not sharp. It's like looking at old photographs instead of living beings.

"It's her!" one hisses.

A few others burst out in a strange, gleeful cheer that hurts my ears.

As I back away from them, I trip and land against a tree trunk. The air races from my lungs. I'm trapped.

One grabs onto my arm, his touch like ice. "Yes, we've been waiting for you to make your appearance." From up close, it looks like his face is melting.

Two more creatures take hold of my arms.

"Finally. After all these years. Welcome home, Gabriella."

CHAPTER THREE

One of the shadowy figures steps closer. "You're just what I pictured. Exactly." His voice is strange, ancient. Words roll off his lips in an unfamiliar cadence. He leans closer and taps a long nail against my cheek, raising the hair on the back of my neck.

"Everything we've hoped for ... waited for," another chimes in.

There are too many of them. My kung fu moves might have worked on Michael, but I'm no Chuck Norris. I certainly can't wiggle from their clutches and deliver a round-house kick. Taking out four at once like they show in the movies is highly unlikely. I want to rail against them, but my mouth clams up. My throat freezes in their horrifyingly magnificent presence.

A commotion erupts on my right. Hissing, spitting—the creatures turn and advance. One still grips me tightly, his nails mining into the tender flesh of my upper arm. I crane my neck and catch sight of Michael. Gratitude surges through my veins. He smashes his shoulder into a pack of them. Surprised, they tumble like unsteady bowling pins. Without hesitation, he lunges at the one holding me. He lands a punch to the creature's temple and it howls and spits, releasing me.

Ten minutes ago, I might have been afraid of Michael's intentions, but I'll take the company of a possible murderer to whatever these other creatures are.

Wide-eyed, Michael crashes forward and shoves me. "Run!"

He doesn't have to tell me twice.

Like I'm on the starting blocks at the State Championship, I take off. Michael's right at my heels, but the others—the shadow people—thunder after us. Branches snap and animals charge away as the otherworldly beings thud over bushes in our wake. Wet dirt and decaying leaves churn under our feet, shrouding us in a dense, earthy smell. I turn to the left, away from where the creatures first came from, but Michael snags my arm.

With a jerk, he shouts, "Not that way! Run toward the portal."

Portal?

There's no time to ask, or waver, so I follow. A minute later, we arrive at the mouth of another clearing. The ground is unnervingly bare. In the center is a tree that once probably stood proud and tall, but now it's half fallen. Its trunk forms a near-perfect arch, which illuminates as we draw near. The glow in the center ripples like water. Static zips through the air.

Michael's almost there, almost running into the space under the arch. But a searing pain around my wrist stops me. The bracelet begins to heat up.

"Michael...?" He doesn't stop. "Michael!"

He hears me now and twists around. "Hurry."

The ground behind me shakes. The shadow people have found us. Their chests heave from either exertion or anger.

I stumble toward Michael, and he catches me by my elbows. My hands splay across his chest. I feel the rapid pound of his heart. That's when he catches sight of my bracelet, which is now shining.

His brow rises. "It can't ... I don't believe...."

He throws his arms around me. When I freeze in time, he's there with me. The shadow people reach for us, but they miss as we fade. Their wails echo as the air around us closes in. Tight. Muggy. I hate this.

Once again I feel a strong tug and the sensation of falling. For a moment, there is no sound at all, yet in a flurry something—maybe other people traveling in time—brushes against us in the blackness. There's a murmuring that I didn't notice last time. What are they saying? The words whoosh by too quickly.

Just as quickly as it starts, it stops. We collapse against something hard and cold, stone—a building.

"I didn't think that would work. It shouldn't have." Michael's beside me. "It never has before."

I blink rapidly. It's so bright outside. Voices mixed with the sound of traffic draws me out of my daze.

Michael's already on his feet when I finally clear my vision, his hand thrust toward me. "Come on, we need to get you out of sight."

Rejecting his help, I shove up from the ground on my own. My breath catches in my throat. Moments ago we were in the middle of the country, but before me now sprawls a city. That, or it's the set from an old black-and-white movie. Horses pulling carriages clomp down the cobblestone street, a boy on a bicycle with a messenger bag whips around us, and a policeman in a heavy-looking coat directs traffic on the corner. Old-fashioned cars on thin tires rumble through the intersection. The sun, close to high noon, pulses heat over the edge of the buildings that line the street.

"Where are we?" I don't even try to hide the awe in my voice. A million questions spring to my mind, but I can't find the words to voice them. This is all too weird. My brain actually hurts a little. Possibly an effect of time travel—that, or it's just plain tired of trying to wrap itself around the situation.

Michael points to a sign in the road. *Wall Street.* Then he ducks beside some stairs and motions for me to follow. I glance down the street again, and I'm left in the same position as before. If I break into a run, where will I go? To the cop? No way. While I don't know much about history, I do know that they used to not hesitate before locking a person in an insane asylum. Especially someone spouting time-traveling madness. Besides, the chill induced by the shadow people still clings to my skin. Michael saved me from them. I can trust him—for now.

I crouch beside him.

He turns to me and studies my face with an intensity that makes me drop my gaze to the ground. Seconds later, he clears his throat, drawing my eyes back to meet his.

"You're Gabriella Creed, aren't you?" He shakes his head, flipping some of his hair out of place. "I'm so stupid. I should have known right away."

Tension floods my body. "How do you know my name?" I bite my tongue before asking him if he's a stalker.

"They called you Gabriella back there."

I lick my lips. "But they didn't say my last name."

"Still, I should have known."

A group of people pass near where we hide. Michael wraps his arm around my waist and drags me further into the building's shadow. It's then that I notice the pungent smell of trash and fish. Right, New York doesn't have alleys. I really miss Chicago.

Once we're safely hidden, Michael releases me.

I scrunch my nose, taking small breaths through my mouth. "But why? It's not like we've met before."

"No." He rubs his jaw. "We sure haven't." Clearly straight-to-the-point answers are not Michael's strong suit.

"Yet you know who I am, why?"

He shakes his head, letting me know the topic is closed for discussion. Crossing my arms, I level a glare in his direction. Michael shrugs back. Oh well. I can play nice, but only because I need his help. If he stops being useful, I'm out.

"What were those things? Those creatures in the forest."

"Shades." He lets out a sigh. "Hey, back there, did you wish to be somewhere else?"

"When those scary things were hot on our trail? Absolutely."

Slowly, Michael reaches over and touches my bracelet. "May I?" He doesn't wait for an answer. He cups my wrist in one of his hands and twists the metal around to examine every inch. When he arrives at the section snug against my inner wrist, he taps on a small black mark on the bracelet. "Fascinating," he mumbles. "None of the rest of ours has this."

Michael's lost in his own thoughts, so I consider him. Now that I'm seeing him in daylight, I can make out all his features. His lips are thin. His eyes are gentle. The skin around them crinkles the couple times I've caught him laughing. For that matter, the fact that he has smiled at all during our exchange speaks to an even-keeled personality, someone who smirks at danger yet takes action when the stakes are high. If he's not intent on killing me after all, then he might be someone worthy of friendship. The jury's still out.

The edge of his thumb brushes against my wrist. His touch shoots electricity up my arm. My heart thuds erratically. I jerk my hand from his and the feeling stops. I look at him, and he's examining my face. His eyes narrow, but not in an angry manner. No—they're curious, full of silent questions.

Michael inches away, putting space between us. "It doesn't happen like that."

"What? The time traveling?" Heat rushes up my neck, either from my reaction to Michael's touch a second ago or from voicing pure absurdity. It's a toss-up.

Relief washes over his features. "Of course, yes, the time traveling." He lifts his arm, tapping the metal bracelet on his wrist. I failed to notice earlier that he wears a matching one. "We have no power over when and where in time we're pulled. We stay in a place until we accomplish our mission. Then we either return to Keleusma through a Portal or we're pulled to wherever we're needed next. Never by our own power, not like you just did. It's not possible."

I tuck my bangs back behind my ears. "But I didn't *do* anything."

"They feared that you'd be special ... powerful. They've been debating it for a generation." His eyes rake over me.

"Me? Special? I'm hopelessly ordinary. I'm clumsy. Bad at math. Completely normal in every pathetic way." I jab him in the ribs like I so often do to Porter. "Maybe you completed your mission. Didn't you say you shift once a mission's complete?"

"No." He cups his face in his hands. "I know I didn't. I was supposed to save Pinkerton. He's going to be captured at some point. My mission was to spring him or to make sure it didn't happen. I didn't get a clear reading."

My brain hurts from the string of riddles. "But before ... I mean, you seemed surprised to find out who that man was."

"I was. I didn't know ... didn't *feel* what my mission was until after you kicked me. When I hit the ground a thought coursed through me—*save Pinkerton*. In that split second, I had to decide if I should follow you or fulfill my calling." He mumbles, "I messed up."

"You saved me from those things."

"Shades. I suppose that's important too, but I've never failed a mission before. There are long-term consequences."

"You'll get in trouble? Is there a Shifter police force or something?"

Michael turns pleading eyes on me. "It's not just about me. There'll be effects for everyone. Don't you get that, Gabriella?"

"Honestly? I don't get any of this." My leg cramps, so I stretch it out. "And it's Gabby."

"Hey, don't do that. People might see you." He motions for me to scrunch against the wall again.

"Are we supposed to stay hidden all the time?"

"Just you. You'll scare the good citizens of New York in that outfit."

Fuming, I look down at my plaid button-up and jean shorts. My hands automatically form fists. "And you're the master of style? What, in a black t-shirt and jeans. Please. The boy bands of the world called, they want their outfit back."

A muscle on his jaw pops. "You're impossible. It wasn't an insult. You look good. Believe me, more than good, but let's just say my clothes blend more with the time period than yours do."

More than good?

Ignoring that, I thrust my hand to indicate the traffic on Wall Street. "These guys are all in suits."

"My clothes are from Keleusma. If I walk out onto the street, the people will see me dressed how they are."

"How is that even possible?" I cross my arms. This has to be a dream. And if it is, I have to commend my subconscious. It deserves a cookie. Michael's pretty cute for a made-up person.

He shrugs. “People see what they want to see. It’s always been that way in human history.” Then he freezes. His eyes focus off to the distance, and he tilts his head. Like he can see and hear something I can’t. I want to clap to break his daze.

Michael’s trance snaps. “What day is it? We’re wasting time.” He shoots to his feet. “Stay here, I need to find a newspaper.”

Before I can answer, he’s gone. I hunch, drawing my knees to my middle. What if those shadow people—those Shades—are here? I suddenly don’t want to be separated from Michael, ever. I hate the thought of depending on someone, but I’m in over my head. If I stand any chance of making it home, I need information and Michael’s my personal Obi-Wan Kenobi. Now, why couldn’t I have been paired with Ewan McGregor? *Red Rover, Red Rover, send Ewan right over*. I would have trusted him instantly.

Craning my neck, I spot Michael across the street. He’s talking to a small boy hawking newspapers. Seconds later, Michael’s eyes flash to mine, and I notice he’s gone pale. Jamming his hands in his pockets, he dodges a carriage. He makes his way back to the stairs where I hide.

His voice holds an urgent tone. “It’s September 16, 1920.”

My brow scrunches. “Okay.”

“It’s September 16, 1920 ... on Wall Street.” He jerks a thumb toward the street sign like I’ve forgotten.

I rise to my feet, brushing off my shorts. “Is that supposed to mean something to me?”

"Your dad didn't even school you in history? This is unbelievable." He grabs fistfuls of his hair. The poor guy is going to go bald if he has to spend any more time with me.

I pop my hands onto my hips. "Why would he? I hate history. My friend Emma and I passed notes just so we didn't fall asleep during class."

He takes my shoulders. "Don't you understand? Your history is your future."

"It doesn't have to be." I pull away. "I don't agree with that."

"It doesn't matter." Michael pinches the bridge of his nose. "We have less than five minutes to find a man named Thomas."

"Five—" I try to take a step back, but run into unyielding stone.

"Don't speak. There will be a bombing. A huge one. We need to find him and keep him safe. I have a feeling he's inside the bank being targeted. Then I need to catch the bomber. This act of terrorism has never been solved. Don't you see? We can change that today." His eyes blaze with intensity.

"How do you know?"

"It just came to me. Don't worry. It'll start happening to you soon enough. No more questions. Stay here for now. I can't deal with people seeing you yet."

Then he leaves.

I notice my hands shaking and tuck them into my armpits, but my knees wobble, too. I'm afraid my legs will buckle any second, so I slump against the wall. *A bomb?* Could I really die in another time? Is that even possible? I wish I'd followed

Michael, even though he told me not to. He needs to stop leaving me alone.

I scan the streetscape, and my gaze lands on a little girl walking hand-in-hand with her parents. They turn toward a store, but the little girl pulls back. The father goes down on one knee and hugs her.

It makes my thoughts bounce to Dad. He's alone now, maybe forever. My eyes swim with tears.

The father gets back up. The little girl nods. The man and woman enter the store, leaving the little girl on the steps. She's smiling, swinging her tiny feet in time with a song she's humming. I really must be in another time period, because in my world, no child is safe left alone.

A clip-clopping, old bay horse blocks my view. A man with his hat pulled low leads the horse and buggy slowly westward down Wall Street. I squint. For a moment, it almost looked like a Shade hobbled beside him, but it has to be a trick of the light. Or I'm paranoid.

I jump when Michael bursts around the corner. He's dragging an older man who sports an impressive white mustache. Michael shoves the man up the stairs. "Quick, Gabby, there's only seconds! Get inside."

Seconds? My eyes immediately go to the little girl. Before I have time to change my mind I'm sprinting across the street. A horn blares, tires skid. I hurtle out of the way.

Michael's inside now, probably making the man, Thomas, duck under a desk or behind a cement wall.

I wave my arms, yelling, "Run! Take cover! Bomb!" Hopefully some of the people will notice and be spared. To my relief, a few people scatter away.

Without breaking my run, I grab the little girl and tug her down in front of me. She screams. We tumble to the ground, and I position her against the wall. My body blocks her from the road.

I snap my eyelids shut, waiting for the explosion. I hear only the sound of my heart racing in my ears.

In my head I say good-bye to Dad.

CHAPTER FOUR

Quick footsteps sound from behind and Michael throws his body over me and the girl. He braces both hands on the wall near our heads, forming a human shield.

Less than a heartbeat later, a large boom echoes just down the street. It's followed by screeching tires, punctuated by terror-filled cries. The force of the blast slams us into the pavement, making me bite my lip. A warm, metallic taste swirls in my mouth. I hear air whoosh from Michael's lungs. His head bangs into mine, but his fortress-like arms hold fast around us. I pull the girl tighter against me and shut my eyes so tightly it hurts.

People shriek.

Windows explode, showering glass into the mayhem. Unknown fragments tear through the air. Metal clanks across the ground.

A moment of eerie silence follows.

The little girl trembles in my arms. High-pitched ringing clouds my hearing, and I realize I'm shaking too. A heaviness that I can't make out shoves at my back.

The world rushes back in. People are screaming and wailing. Others run down the street. The smell of burning hair and fuel makes me gag.

The door to the store we huddle near flies open. A man stands on the stairs. "Mary!" He grips the railing, his knuckles turning white. His knees wobble on the next step.

Recognition washes over me, but not before the little girl springs from my grasp.

"Papa!" She launches up the steps.

Her father envelopes her in a fierce hug, tears in his eyes. He cups his hand to the back of her head, protecting his daughter from the terrifying image of carnage the eruption left on Wall Street.

Straightening my spine, I brush glass off my legs then sway backwards. But I freeze when limp weight presses against me. *Michael.* He wails in pain. The sound is harsh and short, like he's biting it back.

When I turn, he moans again, his body sagging. "Michael!"

"My back." His eyes are closed tightly.

My gaze rakes down him. His shirt's on fire. I jolt to my feet. Without thinking, I start smacking at the small flame racing up his back. It extinguishes instantly. Michael yelps in protest, but I don't know how else to help.

I drop to my knees beside him. "What can I do? Tell me what to do."

Sweat breaks out across his brow and upper lip. His shoulders convulse. Before I know what's happening, he leans toward me, and I cradle his head on my knee. There's soot in his hair and a large gash across his left cheek. Will it leave a scar? I hope not. He shouldn't have to look in the mirror every day for the rest of his life and remember me. The fact that I didn't follow instructions shouldn't mar him. Using the bottom of my shirt, I press it to the cut on Michael's face to stop the bleeding.

He winces. "Is Thomas safe?"

That's when I look up. The bloodshed strewn across Wall Street makes my throat clam up. What's wrong with humanity? Why do we do this sort of thing to each other? There has to be a better way to get a point across. Some way that doesn't involve needless and cruel murders. Senseless destruction.

Smoke hangs in the air like a funeral shroud. Cars are flipped on their sides, packages spilling from their trunks. People lie in the street, moaning, crying, bleeding. Others run to their aid. Chunks of entire buildings are missing. I see an arm on the ground that's not attached to a person. I swallow down a wave of bile.

At least the building across the street, where Michael stashed Thomas, looks sound. "If he was in there, then he's safe."

Michael closes his eyes. He's shivering even though it isn't cold outside. I wish I knew first aid. Why did I decide to work at Slushy Stop instead of becoming a lifeguard or something useful? Making frozen confections will hardly come in handy as a Shifter. I'm useless to Michael.

Instinctively, I run my hand over his forehead and down his hair. "What now? If you saved him, shouldn't we shift? Maybe it'll move us to a hospital."

"It doesn't work like that." His teeth are clenched.

I keep trying to soothe him by combing my fingers through his hair, but anxiety works like a horde of ants in my stomach. I'm so completely unable to help. It's the same way I feel when Dad gets plastered. I usually lock myself in my bedroom and draw the covers over my head until he sobers up.

But I can't do that with Michael. I can't hide from his pain. It's my fault he's hurt. Besides, he saved me when I was in trouble.

Tears pinch out of my eyes. "Then how does it work? How do I help you?"

"Honey." His lips barely move.

I'm not a fan of endearments, but now isn't the best time to pick a fight. I nod, hoping to encourage him. "Yes, tell me what to do."

"Honey."

"I'm here," I whisper and offer his shoulder a companionable squeeze. Maybe he just needs someone beside him for a moment.

Michael rolls off of me with a heart-tearing moan, palms landing on the ground. Ugly blisters are rising on his burned back. Tears scorch my eyes. The smell of burnt flesh is more than I can handle, but I have to. He's trying to stand, but his legs wobble. Making sure to place my arm where there are no burns, I wrap it around his middle. He drapes an arm across my shoulder.

I catch his deep gaze and want to make the lines etched in his brow go away. "On the count of three, stand."

"One ... two ... three."

Michael grunts, and I can tell he bites back a howl, but I get him to his feet. His fingers dig into my shoulder, making me turn my head to look at him. His hot chocolate eyes flood with concern. "There are so many people hurt. We have to help them."

Once again, I'm convinced he's insane. "You're in no condition to play doctor."

Police officers surge past us, on their way to Wall Street.

"But it's what we're made for. We're supposed to help ease human suffering." His teeth start to rattle. Shock? "Or else they win." He points, indicating the havoc caused by the explosion.

I squint. Then I see them. The shadow people—Shades. They're limping out from the shadows cast by the buildings, but the people don't seem to notice them. Shades move closer to the ones that are injured and crying, and they bend close to their faces—sucking in the air.

A tremor works its way up my spine. "Wh-what are they doing?"

Michael leans more of his weight into me. "They feed off human despair. They're growing stronger."

We need to get out of here before they see us. "Tell me where to take you."

He nods. "You're right. We can't let them see you. Leave me. Just run, Gabby."

I tighten my arm around his middle. "I'm not leaving you."

The door to the storefront jingles, and the family from earlier shuffles outside. Mary's father has her in his arms, her head buried against his chest. Her mother gasps as she looks down Wall Street. She dabs at her eyes.

Mary's father approaches us. "Are you the ones who saved my girl?"

He's a towering sort of man. I gulp. "Yes, sir."

He hands Mary to the mother and reaches for Michael. "Here, I can help him. Our vehicle's around the block."

I don't have time to argue. Michael hobbles beside the man and I fall into step with Mary and her mother.

Don't look back. Don't look back.

Within minutes, we're in their old style pick-up truck. It rides low and in the back, where Michael and I are, the sides are made from wooden slats. Michael's lying on his side, his head on my thigh again. Even though I have a blister growing from when I slapped out the fire, I rub the palm of my hand back and forth on his shoulder. Every bump in the road causes him to groan.

"Michael," I whisper. "What year was burn cream invented?"

My words elicit a small smile. "Not yet. Shh." He closes his eyes.

The truck rumbles past the city limits, and fields roll into view. I'm sure in my time there aren't farms so close to New York. It's surreal, seeing a field and the city in the same instance. I peek at Michael's oozing back—charred flesh—and wish I hadn't.

We turn up a long drive, and the truck stops. The man helps Michael out of the truck, and I follow them into their home.

The house is small—one story—a kitchen, a family room, and a bedroom or two. Mary's mother sets water boiling and hands me a jar of amber goo.

"Here," she smiles at me. "This will help your husband. You may have him lie on the table." She presses a wet rag into my hand. "My daughter has experienced a trying day, and I'm disturbed too. I'll see to my family and you see to yours." I can tell she ties to smile and just can't.

"My husband?" My voice ratchets up five decibels, but I catch Michael's gaze. He shakes his head subtly. Two young people traveling together. I guess it's best if they assume we're married. I run my tongue against the back of my teeth. "And what do I do with this?"

Before I can finish my question, Mary's mom backs out of the room. I turn to Michael.

"Don't mind her. She's being proper. They won't come in here again." He's trying to struggle out of his shirt without yowling. I cross the room and help ease the fabric from around his wound as we slip it over his head. Evidently they have a gym in this Keleusma place, because Michael's more ripped than I would have guessed. I try not to get caught gawking as I help him onto the table. He lies, stomach down.

I freeze. "I don't know if I can do this. Help you."

"You can." His voice is so soft. How can he do that? Use his strength to sooth me when he must be in an incredible amount of pain?

I swallow. Hard. "Okay. Tell me what to do." My hands shake.

"Make sure there aren't any pieces of my shirt stuck in the burn. Then use this." He taps the jar of goo.

I pick it up and unscrew the lid. "Is this stuff safe to use?"

"Honey? Sure."

I dab at his back with the damp cloth, biting my tongue and blinking my eyes to keep back the tears that are burning to drop. Michael grips the edge of the table. I wouldn't be surprised if he's holding hard enough to leave marks. I should have found a stick for him to bite before starting. That always seems to work in old movies.

The muscle in his jaw pops. "Now, honey."

"You don't have to keep calling me that." I pour a glob of the goo onto his back.

"Not you. In the jar. It's honey. Only thing to help with burns," he says between pained gasps.

I'm glad he can't see my face. My cheeks flame with embarrassment. Of course he wasn't calling me honey.

There's a light tap on the door, and Mary's mother walks into the kitchen, averting her eyes from Michael's back. She lays a wad of fabric on the counter. "These are clean. You may use them as bandages." She hesitates at the door. "I have this for you as well." She holds up a bundle of clothes. "I noticed that something happened to your clothing during the blast."

I look down at myself. Besides some soot and scrapes, I'm fine.

Oh, right. Modesty in the twentieth century. My shorts are acceptable by my standards, but to her, I probably look like I'm in my underwear.

"Yes, um, thanks." I slip down into a seat again, hiding myself behind Michael.

Mary's mother sets the clothing beside the fabric scraps on the counter. "Thank you for saving my daughter. We can never repay you, but please let us try. You're welcome to stay here until your husband has mended. We don't have much. No spare rooms or beds to offer, but I'll bring some quilts. Will it suit to leave him on the table?"

I nod and she disappears.

When I look back at Michael, he's studying my face. I tuck my bangs back behind my ear. "Do you need something else? Are you in a lot of pain?"

A slight smile tugs on his lips. "I told you you'd scandalize them."

I cross my arms and glare at him.

He shuts his eyes again and his shoulders rise with a long breath. "Actually, there is something you could do."

"What?"

"When you ran your fingers through my hair—that felt nice. Distracting."

I lean forward and slip my hand into his mocha hair, smoothing it back into place. Its slightly damp, but soft.

After a while, Michael's breathing is deep and even. Hopefully he's fallen asleep. I relish the silence for a minute. I guess everything's happening so quickly, my mind hasn't had time to process. But in this free moment, I fight the urge to run out the front door and leave Michael again. Not because

I'm afraid of him any longer, we're past that now. I just can't deal with this.

I shove back from the table, but Michael's hand snakes out and grabs mine. "Hey, you said you wouldn't leave me."

Guilt claws at my stomach. "I won't." I sit back down. "Could those people on Wall Street see the Shades?"

Michael props his head in his hands. "No. Only Shifters can see them. I've heard that normal people can sense them, but I don't understand it all."

"So you're saying, back in my time, there are Shades wandering around? Wouldn't I have been able to see them?"

"Have you ever walked into a room and felt the creeps but couldn't place why? Or been somewhere that suddenly went cold? Have you ever had the feeling that someone was following you, and no one was there?"

Only all the time. I bite my lip, nodding.

"That means Shades were nearby. I never sensed them when I was still normal, but then, I wasn't a threat to them."

"Are you saying I am?"

"I'm saying I don't know." He closes his eyes.

I can hear the fire in the next room crackling, and the floor boards creaking with tip-toed steps.

I clear my throat. "Why haven't we switched—er—shifted? Is there something else left to do? Tell me, and I'll do it."

He blows out a long stream of air. "It doesn't always work like that. Sometimes you do what you're supposed to, and you still have to wait until he's ready to shift you."

"Hold on! *He*—as in, someone is controlling all of this?"

Michael laughs softly. It must have hurt because he groans. "Did you really believe you were in control?"

My hands ball into fists. "Who then?"

"Why are you so upset?"

"I don't believe in someone else calling the shots in my life."

"Well, learn to." His eyebrows lower. "I assumed you heard him."

"If you're talking about the 'leadings' you mentioned earlier, no."

"But the little girl? Didn't you feel a nudge to save her?"

"If by 'nudge' you mean did the right thing to do whiz through my mind, yes. I did the only decent thing that could have been done. But I don't think that's what you're talking about, is it? Michael, you need to start giving me plain answers because I can't stick with you if you don't. I think I've done well so far but—"

He taps the table. "One, if you don't stop talking and just let yourself be quiet every once in a while, you'll never feel a leading. Two, you're driving me crazy. Let's just not speak for a little bit."

"But—"

"Not speaking." He sighs.

I work my jaw back and forth. Maybe I should leave him. Leave all of this. Go and live on my own without having to worry about another person. *Right*. Then let the Shades claw me again. Not likely.

I close my eyes, willing myself to take ten deep breaths, one after another. Mary's mother comes in again at some point. Tells us they are going to bed now and that they'll see us in the morning. I block everyone out and see only darkness.

"Gabby." The whisper wakes me with a jolt.

I must have fallen asleep in the chair because it's now dark in the kitchen. Michael's beside me, a make-shift bandage tied around his middle. "Sorry if I scared you, but we've got to go."

I rub circles over my eyes. "But the woman said we could stay as long as we wanted."

"This isn't a vacation, Gabby. We've got work to do. Come on. I need you to be my crutch again." He motions for me to stand.

I stretch. "Shouldn't we at least say good-bye to the family? Thank them for helping?"

He shakes his head. "It's better this way. Less questions."

"We can't go out there with you hurt like this. It's not like I can protect you."

"I don't need you to, just crutch-duty."

I growl as I wrap my arm around his middle. It's probably considered poor manners to question my Obi-Wan, but I can't help it. "Where are we off to, oh Wise One?"

"There's a portal nearby. I can sense it. Can't you?"

"I sense that I'm hungry, and that's about it."

He juts his chin toward the door. I unlatch it, and we're outside. The sky drapes like rich black velvet above the earth. Pinpricks of starlight push through the dark canvas, offering small beams of hope. The air smells damp as we pick our way across a knee-high field. I can't relax. I scan the horizon over and over again for signs of Shades.

"Where are we going?" I whisper.

Michael points at a grouping of trees. When we stumble closer, I see a tree that's bowed to the ground to form an arc. Just like the one earlier, a glow illuminates the space between the ground and the trunk.

Static electricity zips around us. "It's a portal, right?"

"Yes." Michael sounds relieved. "Now we step through."

My palms sweat. "Where will it take us?"

"To Keleusma."

CHAPTER FIVE

Light ripples around us. This is different than shifting. When you shift, it feels like your lungs want to burst out of your mouth. It's uncomfortable. Almost torturous. Whereas walking through a portal brings on the sensation of traveling in a high-speed convertible with the top down. I can't wipe the smile off my face. I want to laugh. A bubbly feeling tickles my stomach, like I've drunk too much pop. After a few moments, the brightness fades away and we're bathed in a pink-orange splash of setting sun.

We stand in front of a large, old warehouse. The roof sags and spiraling graffiti paints the walls. Swallows have made a nest in the base of a broken lamppost. The surface of a nearby lake is crusted with sprawling algae. A dank, marshy smell fills the air. Foot tall weeds shimmy through cracks in the concrete walkway.

This is the place Michael mentioned with such reverent awe? Maybe it's like the leadings, and I can't see what it really looks like yet. But Michael sidesteps a pile of crushed cans, so clearly he can see them. He winces with every movement. Most of his weight presses against my shoulder. I won't be able to support him much longer.

I tighten my hold on him. "Malfunctioning portal?"

"Naw, this is Keleusma. We're here." He grits his teeth, making the muscles in his jaw form a grim line.

My nose wrinkles. "I expected something, I don't know, a little ... grander."

He raps on the door. "We can't afford the Norms getting curious. Everything about the outside repels them. Remember, they see what they want to see."

With a lurch, the front door swings wide open, and I gasp. Inside, this could be the lobby of a five-star resort. A two story waterfall crashes onto a catacomb of stones in the center. The mammoth room is full of plush carpeting and richly upholstered couches. People scurry across the expanse.

Despite his pain, Michael smirks. "Welcome to our sanctuary, Gabby."

I help him over the threshold. The door shuts behind us. I'm struck with a crisp smell of citrus and mint. Do they have it pumped through the air? I peek around for vents. "What is this place?"

"It's where we train, relax, learn. Some Shifters even live here."

A wispy girl with long blonde hair, alabaster skin, and enormous china-blue eyes jogs toward us. "Michael? I was afraid you'd never return. Oh, goodness, you're hurt." Sidling up to his free side, she eases him from my grasp. "Your back looks terrible! You must be in so much pain."

Michael grimaces at the girl. "Don't go into mama hen mode on me, Lark. I'll live."

Her eyes grow wider, which I honestly didn't think was possible. "I'm taking you to the health center this instant. And I'm not going to listen to any arguments otherwise." She pouts. Her cheerleader voice is already nettling my nerves.

I stand behind them, my fingers knit together. What am I supposed to do? I scan the room. Everyone has stopped what they are doing to stare at me. Some have their brows drawn together. Others appear to be holding their breath. My gaze plunges to the ground. I'm probably just being sensitive. They don't even know me. Most likely, they're shocked to see Michael injured. And if they have a thought about me, it's probably how ridiculous I am for letting Michael get hurt. Besides, how many Shifters are there in the world? Certainly they can't know every single one of them. They can't know I'm new. Can they?

Michael and the blonde have continued walking down the corridor. Squaring my shoulders, I hurry after them. The toe of my shoe skids on the polished tiles in the hallway. Momentum tips me forward, and I tumble onto the floor. My knee burns. Shoving my bangs out of the way, I peek upward and everyone's gawking. Well, everyone but Michael and the girl. They're still hobbling down the hall together.

Like I don't matter.

No one offers me a hand up or asks if I'm okay.

Fine. I shove to my feet and thrust my hands out, palms-up. "Show's over, folks."

Groups of people part for me, like they don't want me to touch them. Seriously, do I smell? I casually lean my nose to catch a whiff of myself. Not my worst. I jog faster after my errant Obi-Wan.

Ahead of me, Michael leans and says something to the blonde. He must mention me, because she stills and turns, as if seeing me for the first time. She blinks repeatedly.

Her mouth drops open. "I don't believe it. I mean, people have been whispering for years. But I always figured it was just talk."

Michael sends an encouraging chin nod my way. "You need to come with us. Since you're new, the medics will want to run tests on you." He squints. "When'd you get the shiner on your knee?"

Oh. When you were busy flirting with the size-zero blonde.

But then my brain clamps onto something he said. Tests? I swallow hard and look at the girl—who hasn't closed her mouth yet. "Hi, I'm—"

"I know who you are," she whispers. Her eyes are still bugging out.

"Yeah, that seems to be going around. Now if only someone would tell me why." I give Michael an *is-she-from-the-loony-bin* look, and he nudges her back to attention.

She closes her eyes, and shakes her head like she's shooing away mosquitos. Then she looks right at me. "I'm Lark Anderson. Pleasure to meet you."

"Medical ward?" Michael grunts.

We tread down a hallway in awkward silence. At least to me it's awkward. I want to ask Michael why people are staring. Why do they stop talking when I walk past? But I'm not going to open my lips until I have a better feel for the Lark situation.

Keleusma sprawls in every direction. The exterior of the warehouse must be a trick of the mind. On my left, we pass a gym. A few people run on a wide track, and others lift weights. Loud clangs resound as two men in the center wield swords against each other. Are those real? They sure sound legit. Will I have to learn that? I scrub my sweaty palms over my thighs.

The pungent aroma of garlic trickles from the westward-facing hallway. A cafeteria? My mouth waters and my stomach grumbles. This morning's charred pancakes are only a memory. What will Dad do for dinner? A lump the size of Russia bobs in my throat.

When we turn the corner, the wide doors of a horse arena are open. A petite, red-headed woman rides a giant, spotted Clydesdale. Sand splatters with each hoof fall. The woman takes the beast over an impressive jump. On the far end of the enclosure, a boy about my age guides two fierce-looking black horses harnessed to a carriage.

I've been rubbernecking again, so I jog around another bend and catch up with Michael and Lark. Lark presses an orange button on the wall, and an automatic door whispers open. A strong bleach smell and something antiseptic stings my nostrils. For a moment I can pretend I'm back in my time, because it looks like any other hospital. People in scrubs descend upon Michael.

Lark launches into a string of questions as she flaps around Michael's attendants. "You can heal him, right? It hasn't been too long, has it? He won't scar, will he?"

A bushy-haired nurse stops me before I can follow them. "A new one? Well now, why aren't the Trainers following protocol? They're not supposed to send you here unaccompanied."

Lark breezes over. "Sandra, it's not what you think." She pats my arm. "This one's a special case. Fetch Darnell for me, will you?"

Okay, if I was the nurse, I'd ignore or argue with a teenaged girl, but she doesn't. With a nod, Sandra leaves. Lark gestures for me to follow her to one of the exam tables along the far wall, but I hesitate. The room is large, and Michael's at the far end surrounded by a hive of medical staff and machines.

Lark squeezes my hand. "Michael says you're safe. So I'll help you. Take a seat over there, and I'll be right back." She points to an exam table. The crackling paper covering the seat is the same you'd find in any doctor's office back home. For some reason, that little thing calms me, so I hop up.

My feet dangle off the floor. I examine my shoes and chew on the edge of my lip. I've felt alone before—abandoned even—but never so out of place. What if I never belong here? Do I even want to? There has to be a way to get home. My dad might not be much, but at least he cares about me.

I fist my hands. I *will* get back home. No matter what, or who, stands in my way.

An olive-skinned man dressed in white strolls through the doorway and zeros in on me. The look in his eyes makes goose flesh break out along my neck. "I'm Darnell." Bright lights on the ceiling reflect off his shaved head. A pace away, he crosses his arms over an Arnold Schwarzenegger sized chest. "My, my, Gabriella Creed. We'd about lost hope that you'd ever show your face in these parts."

I lick my lips. "You've heard of me? How come everyone seems to know who I am?"

He reaches for my arm, his fingers pressing to find my pulse. "We've heard rumors about you for seventeen years. Mostly speculation. My dear, your arrival will be the talk of the year."

Funny, it feels more like I freak them out.

I jerk my hand away from him. "I want someone to give me answers."

"We all learn things ... in time." He presses his thick lips together and shakes his head. "I certainly don't have all the answers you're looking for. But you will, when the time comes for you to need them." Darnell yanks at a drawer built into the wall and pulls out a gray tube. "You skinned your knee pretty good there."

The way he talks is ... off. Sometimes he talks normally, and sometimes he sounds like someone from a period drama. I can't explain it. But I noticed it with Michael and even Lark. All three of them use words and phrases that I'd never say. Maybe their speech becomes mixed up—lost in time just like they are.

I glare at him. "Yeah, funny, I got that a few minutes ago and not one person stopped to help me. A great bunch of good Samaritans you've got here."

He lifts my hand and squeezes goop into my palm. The blister on my hand from putting out the fire on Michael's back disappears. My vision snaps back to Darnell's face. "What just happened?"

"Put the rest on your knee."

I obey, and immediately my skin begins to heal. My jaw drops open. "Tell me you just saw that happen?"

Darnell grins as he replaces the cap on the tube. "I'm sorry people are being standoffish. You'll have to give them time. This is all new for them."

"Yeah, me too." Understatement of the year.

He reaches for an instrument on the counter. It looks like a TV remote control, except its white. Without asking permission, he presses the contraption against the skin on my thigh. A sharp pain lances through my leg and I yelp, trying to squirm away. But Darnell's faster than me and his enormous other hand holds me still.

"Stop!" I shove on his arm. "What are you—"

"Only one second more. I'm just taking your health readings. Making sure everything's okay in your body. There now." He lifts the white remote away and studies the small screen.

My skin shows no sign of being pricked, no blood, but it kills like he stabbed me. I rub my thigh. "Is it supposed to hurt like getting a million bee stings at the same time?"

"Yes." Darnell doesn't take his eyes from the screen.

"Well then, I guess it works." I curl my toes inside my shoe, making sure he didn't cause nerve damage.

Darnell purses his lips. His fingers furiously press buttons.

I crane my neck to see the screen, trying to think of something to say that will crack his serious exterior. Usually, if you can get someone to smile, that's one step away from getting them to spill the truth. Loose lips and laugher go hand-in-hand. "So tell me like it is, Doc, will I live?"

He stows the device in his back pocket and his coffee-bean eyes lock with mine. "Yes."

"Then why do you look worried? Is something wrong with me?"

"Not wrong. *Different*." He fishes a stethoscope out of a black bag on the counter and places the cool metal against my back. "Deep breath. Okay, let it out."

He's probably going to say I need heart medicine. I'll have to convince him my heart only started racing recently. Like, within the last day. "What do you mean, different?" I glance over my shoulder, trying to judge if he's kidding.

Darnell steps back in front of me. "You're clear to shift, if that's your concern. As for anything else, you'll have to ask The Elders."

If there is someone bigger than Darnell, I'm not sure I want to meet them. I gulp. "What was that contraption you used? I've never seen anything like it."

"That's because it's from after your time. From my time."

I rub my palms back and forth against the fabric of my shorts. The movement serves to ground me. I'm here. I'm real. "The future?"

He scratches his neck. "To us, isn't everything the future? It's all relative."

"Could I be sent there? To your time?"

"In theory, yes, but I don't think you will be."

"Why not?"

Darnell tilts his head. "It's the same reason why you won't shift to another country's history."

Okay. Seriously. He may be a doctor and all, but getting an answer out of him is about as easy as explaining algebra to a toddler.

"Which is?" I bite my tongue before tacking a rude comment on after the question.

"Because Nicholas won't shift you into a situation you can't handle. He's not like that."

"I don't understand how this whole time thing works." I shrug.

"You have to forget thinking about time in a chronological sense. That's the pure human way of seeing things. You're no longer a Norm. See, for us, there is no before and after. There is only a start and a beginning."

"Not tracking."

Darnell tugs a pen from his pocket. "Okay. There is the tip of a pen and the clicker." Holding the pen a foot before my eyes, he taps each side as he speaks. "But say you are some of the ink, well then that's the only part of the pen you know exists. Ink doesn't know what the outside of the pen looks like. It only knows that it's surrounded by more ink. But for me, holding this pen, I can see all of it at the same time. Every inch of the pen. I can look at it from every angle and see each part together. That's how it is for us with time. A Norm is ink—their time *is* reality. It's all they know exists. They can't comprehend the big picture."

My head starts to throb again. Maybe I should ask him for aspirin. "But we can."

"No."

I glower. "You just said—"

"We can't, but Nicholas can. He's outside of time. He sees the big picture."

"That doesn't seem fair. Why him? What makes him so special?"

He folds his arms across his chest. "Nicholas has always been outside of time. We trust him."

"That seems like a bit much to risk your life on."

Darnell sighs. "I do what he tells me to."

I cross my arms. "Yeah? And what does Nicholas tell you to do?"

He raises an eyebrow. "Stay in Keleusma and heal people."

I decide to push my luck. Hopefully muscle-man won't clock me in front of so many witnesses. "How convenient. You get to live at the Ritz while people like Michael are out there risking their lives. Do you know how hard it is for him? He gets tossed somewhere and he has to figure out what to do, and who to save. You're telling me there are Shifters that don't have to do that? Who get off easy?"

"Watch your attitude, Gabriella." He captures me in a fierce stare. "Each of us has a calling to fulfill. Not one is greater than the other. Some of us spend our entire existence in Keleusma. Others shift through time. You need to respect each Shifter's path." Darnell jams his hands into his pockets. "Stay here until someone comes for you."

When he leaves, my gaze instinctively travels back Michael-way. They have him back in a shirt. He's sitting in a chair, drinking something. He willingly holds out his arm. A member of the medical team puts a white remote to his forearm. Michael doesn't even flinch.

"He was the youngest person to ever shift, you know." Lark's voice makes me jolt. "Not even on the right day."

I face her. Has she seen me studying Michael? Playing dumb might be my best option. "Who?"

"Oh, the coy act won't work on me." She beams. "Michael Pace, of course. He first shifted here when he was eleven. Can you imagine?"

"Is that not normal?"

"Not at all. Most people shift between their fifteenth and eighteenth birthdays, but not eleven. That's unheard of."

I peek at Michael, and he's looking at me. I look down, suddenly nervous. "He must have been terrified."

"Who knows?" She flips honey-colored hair over her shoulder. "I can't imagine Michael afraid, but then, I've only known him for two years."

"When did you shift?"

"When I turned sixteen."

I scoot forward on the table, licking my lips. "How did you make it happen?"

"You mean the first time? Don't you know?"

I shake my head.

"You have a chance to shift on each of your birthdays. When someone acknowledges your birthday, then it either happens or it doesn't. I was so disappointed on my fifteenth birthday when I wasn't pulled."

"So you knew it would happen?"

"Of course!" She leans closer. "You didn't?"

"No," I whisper.

Lark rocks back on the edge of her feet. "Wait, your dad didn't tell you?"

I don't answer, and Lark whistles long and low.

Every birthday washes through my mind. Dad makes pancakes, but never says happy birthday. I cried myself to sleep each year, hating the day that marked my birth. The truth hits my gut like a sucker punch. He ignored my birthday because he loved me. He knew, and didn't want this for me. Dad was protecting me.

My throat feels itchy, tight. My vision starts to blur. "What would happen if no one acknowledged your birthday and you passed eighteen?"

Lark twirls a piece of flaxen hair around her finger. "I don't think you'd ever become a Shifter. But that's nonsense, it would never happen."

I work my bottom lip between my teeth. "I guess not."

She hands me a small bag. "I brought you clothes. Go ahead and put them on."

"In front of everyone? No way."

"You're funny." Lark laughs, pointing at a door to my right. "Bathroom's right there."

Closed away from everyone, I grab the cool edge of the sink and let the chill seep into my bones. "This is real," I whisper to my reflection. "Just play their game, follow their rules, and find a loophole home." I change out of my old clothes and pull on the set Lark gave me. Close-fitting, dark jeans and a black V-neck shirt. I examine the fabric under the light. It feels like the same cotton blends we wear in my time.

With a fortifying gulp of air, I open the door.

Lark's there. "Looks like a good fit."

"Sure." At least I'll blend with everyone else. No more Where's Waldo for me.

She nudges my side. "Michael's watching you like a hawk."

Without thinking, I glance back at him. Sure enough, he's looking at me. He lifts his glass in a salute, smiles, and downs it.

My cheeks blaze as I remember thinking he was calling me honey. "Will he be okay? The burn was awful."

"It's probably only a scar now. If you got him here fast enough, it's healed. One more adventure story for him to add to his list." Lark winks at me. "He's cute, isn't he?"

"I guess so." My fingers bite the fabric on the exam table.

"Too bad he's off limits."

CHAPTER SIX

"Off limits?" I hate the squeak in my voice.

She shrugs. "Sometimes I really do hate the Pairing. But hey, rules are rules. Besides, I have Eddie waiting back home, so I have nothing to be upset about." Lark hides a giggle behind her hand.

Pairing? Something cold fists around my heart and squeezes. I glance over to Michael. He meets my eyes, holds up a finger, mouths "*one minute*," and turns to talk to a doctor.

Lark pokes me. "You do have a Pairing, don't you? I wouldn't ask since everyone has one, but you're so strange. It makes me wonder."

If these people don't start speaking English.... I swing my feet, drumming them against the table. "Um, sure."

Lark seizes my shoulders and looks me dead in the eye. "You've got to be kidding me. How *green* are you?" She gives me a little shake.

I roll my eyes and wiggle out of her hold. "Well, considering I just learned what a Shifter is less than a day ago, I don't know why you would assume I know everything else."

"Okay! We can solve this." Lark claps once. "Back in your time, is there a boy who has been your friend your whole life? Someone you do everything with. He'd be a guy you have a natural, easy friendship with."

No! No! No! Not here too. A recording plays in my mind. It clicks through every person who has every told me Porter and I will end up together. Shooing the thoughts away, I swallow hard and nod once. "Porter Jensen."

"Ah-ha! Porter is your Pairing."

"Meaning?" But it's obvious. Marriage? To Porter? I inwardly cringe. That would be like marrying a favorite dog or a comfy pair of socks. I can't. I won't.

Lark laughs, her blue eyes sparkling. "You two will get married, of course."

I sit up straighter, not because of the Pairing, but because of what Porter means. He's in my time and it sounds like Lark's saying I get to go back. "Then there's a way home?"

"Sure. You always go to where you're most needed, so as long as there's something to pull you back home, you will. A Pairing guarantees that. You're meant to be together. It's been destined since before you were born."

"I don't believe in stuff like that." I catch Michael's gaze, and he sends a wink my way. For some reason, it makes me feel off-balance and dizzy, like the beginning of the flu. Does he have a Pairing?

"It doesn't matter what you believe. That's how it works. It's the only way for a Shifter to be born. One Shifter plus one human—together make a new Shifter." She shrugs. "Those are the rules."

I slide off the table, landing with a thump on the ground. "Wait. Then is my dad a Shifter too?"

"No, fully human, has to be since we know your mother was a Shifter. The only humans who know about Shifters are the ones we end up marrying, but they are promised by the Seal, which makes them physically unable to tell anyone but their offspring."

The information shudders through me. My gut twists in a knot, and acid burns at the back of my throat. I take a step back. "You're wrong. My mother wasn't a Shifter. She died. There's no way—"

Lark arches an eyebrow, advancing toward me. "What'd she die of? Did you see it happen?"

I thrust out my hands to block her progress. "You're sick! She died in a plane crash. She was so mangled it had to be closed casket. Satisfied?"

"Closed casket?" She taps her foot. "Convenient. Listen, Gabby, your mom was a Shifter. For you to be a Shifter, she had to be one."

"Have you ... did you ever meet her?" My hands shake. I try to hide them behind me. "Is she here?" My gaze instinctively darts to the health center's doors. What if I snatch a glimpse of her? Rosa Maria Creed. Long raven hair bobbing as she fast-walks past. Despite all the years, I'd recognize her from all of Dad's photos.

I raise my chin. I'd grab her, yell at her, and yank her back to Dad.

Maybe hug her too, somewhere in there.

"No. I'm sorry." Lark frowns like she really regrets telling me. "But she was a Shifter. I can promise you that."

"I was just a baby at her funeral, but I've been to her grave."

"All a hoax. I can't believe your dad did it, though." Lark shakes her head. "He should have told you. He's supposed to have trained you in combat, history, debate, horseback riding." She massages her temples. "He's supposed to tell you all about shifting and have you prepared by your fourteenth birthday. It's part of the deal, when someone falls in love with a Shifter."

"Are you saying I'm not human?"

"No, you are. You're just a Shifter and your dad, we call him a Norm. The Norms of each time just go through their appointed lifespan and do whatever it is they need to accomplish. The Shifters, we get pulled through time to wherever we're needed. Norms don't have that power—most don't even know it exists."

I'm about to say something, but my voice sticks because two gigantic men in teal uniforms burst through the health center's main doors. They march toward me. Both look bulldog-mad. My gaze scours the room, trying to find a route of escape. Who are they? What could they possibly want? I glare at Lark. Has she been stalling me this whole time? Note to self, stop trusting people.

The uniformed man with the better tan nods at me. "Gabriella Creed."

I could pretend not to speak the language, but Lark-the-super-rat would most likely blow my cover.

"That's me." I shuffle to get away. My back slams into the high counter, sending medical equipment crashing to the ground. Green liquid pools from a shattered glass bowl, and a metal instrument rattles against the tile. Everyone in the room stills, turns. One of the Teal Team grabs my arm, his fingers digging clear to my bones. I wince and attempt to wiggle free.

"Hey!" Michael jostles away from his nurses and crosses the room. "Let go of her!"

"Not your fight, Pace. Back down." Number two of the Teal Team pushes Michael away.

I thrash against my captor. "Leave Michael alone! He's hurt."

Michael pries the man's hand from the neck of his shirt. His face is red. He takes two deep breaths. "Since I'm her trainer, this is my fight."

"Not when it deals with the Creed bloodline, it isn't."

Thug Number One holds my wrists tighter than any handcuffs could. Fighting a whimper, I move to land a heel into his foot like I did to Michael when I first met him, but my captor simply laughs.

"Nice try, little girl." He blocks my foot with his leg and crushes me to the ground before I can make a noise. Air spills from my lungs in a loud whoosh. My chin glances off the tile. He slams a mammoth hand down on my upper back, hard. Chiropractics might be in his future.

Michael inches closer, his hands up in a gesture of surrender. "Seriously. Jason, Ben, no reason for force. She's scared. She doesn't know what's going on."

His voice takes on a pleading tone. A look comes into his warm chocolate eyes, like he's talking to a spooked horse, calming. "Hey, Gabby, you're not going to struggle anymore, right?" He takes a few more cautious steps forward, passing the second thug. "Go ahead and let her up. You guys can hold me responsible if she does something." Michael crouches beside me, his hand extended. "Take my hand. I promise I'll stay beside you. No matter what, okay? You're safe."

My teal captor allows me to sit up. I scrub my hand over my face, rubbing where the tile floor made my cheek cold. "Where are they taking me?" I look to Michael. He turns with his eyebrows raised to the tanner thug.

"The Elders," says the man who I think is named Ben.

Michael smiles at me, offering his hand again. "I was going to take you to The Elders anyway. We might as well go with them. Don't need them grumpier than they already are, right, honey?"

"Don't call me that." Teasing me in my moment of need!

"You didn't seem to mind before." Mirth is written in the quirk of his lips.

I scowl at him. His barbing doesn't warrant an answer. Still, I slip my hand into his, and he helps me gain my feet. Something scuffs on the floor behind me, and I lurch toward Michael for safety, my free hand fisting into his shirt.

"It's just Lark," he whispers.

One of the men in teal levels a menacing stare in her direction. "Don't know if you should come. What will your father say?"

Lark juts out her chin. "Why don't we go and see."

"Suit yourself," the teal men mutter in unison.

With a uniformed man on either side, we're ushered out of the health center and into the hallway. A hush still covers the room, every eye on us.

Michael tugs my hand. "Don't worry."

My tone is low. "I'm getting the feeling this isn't normal."

He shakes his head, his eyes close for a brief moment, and he smiles. "Nothing about you is normal. Trust me."

I gulp. I'm not sure if it's the possible terror of whatever The Elders will do to me, or if it's the shocking heat surging through my body—starting exactly where Michael grasps my hand. *Grow up.* I should be more concerned about my possible future demise. But the fact that this guy willingly walks beside me into a situation that could get him into trouble, fills my senses.

His voice shatters my scattered thoughts. "Did you hear me?"

Busted.

"Um, sorry ... thinking about death."

He squeezes my hand. "It'll all be okay, you'll see."

"Of course it will be." Lark elbows in. "You're with me. It's not like my dad's going to do something to you in front of me."

I arch my brow. Based on the force of the Teal Team, I'm guessing The Elders have a lot of power around here. "Can't he just order you out of the room?"

"Well, yes, but—" Lark plows right into one of the uniformed men's backs. "Oh, we're here."

I wish I'd memorized the turns we took to get here. Something tells me I'm not being hauled to The Elders for tea and cookies. How can I have any hope of escape if I don't know where I'm going? I dig my nails into the back of Michael's hand, willing him not to leave me.

A man in a long dark robe, like the ones worn at graduations, stands near an ornate wooden door. He wears a strange expression, regretful, like he just skinned a puppy. With a sigh, he unlocks the large, intricately carved door and pushes it open for us.

If I thought the entrance of Keleusma passed for a four-star resort, this chamber must be where the millionaires vacation. The crimson chairs in the room are opulent to the point of being ridiculous. The armrests seem to be fashioned from gold. We inch across carpeting that might as well be made of grass. I hear trickling, the sound of a steady river. Three giant rainbow-feathered birds soar in a circle near the glass ceiling. Outside, the dying sun bleeds into the coming night.

"Bring her forward," a distant voice booms. That's when I notice the long desk on the far side of the room. Four people sit behind the polished surface, each resting their chin in their hands, measuring me as I walk forward. My knees are shaking, but I don't want them to notice. If my father taught me one thing, it's not to let anyone push me around. Ever.

With that though, I release Michael's hand and square my shoulders.

Michael glances at me, questioning, but I look away. How long have I taken care of myself? I don't need him. What I need to do is stop depending on him. On anyone. That only brings trouble, disappointment. Dad depended on Mom once, didn't he? Look where that got him.

It doesn't matter, anyway. The over-muscled members of the Teal Team marshal Lark and Michael off to the side, while I'm left front and center.

Two women with dark corkscrew-curly hair sit side by side. Their facial structure matches perfectly, their dark eyebrows and pale skin, identical. Twins? Beside them is a stern-looking man with pale hair and piercing blue eyes. The final person is a rumpled, older woman. Her gray hair is a fuzzy crown. She's the only one smiling. I imagine her to be the kind of lady with hordes of feral cats roaming her home.

The blond man, who I assume is Lark's father, clears his throat. "What brings you to us, Gabriella?"

"Your muscle squad, sir." I jut my thumb toward them.

His pale lips form a grim line. "I meant, your pull, my dear. We knew it was your birthday. We prepared Keleusma for your arrival as we have the last three years, but you didn't show. Picture our surprise when we discovered you shifted to another time. Now, what I need you to tell me is, how did you do it?"

I take a step closer. "I don't know. I don't know anything."

"I don't believe her," hisses one of the twins.

Lark's father holds up a hand to silence her. "It would behoove you to be honest, Gabriella. Tell me, child, are you, or are you not, working for your mother?"

Air suctions from my lungs. My hands fumble together. "My mother is dead."

"Lies," mutters the other twin. They remind me of snakes.

I ball up my hands at my side. "She *is* dead."

The man smirks as he jots something onto the tablet in front of him. "Of course, dear. Now, tell me, have you heard from Erik at all? It's okay to be honest. No harm will come to you."

Erik? I try to go through all the information I've learned in the past day, but don't remember hearing the name. "I don't even know who that is."

Lark's father pins me with an icy stare. "I see. And what about Nicholas? Have you talked to him?"

"No. I never even heard of Nicholas until a few minutes ago."

"So." Lark's father taps his pen against the table. "When you risked the lives of two Shifters to save that little girl from the bombing on Wall Street, you did that without direction?"

Only under the direction of what is right. I narrow my eyes at him. "I guess so. Yes."

He curses, banging his fist on the table. The four glasses of water rattle. "You foolish child!"

"Father." Lark's voice breaks in. "She didn't realize. How can we expect her to know what no one ever told her? It's not fair to hold her to the same standard as someone who grew up knowing all our rules."

Her father glowers at her, and his cheeks burn red. “Why are you here? Remove my daughter.” He beckons the Teal Team. They grasp Lark by both arms and show her out of the room. I glance at Michael, steady Michael. He smiles, but it doesn’t meet his eyes.

My nails dig into my palms. I know my knuckles are growing white. “The little girl would have died if I didn’t do something.”

Lark’s father waves his hand, dismissing my words. “That’s of no consequence. If she wasn’t in the plan, then she’s not worth risking a life to save. Understood?”

I stalk toward the table. All four Elders sit up straighter. “No, actually, I don’t understand. Who are you to make that call? How can you say one life is worth more than another?”

“You have to follow what we say. The rules were made for the good of all Shifters. If you aren’t led to save someone, you don’t. It’s that easy.” He grinds his teeth, growling more than speaking.

I rest my hands on the edge of their table, lean forward. “Well, I disagree.”

Both of the twins shudder.

“She’s dangerous.”

“She’ll ruin us all.”

Lark’s father points at Michael. “Come here, son. Let’s have her see what her emotional whims allowed to happen.”

He’s whispering something to the twins while Michael makes his way to my side. The twins spring to their feet and bound around the desk. They turn Michael around, and wrench his shirt up so I can see his skin. An ugly scar the shape of Pangea mars half of his back. The sight of it makes my stomach flip. Why didn't they heal him completely? Without thinking, I reach to touch the scar, but I stop myself before contact. I let my hand fall to my side. "It's still there."

"Still there." Michael meets my eyes over his shoulder.

"Does it...?" I look down at my shoes. "Does it hurt?"

Michael gently tugs his shirt free of the twins and flattens the fabric over his back again. He turns away from them and steps closer to me. "It's a scar. I'll always have it. But it doesn't hurt."

"Oh, Michael. I'm so sorry, when we were at the health center, I thought—"

"I'm fine. It's nothing." He lowers his voice. "It was worth it."

The cat lady sighs. "I like her."

But Lark's father speaks over her. "You didn't get him back to Keleusma quickly enough. He's damaged forever because of your rash actions." He stands. "I hope this helps you understand our decision."

Michael angles his body in front of mine. "What decision?"

The Elder grins for the first time, light flickering off his wolf-like fangs. "Ben, Jason—seize her."

CHAPTER SEVEN

Florescent light ekes through the slats at the top of the cell. What I hope is water drips from a leak in the ceiling. The beat of it landing on the ground drives me batty. Uneven wood nips the palms of my hands. I pound on the door anyway.

"You can't keep me here! This isn't fair! Let me out!" I yell until my throat goes hoarse. No one answers. No one's going to. Big waste of energy. I prowl the tiny room, trailing my fingers against the icy walls, hoping to find a crack, a blemish, somewhere to tunnel. It could happen. Edmond Dantes used a spoon to dig his way out in *The Count of Monte Cristo.* Sure, it took him fourteen years, he had a crazy old man helping him, and he was burrowing to get back into a world full of people who betrayed him.

Minus the old man, my situation is not that much different, really.

At least Edmond's father didn't lie to him about his mother's death.

Time has become useless in this dark hole. Ten minutes may have passed, or two days. I don't know. Anxiety chased hunger out the door a long time ago.

As if they're a group of toddlers that can't be trusted, I yank my thoughts close. They can't wander. If they don't wander, I won't be able to contemplate what The Elders plan to do to me. Why they hate me.

I crumple against the wall and slide until I'm on the ground, knees tucked close to my chest. I shiver as the cement leeches all my heat away. Okay, maybe there's a fear factor there too. With my cheek resting on my leg, I zone out with my gaze on the wall. What did I ever do to deserve this? Where is their leader—this Nicholas—who supposedly moves the Shifters through time like puppets? Is he angry with me too? Or is he just a made-up pawn? Powerless. Fake.

No different than me.

"Where are you, huh?" I pop to my feet. "Oh, great, mighty ruler." Sarcasm drips from my lips. "You like this, don't you? Making me become a crazy woman. Talking to myself. Thinking you can hear. Thinking you're *real.* Well, you're not." I prowl the small area like a lion in a zoo enclosure. "If you were, I sure wouldn't be locked here. And men like Lark's dad wouldn't have power. And people like Michael wouldn't get hurt. But you can't do anything. You're a crutch, a phantom. Someone to blame problems on."

I fall silent when metal scratches against metal. Someone's unlocking the door. I bite my lip. Pounce on them? Or cower in the corner? I choose the middle-of-the-road approach, standing in the center of the room, a deep breath locked inside my lungs. Self-defense lessons flood into my mind. Not that I know where to run if I get out of here.

A young, spindly man with circle, wire-rimmed glasses ambles into my cell, food tray in hand. Spices and the smell of cooked meat accompany him, filling the small area. The door closes, and clicks. Locked.

"Who were you talking to?" He grins at me. Maybe he's twenty-five, thirty?

My arms fold over my chest. "Who are you?"

"My name's Eugene." He tries to hand me the tray. Warmth curls from a bowl of chili. My mouth salivates. Everything in me screams to devour the food, but what if Lark's father sent him? What if it's poisoned and makes me die, foaming at the mouth? Chili wouldn't rank first on my list of choices for a last meal.

I shove the tray back at him. "Well, *Eugene*, you can tell them to stuff it until they let me out of here."

"A hunger strike won't help you accomplish much besides a grumbling stomach. Maybe a headache if you hold out long enough, but that's about it. It sure won't get you out of here." He shrugs. "If it means anything, I promise I'm one of the good guys. At least, I mean, I'm on your side."

"My side? And tell me, what battle are we supposedly fighting?"

His eyebrows dart up his forehead. "Good and evil. The fate of mankind."

Great, just great. What exactly does this man think I'm going to do for a bowl of chili?

I rock back on my heels. "Riiight, so nothing all that important."

He shakes his head. "What matters is, I think you're part of the right team, whether you understand that yet or not." He smiles, and it's so soft and kind and reminds me of my dad when he's apologizing. Something large knots in my throat and I try to swallow it down.

How can he say such things about me? As if he knows my deepest desire to be special ... to matter. But it's nice to be believed in, even if the hope is false.

Hunger overtakes reason, and I scoop up the generous slab of cornbread and take a bite. I let the chunks melt in my mouth, linger on my tongue. Delicious buttery heaven.

Eugene chuckles at my eagerness. He motions me toward a concrete slab built into the wall, which makes a sort of bench. I guess that's where I'm destined to sleep tonight. No blankets or pillow provided. These Shifters sure are pleasant people. When we sit, Eugene slides the tray onto my lap. I dig into the chili and it warms me momentarily. After a few bites, I inch to the very edge to put the most distance between us.

Resting his elbows on his knees, Eugene rubs his hands together. His glasses are so smudged that I doubt his ability to see through them at all. Without looking at me, he says, "He can handle being yelled at, railed against. It doesn't bother him."

"Who?" I mutter around a mess of beans.

"Nicholas."

"It's hard to yell at someone you don't believe in." I wipe my mouth with the napkin and throw the rest of the cornbread into the bowl of chili.

Eugene waggles his finger at me, good-naturedly. "Keep telling yourself that. Maybe if you say it enough, you might even start to think that. But I doubt it. Besides, Nicholas hearing doesn't depend on your belief. Not yet."

I don't want to talk about whoever Nicholas is. If he has something to do with The Elders and this situation I'm in, he clearly has it out for me too. "So who are you, in the big picture of Shifters? Kitchen boy?"

"Naw, more like computer whiz." Eugene yanks his glasses from his face. One side catches on his ear, and he has to pull again. Finally off, he rubs them on the tail of his shirt and puts the glasses back on. If it's even possible, they look dirtier.

Finished, I set the tray on the ground. "Let me guess, you did something awful and your punishment was to bring me dinner."

His voice takes on the tone of a game show announcer. "Oh no, folks. It looks like Contestant One loses the prize. Shame too, it was an all-inclusive trip to the Bahamas." Eugene gestures to a fake audience. "Should we give her another try?"

"How about you just tell me?"

"It's so much less fun, but if you insist." His face drops back into a solemn expression. "It's simple. I'm here because I wanted to meet you. I asked for the honor."

I inch to face him, my eyes narrowing. "But you don't even know me."

Eugene leans back, crosses his ankles. "You're right, but I want to."

"Why?"

"Because, Gabriella, I believe in you."

"That's crazy. Besides, there's nothing worth believing in here." I shoot to my feet and pace away.

He shakes his head so hard I fear for the health of his brain. "That's not how I see it."

I lean back against the wall. "Yeah, well enlighten me, computer whiz."

"Some of them think you're dangerous. The Elders, and some of the others too."

I make a show of glancing around the cell. "Yeah, I picked up on that."

He shuffles his feet. "Let me talk. It's just because you present something new, something they can't explain away. I happen to think that doesn't necessarily make you bad. There are a lot of us who feel the same way. I saw Darnell in the mess hall. He's not supposed to, but he showed me your blood reading. You're different, Gabriella. Special."

"But I'm not."

He leans forward. "You are."

"Why me?" I take a step closer. "What's wrong with me?"

"Nothing's wrong. You were created this way. Born to accomplish something out of the ordinary. That scares people, terrifies them. But not everyone. There's a group—a fraction of us that support you." Eugene's voice is low.

Supports me? This is starting to sound like war. Icy terror skitters across my spine. I open my mouth to speak, but the words stick in my mouth, because my cell door swings open again. What now? Have they come for Eugene? Angry at him for bringing me food? I'm expecting a Teal Team guard, but instead, marvelously, there stands Michael.

A sense of calm blankets my heart.

I can't explain it, but we're like North and South ends of a magnet. Instantly attracted. Meant to stick together. The look in his eyes tells me he'll always come for me, no matter what. I don't know why I didn't sense it when we first met. My first instinct now is to lunge at him, toss my arms around his neck, and hug tightly. That, and then admonish my Obi-Wan to never, ever, let me out of his sight again. But my muscles freeze because Michael looks angrier than a bull that sat on a bee. It wouldn't be surprising if he started pawing the ground. Seriously.

The width of his shoulders seems to have grown. He takes up the whole doorway. His dark hair has gone limp, cascading into his eyes. Even still, his glare is unmistakable. Something boils in his chocolate eyes, deep and menacing. Bathed in shadows, he looms like a dark angel—come for vengeance. Michael's intensity would frighten me, if his look was aimed my way. But he's focused on poor, squirming Eugene.

Michael's lip pulls up. "What are *you* doing here?"

I pop to my feet and begin to ramble. “Oh, me? Thanks for asking. There was this creepy meeting with Lark’s dad—who I think has some serious mental issues by the way—and he—”

Michael silences me with a look. His eyebrows are drawn low.

Eugene’s foot nudges the tray on the ground. “I brought her dinner.”

My dark angel folds his arms across his chest. He leans a shoulder against the door frame. “And you’re still here—alone with her—because?”

I hold my tongue this time.

“Because, last time I checked—Keleusma and us Shifters for that matter—are free to do as we want.” For a skinny guy, Eugene can sure puff his chest out when he needs to. He snatches up the tray, and does a sort of an awkward bow to me. “It’s been a pleasure, Miss Creed. Until I see you again. Take care.” Eugene makes a move for the doorway, and Michael steps aside and lets him into the hall.

I wait for the sound of Eugene’s footfall to die before squaring my shoulders toward Michael. He’s not going to get my originally planned warm welcome. Not when he was rude. “Okay, and what was the Mr. Creep act for?”

Michael relaxes his stance and shoots a smile my way. “He’s an odd one. Sorry if he said anything weird to you. When it comes to the technical problems around here, he’s our go-to. Otherwise, Eugene’s known to talk a lot of nonsense.” He takes a step closer. “He didn’t say anything strange, did he?” He takes my elbow in his overly warm hand and gives a squeeze.

Can I trust Michael? A fist tightens in my gut. I jerk out of his touch. “Honestly, everyone here talks in riddles. Present party included.”

“Well, I have something to say that’s perfectly clear.” He grins at me, and for the first time I notice he has a dimple, but just one, on his left cheek.

I work my jaw back and forth. “I’m all intrigued.”

“You’re free, Gabby. Let’s get you out of here and to your new room in the residential wing.”

He doesn’t have to say another word. I bolt to the door. Michael’s boisterous laugh follows me down the hall, and he has to jog to catch up. “Hey, slow down, Trigger, you don’t even know where you’re going.” He lays a protective hand on the small of my back, guiding me to the passageway on the left when I was aimed for the right.

“Let go.” I jerk away from his touch.

He stops walking. “I’ll apologize, if you tell me what I did wrong.”

“Why were you so rude to Eugene? He came and helped me and you didn’t, so—”

“Wow. Well, I’m sorry. I was busy petitioning The Elders on your behalf. I mean, if you’d like to still be in there...”

No wonder. I should have known he was trying to convince them to let me go. I gulp. Now I’m the one who should apologize for being rude. “Thank you. Whatever you did, it worked.”

“Follow me.” He brushes past me and heads down another hallway.

I now have to jog after him to keep up.

He motions toward an elevator and ushers me inside. When the door whooshes shut, he looks my way. “I just asked them to seek guidance from Nicholas. They listened.”

“Funny, I tried to talk to him and heard squat.”

He scans a card over the reader in the elevator. “Maybe you were talking so much you couldn’t hear him.”

“Unlikely.” I shrug. “I take it he doesn’t want me rotting in a cell?”

“Nope.” He leans toward me, and shakes his head. We’re so close inside the elevator. He must have showered since the last time I saw him. Michael smells like pine trees with a touch of peppermint.

I’m suddenly worried that I don’t smell as fresh as he does. I take a step away, and lean against the far wall. “What then?”

“The same thing he wants from all of us. He wants you trained and working. Nicholas is all about taking action on things, not sitting idly by.”

The elevator wobbles to a halt and the doors ease open. I grab Michael’s arm. “Take me to him.”

“To who?”

“To Nicholas. I’m sick of all this second-hand information. I want to talk to him, face to face. I have so many questions.”

He tugs me out of the elevator before the doors slide shut. “You can’t see him. It doesn’t work like that, Gabby.”

“Really? What? Am I not good enough for him?”

"No, it's not like that at all." He pinches the bridge of his nose. "*I've* never seen Nicholas. The Elders have never met him, either. No one has."

"But that's ridiculous." I stop walking, forcing Michael to turn and look at me. "So all these people, this whole place, follows the orders of a man you don't even know."

"Careful, Gabby." His gaze darts up to the ceiling, scans as if he's searching for something, then lands back on my face. "It's called trust. You should try it some time." Michael swings around and punches a code into a keypad on the wall. A door whispers open.

There are groups of people walking in a large corridor. We can't continue our conversation without being overheard, and something tells me I don't want to be heard arguing Nicholas's merits, or lack thereof. Unless I want a one-way ticket back to that cell. No thank you.

"Your room is just this way. Girls ward, number 309." Michael withdraws a purple keycard from his back pocket and hands it to me. "Go ahead. Use it."

"Are you allowed here?"

"Sure. Because of the Pairing, they aren't too strict about keeping us out of each other's residential area. There isn't much to worry about there."

"Right. Of course." I wave the card in front of a black box on the wall. There's a clicking sound, and then the door rolls open to reveal a spacious bedroom with a small sitting area. My first thought is that the cat-lady Elder must have decorated the space. The bedspread is an eye-piercing orange, complete with flashy pink pillows. Avocado green walls scream to be repainted, and a loud floral-print couch does nothing to improve the look. An overpowering scent of roses accosts my nose.

Michael steps in behind me. "Wow, sorry. The last girl who had this room grew up in the seventies. She had a flare for the eccentric. I'm sure you could change it if you want."

I finger a string of beads hanging in a curtain from the ceiling. "What happened to her?"

He glances at me over his shoulder as he walks to a ledge on the wall. At first, he doesn't say anything, just traces his fingers over the wooden shelf, gathering dust. With a long blow of air, he sends dust moats waltzing across my new room. Then he turns back to me.

"She died, Gabby. People die."

I take a step in his direction. "Of old age. Something like that?"

"No. Cathy was twenty, I think. She died shifting. Last we heard she was in the midst of a typhoid outbreak. It happens. That's why the Elders cautioned you."

"I'm so sorry about your back." The words spill out before I can rein them in.

Michael shakes his head, inching closer. "I didn't mean—"

I lick my lips. "It was my fault. I should have listened to you."

"You saved a child's life," he says. Michael's close enough to smell again, fresh like the sunshine splashed outdoors. Using one finger, he tucks a chunk of bangs behind my ear. His light touch sets loose an army of traitorous butterflies, beating their wings against my stomach.

I have to lean closer to hear him as he lowers his voice. "And when I look at that scar, or feel it pull, it'll only make me think of you."

Um, lungs—take a breath already. "Is that a good thing?"

His dimple comes back out to play. "Very good. Sleep now, Gabby." He takes a step toward the open doorway.

I fight the urge to grab his arm. Yank him back. He's the closest thing to home right now. "You can't just leave. What happens in the morning? Will you come for me?"

He smiles, and his eyes are only half open. "I'll see you in the morning." Michael strolls back to the hallway, but at the last second, he turns and points to the ledge on the wall.

I notice a piece of paper that wasn't there before. I'm already pacing toward the wall when I hear the door close. Michael's gone, and somehow the room feels colder. Trepidation nibbles on my heart as I unfold the paper and scan the words:

Be careful. Don't ask any more questions. The Elders are watching you.

CHAPTER EIGHT

Loud pounding on the door wakes me with a jolt. I snap up in bed, pulling my covers to my chin like a shield. What now? Did I do something wrong? I can't think of anything. Why would they come for me again?

After Michael left last night, I paced my room. Folded his note and tucked it into my back pocket. I tried to figure out how to work the overly technical shower in the bathroom and failed miserably. In the end, I curled on top of the bed, and sleep tiptoed in quicker than I would have imagined possible.

My eyes dart around the room. There's no place to take cover. Unless you count ducking behind the couch or hiding in the bathroom. Besides, they probably slipped a tracking device under my skin while I slept. The Elders seem the types.

The door opens before I can compose myself.

Lark saunters in, shaking her head as she surveys me, her hands on her hips. "Still in bed. What are we ever going to do with you?"

I glare at her and flip down my covers. "How did you get in? I locked the door."

She waves a black keycard. "Elder's daughter comes with the occasional privilege."

"Well, that's just great." When my feet hit the chilled floor, I snatch them back up. A rug would be a nice touch. An eggplant-colored one would match this wacky room.

Lark wrinkles her nose. "Gross. I can't believe you slept in your clothes."

"It's not like I had a choice." My muscles flex, bracing against the cold as I touch my feet to the ground again.

"You have a closet full of stuff right there." She points at the wall.

The wall is just that, a wall. No door handle, nothing to hint at a closet, just peeling avocado paint.

I tap my finger on my chin. "Are you sure?"

"You're hopeless, completely hopeless. How will you ever figure out what to do when you shift?" Lark strides to the wall and presses her palm to it. A wave of light flickers over her, and a door appears. She pushes it open. "Voila! Plenty of clothes." Her eyebrows are lowered when she turns back around. "Tell me you showered."

I stand. "I wanted to, but I couldn't figure it out."

"Ugh. Swipe your card. There's a slot by the soap tray." She pushes a pillow off the couch and grabs a seat. "Go. I'll wait."

First, I stumble into my walk-in closet. Rows of matching shirts and pants line one side. On the other, there are drawers filled with underwear and pajama-type clothing. I snag a change of clothes and head to the bathroom. She's right. There's a small slot I didn't see before, right under the empty soap tray. I slide my purple door card in.

A touch screen appears on the wall with buttons for different kinds of soap, shampoo, and conditioner. I pick apple blossom, and small bottles appear out of the wall and fill the soap tray. Another button gives me a razor and shaving cream. Lark's waiting, so I try to hurry, but I didn't realize how tight my muscles were and how good the warm water would feel.

I stand there. Eyes closed. As if the water can wash away the deep knots in my back. But it can't. Nothing ever will. Less than two days ago, I stood in my small kitchen with Dad. Can that be right? Will I ever get back home? Tears trickle down my cheeks, mingling with the green shampoo. Hands braced against the wall, I drag humid air into my lungs like a drowning victim. *Get a hold of yourself*! Lark can't hear me. I don't want word getting out that I'm prone to breakdowns. A liability. Weak.

After toweling off, I yank on my clean clothes and braid my wet hair. A few splashes of cold water from the sink helps take away the blotchy hints of crying. I reach for the door, raising my chin. Movies always depict the resilient hostage as the one that survives. The other Shifters need to think I'm strong—indifferent to how horribly I've been treated. It's the only way to find a chink in their armor. The only way I'll get home to Dad, Porter, and Emma. All that matters.

Lark's on her feet when I come back into the room. "Great. Clean. Let's go."

I toss my wad of dirty clothes near the unmade bed, and follow her to the door. A moment before she opens it, Lark spins around, facing me. "I'm sorry about my dad yesterday. He ... he can be a bit much."

"I really don't think I should say anything."

She gives me a meek half-smile. "It's not like that. It doesn't have to be. Just because my dad's one of the Elders, it doesn't mean I agree with everything he does." Her last words are barely audible.

The only answer I can give is a nod. She looks sincere, right into the depths of her crystal blue eyes, but one word against her father's not about to buy my trust. For all I know, she's a set-up. I'll take actions over words any day.

Reaching around her, I press the button that opens my door. "So what's on the agenda today?" I brush past her. She has to double-step to catch up, but I don't wait.

"You start training."

"Okay, what exactly does that entail?"

"Oh, everything." Lark shrugs. "Guns, combat, horse-back riding."

People sweep past me in the hallway. Yesterday, they seemed afraid of me. Today, they keep their eyes on the ground, or on each other, seemingly deep in conversation. Or they're ignoring me. Or they couldn't care less about me. Wow, I think way too much.

I focus back on Lark. "Why is horse-back riding so important?"

"Hmm, I don't know. Maybe because since the beginning of the world, the horse has been the main way humans have traveled. Cars didn't start being used until the late 1800's. Even then, most people still rode horses. If I'm right, a lot of the world still rides horses in the time you're from." She guides me to the entrance of the horse arena and flings open the doors.

That brings me up short. "My time ... so you're not from then?"

Blonde hair flies as she shakes her head. "A bit before your time."

No wonder she talks weird sometimes.

Michael's on the far end leading a reddish horse. He raises his hand in welcome when he sees us, like we might miss him, even though he's the only person there.

I seize Lark's arm, stopping her. "Can you train me? It doesn't have to be Michael, does it?"

She peeks over my shoulder toward where he stands. "You don't like him?"

Oh, more along the lines of liking him far too much. Just the memory of him tucking my bangs back in place last night makes my heart beat off-kilter.

Lark's eyebrows draw together. "I don't know what happened, but I promise he's a nice guy. Not to mention, easy on the eyes." She winks.

Not helping.

She sidesteps me and eats up the distance between us and Michael. I trail her like a homeless mutt. Lark pats the horse's forehead and eases the reins out of Michael's hands. "So how about I teach Gabby instead of you?"

His eyes dart to mine, full of questions. He hooks his hand on the back of his neck. "Not gonna happen."

Lark's cheeks turn a pretty shade of pink, but I don't think she's blushing. "Why? Why do you automatically get to do everything?"

"Don't make it sound like I'm lording something over you. It wasn't my choice, but I'm her Trainer. I was picked to do this. Nicholas practically tossed her in my lap."

Wasn't my choice. Tossed her in my lap. His words pierce, burrowing deep beneath my skin like long wooden slivers. The pain's probably for the best. If Lark's right, then it means Michael has a Pairing waiting for him in his time. Even if I'm not crazy about Porter, I should respect Michael's Pairing. The warm feeling I had yesterday when he held my hand can't be right.

I take a half step forward, skirting the horse, whose radar ears follow my movements. Creepy creature. "Um, in case you forgot. I'm standing right here."

Michael tightens a strap along the horse's stomach. The horse stomps on the ground a couple times, kicking up dust. "Let's get you on."

I back up. "If you don't even want to be my Trainer, why can't Lark teach me?"

Michael's jaw drops, he closes it, and opens it again. "Wait..." He throws his hands to the side. "Don't tell me you're offended by what I said. Girls are so weird."

Lark stands at an angle, crosses her arms, and juts out her chin. "You *did* say that training her wasn't by choice. That doesn't sound like you're all warm and fuzzy about the job."

He runs his hand through his hair. "That's not what I meant. Stop bending my words."

I bite my cheek. "That's what I heard too."

"Well, we'll have to have Darnell check your hearing later. Lark, you can head out." He points at me, then the horse. "You, horse, now."

Lark faces me and gives my arm a squeeze. "Just ignore him if you can. I'll see you later. You'll need my help with the bomb making. Even he'll admit that I'm way better at that than he is." She flips her hair over her shoulder and strolls out of the arena.

Bomb making? My heart sinks.

Michael clears his throat. "All right, Gabby, we don't have all day."

I knit my fingers together. "How about we start with something else?" Guns sound easier than horses. More predictable.

"Don't tell me you're afraid of Polly? She's an old mare. A pet kitten would be more dangerous than her."

Once when I was younger, Dad brought home a pet rabbit. Thought I needed company. A day later, ten-inch scratches on my arms proved that me and animals don't mix. Emma took the demon bunny off our hands. We've never had another pet since.

I kick the toe of my shoe into the sand. "Well, Polly keeps moving her ears in circles like she's possessed or something. I don't trust her. Besides, kittens have claws. So they don't exactly fall into the harmless category in my book either."

He strokes Polly's shoulder. "That's how a horse senses their surroundings. See, her ears are up now. She's safe. Horses are good like that. They'll let you know if they don't like you. Or don't trust you. If that was the case, Polly's ears would be flat against her head."

"Let's make a deal. If I shift to say, something B.C., then I'll just walk."

"Yeah, that's not going to work." He holds out his hand. If I don't do as he asks, he'll probably grab my hand. That can't happen. My eyes meet his, and Michael gives me a heart-robbing smile, which really doesn't help. My heart beats a little faster. I clench and unclench my fingers.

I stalk forward and grab the foot piece on the saddle. "Fine. Now what?"

"Get your foot in the stirrup."

"All the way up there? I'm sure you could find me a shorter horse. A pony?"

"Here." He crouches on the ground, his fingers knit together to form a step.

Note to self, Michael's not the compromising type.

I slip my foot into his hands, and he gives me a boost. I'm in the saddle before I have time to react. The horse moves its feet, making me list to the side. I grab for the saddle horn, but my sweaty hands slip right off.

Michael strokes the horse's neck, his voice firm. "Steady."

"She doesn't like me." I move to get down, but Michael lays a hand on my calf.

"If you're really that scared, I'll ride with you."

I chew on my lip. "Should I get down? Doesn't the guy usually ride in front?"

He barks out a laugh. "You've watched too many movies." With a nudge, he moves my foot out of the holder and swings up behind me. I slip my foot back into the stirrup. He's not in the saddle with me, so he must be actually on the horse. His arms come up around me, and he grasps my hands as they hold the reins.

"We'll steer together. You wouldn't learn anything if you just held on behind me. Go ahead and give Polly a little kick with your heels."

The horse begrudgingly lumbers forward. We're moving about as fast as a merry-go-round. Even still, I lean back against Michael a little. His solid presence behind me helps quiet my nerves. Well, about riding at least.

When he speaks again, I can feel his breath warm against my ear. "When we were talking to Lark and I said I didn't choose to be your Trainer, I said that so she couldn't fight me. I wanted to make it sound like Nicholas only wanted me helping you. Make it impossible for her to argue, you know?"

The Pairing. The Pairing. The Pairing. Maybe if I repeat it enough… I try to picture what his Pairing must look like. Maybe she's an exotic girl with dark eyes and long, shiny hair. Or a pretty red-head with a smile that makes him light up. Ugh. I don't like her already.

"You ... you didn't want her training me?"

"You're different, refreshing. Is it so bad if I want to keep you nearby? Besides, since you crashed my mission, I feel responsible for you." I feel him shrug.

If we weren't plodding along on a horse, I'd close my eyes—take in his words. No one has ever felt the need to watch out for me. No one ever cared enough.

He mistakes my silence. "Oh, gosh. Tell me I didn't do it again. I didn't mean responsibility like a burden. I meant it in a good way. I'm just ... going to be quiet now."

I take in a few deep breaths. "Believe me. I'm not that easy to offend. You're fine. Besides, you have to talk to tell me how to work this beast."

His arms relax beside mine. A soft chuckle escapes from his lips. "Not a beast—Polly. Lesson one, respect the horse."

"Got it. Lesson two?"

"The secret to working with any horse is they want to know you're worth trusting. If you're afraid, they'll sense it, so you have to shove down your emotions and take command. Once you do that, a horse will do almost anything you ask it to."

Not so different than my plan for the Elders.

"Um, how do I get it to not walk into this wall?" Okay, so we're ten feet or so from the edge of the arena, but I'm not going to wait until the horse bangs into something to ask about turning.

"You pull the reins whatever way you want the horse to go." He takes his hands off mine. "Hold the reins in one hand, like an ice cream cone. Your free hand can either rest on your thigh, or you can hang onto the horn if you want. Then go ahead and turn Polly. She's not the brightest, so if you don't turn her she'll just stop when she gets to the edge."

I feed the reins through my hand like he said, then clutch the horn for dear life. Polly stops before I have time to turn her. I let my head droop.

His hands brush against my forearms. Hope he doesn't notice the goose bumps. "Give her a good kick while you turn the reins."

Following his instructions, I walk Polly back and forth over the arena for the next ten minutes, feeling more comfortable by the end. As I complete a final loop Michael points to the edge of the stables and tells me to park her there. I obey.

The moment we stop, he slides down. "Go ahead and climb off her. Bring your leg over and drop to the ground."

Okay, so Polly proved she wasn't so bad. Easing my foot out of the saddle, I swing the other leg over the horse's back. Michael sets a hand on either side of my waist and helps me meet the ground slowly. I turn in his arms. The pressure of his hands burns into my skin.

Pushing away, I brush my errant bangs back behind my ear. "What's next?"

He takes Polly's reins and leads her through the wide doors of the stable. A man in jeans and a tucked-in T-shirt steps forward and takes Polly from him. Michael turns back to me. "So, what are you already good at?"

I stumble over my feet, sending a cloud of dust up in front of us. "Honestly, not much. I ran track in high school. I came in fourth at State. They don't give awards for that, though."

"And you can deliver some mean karate moves." Michael rubs his stomach like it still hurts.

"Sorry I did that. When we first met—"

"Don't apologize. You had no clue what was going on. I should have realized that sooner." We start walking across the empty arena.

"My dad made me take self-defense classes."

"So he didn't have you completely unprepared."

"That, or we live near Chicago ... high crime rates and all."

Michael cocks his head. "You do?"

"Why, is that weird?"

"It's just ... I grew up near Chicago too. In the same time as you did."

I stop. "Really? Wouldn't it be strange if we had seen each other—back in our time?"

Cracking his knuckles, he turns his back on me. "I haven't been back there in forever."

But Lark said I'd go back because of Porter. My heart plummets into my shoes. "So since you shifted the first time ... you haven't gone back?"

"No. Um, let's go do something else. We're wasting the day."

"Lark said you're special." My cheeks instantly burn. It's word vomit. I didn't mean to say it. But the words are there, and I can't take them back.

"Special? Ha, not likely." His voice sounds hollow, dead almost.

"But you shifted when you were eleven."

Michael rounds on me and his brow wrinkles. His gaze roves over something above my head. "They wouldn't call me special if they knew *why* I shifted."

"No one knows?"

"No one." He turns and strides out of the arena.

"Why did you shift?" I'm a step behind. I don't know why, but I have to ask. Suddenly knowing is the most important thing in the world.

"It doesn't matter." He braces a hand on the wall in the hall and closes his eyes. "Please don't ask again." The anguish marring his face sends a lance of pain deep into my chest. And I have to obey. There's no choice. He's the closest thing I have to a friend here and he looks ... sad.

I pat his shoulder. "Okay, I won't."

For now.

CHAPTER NINE

The next morning, I'm scooping scrambled eggs onto my plate in the cafeteria when Eugene sidles up to me. Now that I see him in the light of day, I guess that he's in his thirties.

He snatches a few sausage links from a warming dish. "The eggs here are passable, but I'd suggest grabbing a pumpkin muffin too. They're out of this world."

I add two small cartons of orange juice to my tray. "How about us? Are we out of this world?"

The corners of Eugene's lips lift as he points a butter knife full of cream cheese at me. "You're one odd girl. It's a lucky thing that I like you."

I lower my voice, tilting my head closer to him. "Seriously, is Keleusma still on Earth, or are we ... you know, somewhere else?"

"Very much still on *terra firma*." He places a pumpkin muffin on my plate, then two on his.

I roll my eyes and turn toward the seating area. "*Terra firma*. Nerd. And you said I was strange."

He's at my elbow. "Sit with me, over here." Jutting his head, he indicates an open table. I'm not really in a situation to be choosy about my friends. Besides, Eugene's lovable, in a dorky, older brother sort of way.

Based on the rest of Keleusma, I figured the cafeteria would be fancy. Plush seats and waitered tables—that sort of thing. Yesterday I discovered that this is just your standard lunch room. Hard plastic picnic tables boasting permanent juice stains line the area. Crude wooden napkin holders sit beside salt and pepper shakers. They look like they were nicked from a late night diner. A grease smell permanently hangs in the air.

On the way to our table, we pass a wall with four giant, framed pictures. The Elders. All of them stare at you while you eat. Lovely. The first is Lark's father. Even captured in a photo, his eyes pierce me and make me feel less than I am. Underneath hangs a gold-plated plaque reading *Donovan Anderson*, which sounds appropriately doom-worthy. Peeking at me next are the twins, Clarissa and Mimi Walsh. Last hangs the cat lady—smiling bright—Beatrix Vaughn. A gaudy banner suspended above them reads: *Thank you for your votes.*

Wait ... people chose these monkeys? My esteem for anything Keleusma goes down the proverbial drain.

I drop onto the bench with my back to the photos and take a bite of my eggs. Willing my throat to swallow, I reach for the pepper. One point for Team Eugene—the man knows his food.

Darnell drops down beside me, steam curling off his raisin-sprinkled oatmeal. Healthy junk. How doctorish of him.

He arranges his silverware and lays a napkin on his lap. “Enjoying your training?”

I take a long swig of orange juice. “As long as horse racing and shooting arrows aren’t in my future, I’ll be fine.”

“That good, huh?”

Eugene fires a warning look at Darnell. “It’ll get better. I promise. Beginnings are always bumpy. Do you know what your plans are for the rest of the day?”

I didn’t realize Lark was standing behind me, but her voice is unmistakable. “Sword fighting and bomb making.” She claims the other seat beside me. “Maybe some history too.”

Great. Nothing like getting maimed today. Or dying.

Michael must have been with her, because he rounds the table and sits next to Eugene. Nudging me with his foot under the table, he smiles good morning. “Pumpkin muffin. Smart girl.”

I peel the wrapper off the muffin. “It was Eugene’s idea.”

Eugene’s cheeks turn red, like I just paid him the highest compliment. He pulls a spiral memo pad from his back pocket and jots something down. I try to see what he’s writing, but his other hand blocks the paper. Then again, Michael did warn me Eugene was odd. I sink my teeth into the muffin. Odd or not, the resident computer whiz is completely trustworthy. Bad eggs. Delicious muffin. I guess that’s all it takes to win me over.

“So.” I clear my throat. “Tell me everyone’s kidding about bomb making.”

Lark does her bug-eyed thing again. “The bomb lessons are for real.”

Pushing my eggs around on my plate, I look down. "I mean, how often can we really run into a time where we'll have to use that skill?" One in a million ... billion would be better. Or never.

Lark snaps her fingers, forcing my gaze back to her. "Do you want to get stuck in a situation where you have to disable a bomb in less than two minutes and *not* know how to do it? I've been there, multiple times. Unlike you, I knew how to handle it so I was fine."

I push the images from the Wall Street bombing out of my mind and point my fork at Darnell. "You said Nicholas won't send me somewhere I can't handle. I'm pretty sure another bomb meets that requirement."

He steeples his hands. "True. But you can handle a lot more than you think you're capable of."

Darnell's words lodge into my mind like a snow-cone-induced brain freeze. I shiver and push my tray away. I fight the urge to kick something. "I don't ever want to touch a bomb. This isn't fair. Nicholas isn't fair. How can you guys sit here and talk about him like he's wonderful when he puts Shifters in these horrible situations again and again?" I meet each of their eyes. "None of you has a choice about where you go or what you do. Doesn't that make you angry?"

Michael fiddles with his cup of coffee, swirling the liquid. "We always have a choice."

I shake my head. "But that's just it! You don't. He treats you like robots. Making you do whatever he wants." My voice is rising.

What's wrong with them? Being out of control is never okay. My father constantly hands over control to his drinks—what does that get him? Nothing other than something to point at and blame, which for some is enough. But not me.

Lark rests her hand on my shoulder. "Maybe we don't have a choice about *where* in time we shift, but we choose what we do in that moment. Say I shift to one of the World Wars and I'm supposed to save someone named Grant. I can choose to save him, or I can do nothing and let him die. It's completely up to me. Now, I'd go ahead and save the guy, but I don't have to."

Eugene scrubs the back of his hand across his mouth. "Lark's right. Our choice is the thing that holds the most impact on the future. If you want my opinion, that amount of responsibility on us feels overwhelming. It's our choice of action or inaction that matters in the end. I sometimes think it'd be easier—safer, to be a robot."

My fork clatters to the table. "How soon do you think I'll have to go back out there?" Translation: is there an opt-out clause?

Michael rests his elbows on the table. "Don't worry. You always shift with your Trainer the first time. I'll make sure nothing happens to you."

Gathering my tray and his, Darnell rises from the table. "You'll be fine, even if you fail or choose not to complete your mission. Nicholas always watches over us. Just stay clear of those Shades and you'll be fine."

Eugene rubs his hands together. "Yeah, and whatever you do, don't ever let a Shade touch you."

Nibbling the side of my cheek, I glance at Michael. He's looking down, tracing his fingers over a purple stain on the table. Clearly, he overlooked telling everyone about our run-in with the Shades. I should respect his silence on the subject. He has to have his reasons. But Eugene's statement turns to ice in my veins, halting rational thought.

Words spill from my mouth. "They already did."

Lark gasps and drops her spoon faster than if it bit her.

Eugene takes off his glasses and cleans them with a napkin. "Are you certain it was a Shade?" He narrows his eyes at Michael.

Just the thought of them causes my hand to tremble as I set down my empty orange juice carton. "Um, truly creepy-looking people who hobble around—their faces look like they're melting."

Brows furrowing, Eugene turns back toward me. "Melting. You could *see* that?"

"Of course, can't you?"

He shakes his head. "Only when their image is captured in a photograph. But when I see one in person, their skin looks normal."

"Same here," Lark pipes in.

I meet Michael's soft gaze. His sad smile. "I don't see them melting, either."

My heart pounds like a kick drum. "What's wrong with me? How come I can see that and you guys can't?"

Lark and Michael seem more than happy to let Eugene do all the talking. He leans forward. "Think about it. Being able to see them like that helps you. It's a gift, really. You'll always be able to notice them right away, whereas sometimes it takes half our mission before we spot them. But you said one of them touched you. Let's go back to that—what happened?"

I tell them about when I first shifted and ran away from Michael. Relive the horde of Shades converging on me in the woods. Their sharp nails. Feel their cold breath. Hear the antiquated lilt in their speech.

"Did they speak to you?" Eugene butts in.

I play with my napkin. "They said, 'Welcome home.'" It's a whisper, but they all hear it. The three at the table exchange horrified looks. Their actions confirm my worst suspicions. I'm weird. An oddity who can't fit in during my own time, or this time. Any time. Michael bows his head, raking his hand through his hair a few times.

With fierceness I didn't know the spindly guy could possess, Eugene reaches across the table and seizes my hand. "They will try to persuade you to go with them. Don't, Gabby, don't ever give in. You're better than that. Don't ever take anything from them. No drinks. Hear me? If they offer you anything or try to take you away, you do everything in your power to get away."

"Of course." I wince because of his hold. I want to pull away from him, but the message written in his eyes is clear. For a reason I don't understand, Eugene cares about me. He's afraid for me. I want to say something. To let him know I appreciate his concern, but the best I can do is, "They're freaks. I don't ever want to see one again."

Eugene releases me then. Hiding my arms under the table, I rub my wrists, willing the blood to return. As my thumb traces over my skin, my mind preforms a triathlon through my scattered thoughts. I'm going to be in situations where I'll have to sword fight other people. Maybe kill someone. Or be killed. I picture myself, hovering over a ticking bomb as a crowd of hostages depend on what color cord I snip. Not only those things, will I also have to ward off scary-looking creatures who want to acquire me?

Life was so much easier only a few days ago.

My muscles scream to get up and run away from these people. This madness. But where will that get me?

Michael's not ready to drop the conversation. "Not seeing a Shade again ... that's not an option. You *will* see them again. There's no way around it. They'll try to talk to you, Gabby—persuade you that their way is better."

"Um, I don't see them succeeding."

Michael shakes his head slowly. "Don't underestimate them. They have a certain kind of freedom that we don't have. A Shade can be really convincing when they want to be."

"Convincing?" I grab my knees to stop them from jiggling.

Lark seems to be biting her lips, but then she blows out a long stream of air that ruffs her hair. "Shades aren't born. They're made. You don't think Shifters get to choose for themselves, but know how a Shade becomes a Shade? A Shifter chooses to become one. That's the only way. They choose to turn their back on Nicholas and leave Keleusma forever. All it takes is one swallow of this drink they call the Elixir and you're a goner. Don't let them get near enough to speak to you because everything they say—the life they describe—it's tempting."

Somehow I managed to forget that Lark—otherwise known as the daughter of Donovan—sat right beside me. Great. Just great. Surely she'll tell her father about my encounter with the Shades. And he'll have me marched right back to the dank cell for, oh, the rest of eternity. Or longer.

She taps my arm. "Come on, we can't put this off all day."

My gaze bolts to Michael. He isn't going to let her take me. Is he? But he gives me a chin-up in the form of a good-bye. "See you later. Have fun."

What did I miss? "Wh-where are you going?"

He turns an apple over and over again in his hand. "Earth to Gabby. You weren't listening at all. There's a meeting I have to go to, so Lark's going to show you the swords." He points to Lark. "Play nice."

Most of the other Shifters have already cleared out of the dining hall when Lark and I leave. She leads me back to the gym I noticed on my first day here. Human sweat and the smell of plastic and rubber mingle together. Along the edges are standard issue weight-lifting and cardio machines. Blue padded mats line the walls. Almost every machine is occupied. Rhythmic, pounding feet of people on the treadmills intertwine with the clinking of metal near the weight-lifters.

"Are all Shifters annoyingly in shape?"

Lark waves her hand in a gesture of dismissal. "Of course we are. We need to be prepared for any type of mission. That means being able to run for long periods of time, out-wrestle someone, and move quickly through obstacles."

I disguise a snort with a cough. Lark wrestle someone and win? It's too ridiculous to imagine. She might be ninety-five pounds, and that's only if she's soaking wet and wearing steel-toed shoes.

In the middle, multiple groups of partners cluster together in hand-to-hand combat. On the left is a boxing ring, but my eyes go right to two men wielding axes. Their grunts and howls echo off the high ceiling. Sparks fly when their axes meet. The sound of metal clanging makes me grit my teeth.

Palm to my heart, I jump when Lark steps into my vision. She thrusts a bat wrapped in fabric toward me. I take it. "We're fighting with these?"

Her hands go to her hips. "If you want to start with axes, we sure can."

Point taken. I follow her to a circle of mats where she runs through the basic information.

First lesson of sword-fighting: always keep your feet shoulder-width apart. Never let them cross. Instead, slide when moving. Doing otherwise causes tripping, and makes onlookers laugh. Live and learn. Second, align your wrist with the hilt, not your thumb. I get this after a few failed tries. Third, block your opponent's attacks using the portion of the sword closest to the hilt so there is power behind the defense. Using the tip of the sword will cause more laughter. Last, swing like mad. Which is easier said than done.

We run through a few slow practice moves. Then Lark smiles, which makes her looks scarily like Donovan. "Now for some real fun!"

She jabs at me, catching me off guard. Forgetting my stance, I totter backwards, arms waving. Before she can get to me again, I bring my makeshift sword in front of me. Defend. I press her back, but she does a circle move and smacks my back with the sword when I'm trying to recover.

"Dead!" She laughs.

Hands resting on my knees, I try to catch my breath. Warm, nasty gym air fills my lungs.

"Again." Lark gets into ready position.

I bring my sword up. Less than a minute later, she cuffs me across the side, and I fall. Ouch. For the record, a fabric-wrapped bat still hurts like the dickens when it's bashed into your ribs. She pulls me up, and we start a new round.

People have gathered around us, cheering and taunting in turn, the latter intended for me. My blood starts to boil. I dust off my pants and bring my sword back into position.

She moves to strike me, but I slide backwards. Now I have enough room to add my lessons from self-defense class into the fight. I shoulder-roll forward and it lands me under her aim. I'm moving too fast for her to keep up. With a groan, I heave the sword and cut her legs out from under her. She drops onto her back. Her weapon bangs onto the floor, rolling out of her hand. I spring forward, straddling her. Press my sword into her jugular.

The sound of clapping snaps me back to my senses. I lift my sword and offer Lark a sheepish grin. After snagging two bottles of water we spend another hour in practice battle. Then she brings me to a place called the education center.

"No bomb making?" I tease.

"Another day." She leaves me in the hands of a wrinkled old man who smells like clothes from a basement. Supposedly he's a professor.

He makes me sit on a rough, wooden chair. As he speaks, I drag my fingers over the wood grain in the table in front of me. A touch screen appears on the wall, and he pulls up images that are a hundred years old. He drills me on historic dates, culture, and manners, wagging his finger mercilessly each time I answer wrong. Hopefully, his finger is prepared for the amount of wagging I'm going to cost him. I feel like I'm back in history class, accept I don't have any friends to pass notes to. I'm stuck here for lunch and dinner. Hours later, I'm thinking a fork to the eye would be a better fate to endure.

Back in my room for the night, I ease the fastening off my braid. Running my fingers through my hair, I examine my area. Someone's been here while I was gone. A maid of some sort. My bed is tidy, and the dirty clothes from yesterday that I left bunched on the ground have vanished. I throw myself onto the couch. Okay, this someone cleaning up after me part I could get used to. At my dad's I was the main cleaner. If I'm lucky, maybe they'll even iron my clothes before bringing them back.

Suddenly I freeze. My eyes go back to where I left my dirty clothes the other morning. Including the pair of pants that held a note in the back pocket—Michael's note. It's gone.

Oh, no. What have I done?

CHAPTER TEN

Breathe. Don't flip out.

They probably tossed the clothes into a pile on the floor of my closet. That's what I do when I want my room to look nice but don't want to actually clean it. I stride across the bedroom and slap my palm to the wall. The light beam waves over me and my closet opens. I paw through the drawers. Glance around for a suspicious lump. Drop to my knees and peek under the dresser.

Nothing.

Without thinking, I leave my room and march out into the hallway. All the lights are off. Looks like Keleusma closes down for the night. From the direction of the main lobby, a vacuum's running, and someone's having a muffled conversation. I slink against the wall and try to find carpeted patches to tip-toe across.

No one said anything about a curfew here. What will they do if they find me out of my room at night? More importantly, what about the note? Hopefully, they'll just think it's some joke and toss it away. But the way people act here, the maid probably brought it straight to Donovan The Terrible. Yes, he deserves the caps.

Terror skitters like marbles down my spine. Not for me. With the way things are going, I'm bound to come to blows with the Elders one way or another. I can figure that part out. Deal with it.

What propels me forward is what they might do to Michael. If it wasn't for him, I'd be the one with a huge burn scar on my back. Maybe not even that, because without Michael, the Shades would have dragged me who knows where. In the short amount of time we've known each other, he has stood in the gap and saved me more times than I can count. I owe him this.

Laundry is usually done in a basement, right? Why do people clean things in the dankest, darkest part of a building? Beats me. But every house and apartment building I've even been in has the washing machines on the lowest level. Does Keleusma even have levels?

I pause a moment, allowing time for my eyes to adjust to the dark. Once I can see, I make my way, feeling against the wall. There isn't time to worry about whether or not there are surveillance cameras. Probably not since this place is supposed to house a bunch of world heroes.... On the other hand, they do have jail cells.

Most of the service-oriented stuff has been located at the easternmost end of the compound. Food prep, a hair-cutting room, and the medical facility are all in this direction. Logic says something like laundry will be this way too.

When I turn the corner, I have to tread across a tiled section of flooring. I step heel to toe, to make the least amount of sound. Darkness floods this area, more so than before. Splaying my hands out in front of me, I feel for any obstacles. But I miss a small trash bin. My shin bashes into it, and the metal rattles on the floor, echoing like a hubcap spinning on an abandoned street. The momentum flings me forward. Arms flailing, I drop to my knees. The trash can falls on its side, rolls ten feet, and lands with a hollow *thunk* against the wall.

Footfalls announce someone's approaching from the residential wing. Seconds. That's all I have. I swallow hard.

My heart's pumping in my throat. Blood pulses like a rock concert in my temples. Frantically, I crawl forward. When I feel carpet under my hands, I claw my way to the wall and gain my feet again. If somebody discovers me, I want to be found standing. Not like a kid on my hands and knees. Although, not being found at all sounds a whole lot better.

No longer caring about noise, I take off at a sprint down the corridor. Behind me are footsteps, closer ... closer. Alarm heightens my ability to see. I hurdle the next stupid trash can. I'm by the cafeteria now. The doors to the dining area are blessedly unlocked. Shoving them open, I rush to a couple of huge shelving units on wheels, similar to a baker's rack, where the clean dishes are stored. I try to move one, but it's far too heavy.

The door to the dining area starts to open. I wedge myself into the small space between the shelving unit and the wall. My rib cage is smashed. Each breath hurts.

A man I don't recognize paces into the room, his boots galumphing on the hard floor even though he walks slowly, deliberately. What will they do to me if I'm discovered?

Hand on top of one of the tables, he peers underneath. In the shadows, he looks behind each large trash can. He even lifts the lids in case I've climbed inside one of them. As he steps closer, I hold my breath, and my lungs burn with a stabbing intensity that makes my eyes water.

Save me. Hide me. Save me. Hide me. The words pound in my mind. Steady and repetitive. Like the soles of a runner's shoes slapping concrete.

The man is less than three feet from me. I can make out his sharp nose and square jaw. Any hope I had tailspins into the ground. Surely if I can see him, the opposite is true too. His head swings my way, his vision bounces over me, and he turns and strolls out the door.

For a few moments I stay in my hiding place, stunned. He's gone. Just like that? Finally I ease away from the wall and stumble a few feet into the open area, away from the shelving units. Sucking in a deep gulp of cool air, I run my fingers over my ribs. I decide to duck behind something for another twenty minutes or so, let the place clear of people searching, and then head back to hunt for the missing note.

Before I can move, a firm hand clamps down on my shoulders. A ring on one of the person's fingers bites into my skin. I spin around, expecting the worst.

And find it.

Donovan shakes his head a few times. Almost as if he's disappointed in me. "What are you doing away from the residential wing?"

Either he materialized out of thin air, or he's been here the whole time. Waiting. Watching me. Both options are equally creepy.

The expression on his face is so fierce, I have to look away. I choose to examine the toes of my shoes. "I ... um ... I."

His hold on my shoulder tightens. "Are you hurt? Did you need to speak to someone?"

I shuffle my feet. Allow my gaze to flicker back up at him and find an odd softness in his eyes. Concern? Pity?

More like a ploy.

Donovan is not on my short list of trusted people. Nor do I expect to ever find him there. Even still, my tongue comes unglued. Michael warned me the Elders would be watching me. In fact, it's silly to think they don't know about the note already. I might as well not get lying added to my growing record of grievances. I open my mouth to speak, but Donovan glances at something behind me.

Lark steps into my line of vision. Hands propped on her hips. "Man alive. You're really terrible at this, Gabby."

So, she helps her daddy hunt down errant Shifters. Pulling out my mental tally book, I place Lark in the traitor category. What's her problem? I want to see her slip and fall into a dumpster full of fish eyes. Seriously.

Donovan lifts his hand from me and crosses his arms. "What's this?"

She giggles. “Nothing to worry about. I’ve been helping with Gabby’s training. And, as you can see yourself, she’s failing both the stealth and snooping exercises. It’s been pretty abysmal. But she’ll get there, I promise.”

I frown. Her words make no sense. Why is Lark covering for me? What does she stand to gain by lying to her father?

Donovan looks back and forth between the two of us. “I didn’t see a note in the training log about a night session.”

“Oh! Sorry, Dad. I completely forgot. Besides, I figured no one would question me.” She bats her eyes. Playing up the daddy’s little princess bit.

His lips tug with the lightest smile. “Yes, I always say you are the best we have on the field. If anyone can get her into shape, it’s you.”

So they’re talking like I’m not here. Lovely. Know what? At the moment, that is perfectly fine with me.

Lark pats Donovan’s arm. “Everyone knows that’s because I learned from the best.”

Finally, his stance relaxes. “All right, you girls head back to your rooms. You sent my entire security team on a mad goose hunt. Training’s over for now. Promise to fill out the proper paperwork from now on and we’ll forget this happened.”

We both nod in unison.

Donovan lays a hand on top of Lark’s head. “I have to go call off the patrol. They’ve all been on edge with the changes and worried in case....” His eyes skirt quickly to me and then away. “If the Shades find a way inside, I don’t know what we’ll do.”

I locate my voice. "Nicholas will protect Keleusma. Won't he?"

Lark's father tilts his head, considering me before he answers. "In theory. But there's always a chance that we can get in the way of what he's trying to do." With that, he wishes us sweet dreams and leaves. His shoes don't make a sound as he strolls away.

For the space of a few heartbeats, I stare after him. He's not so terrifying when he's not sitting behind the table with the rest of the Elders. Alone with his daughter, he's just another normal dad. The exchange has thrown me off kilter. I don't like it. I want to be able to place these Shifters in one of two groups. Trustworthy or evil. In-between ground only makes things more confusing.

Beyond that, the last five minutes shoot a pang of longing through my chest. How is my dad holding up? Does he miss me? Worry late into the night? Will my homecoming soften the lines around his lips too? Or has he drunk himself into oblivion?

I turn back to Lark. "So why stick up for me?" Even as I say the words, I already know the answer. Where's my eraser? Lark's name needs to make a pilgrimage to my Good People list.

"Like I said before, I don't always think he's right about everything."

"Your dad is a pretty intense guy."

She shrugs. "He's been through a lot."

"Still. If you get caught..."

"Don't worry about me. Anyway, Michael made me promise to take care of you."

My betrayal of Michael seizes like poison in my body. Guilt clings to every thought. "He gave me something ... something that wouldn't be good for anyone else to see, and I lost it. That's why I'm out here. I need to find it."

Her eyebrows rise. Questioning.

"I left a note in one of my pockets and now it's gone from my room. If it's found, I think it could cause a lot of trouble for Michael."

"Listen, my dad called off the patrol, but that doesn't mean there won't be people out." She grabs my arm. "Let's get you back to your room, then I'll go find this note."

I wrench away. "Not happening. I made this mess. I should be the one to clean it up."

Lake pulls me up short. "Okay, we need to get something straight. When it comes to you, my dad is right about one thing. You are stubborn and headstrong and dangerous."

Um, that's *three* things. "Then I'll just go by myself—"

She blocks my progress. "Oh, no you don't. You'll hear me out is what you'll do. Know why there is more than one Shifter, Gabby? Because we need each other. We depend on one another to get things done. Once you're a Shifter, there's no going it alone. We take care of each other. I'm sorry about whatever went on in your time that made you hate everyone, but you need to learn there are more people than just you who are capable of managing things."

"I don't hate everyone," I mumble, but my fight is gone.

She thumps her chest. "I know where the laundry is. I know the system and will be able to find the note within seconds. If you're with me, you're a liability. Plain and simple. Besides, how do you expect me to explain why you're wandering around after my dad told us to go back to our rooms? If someone finds me alone, they won't question it."

I'm tired. And know what? It might be nice to let someone else bear the load for once. In silence, we walk back to my room. She promises to be back in less than a half hour.

I shower and change into comfy clothes. Braid and unbraid my hair. Bite my nails. Drum my feet on the side of the couch.

It's the longest half hour of my life.

Lark's smiling when she saunters back through my door. From her pocket she pulls the note and extends it toward me.

I snatch it. "Did you read it?"

"No. Whatever it is, it's between you and Michael. I didn't even unfold the thing."

"Thanks." I hold the note up. "And sorry. I should have trusted you." I fold my fingers over the paper. The corners pinch into my flesh, working like a balm to my nerves. Michael's safe.

She makes a move to leave, but I want to ask her something. I thought to voice my question to Michael, but then he said he hasn't been home since his first shift.

I clear my throat. "Do you ever go home? You know, to your original time."

"Of course." Slouching onto my bed, she sighs. "I'm back with Eddie a couple times a year."

"How do you do it?"

She trails a finger over the wild pattern on my comforter. "You shift to whoever needs you most in that moment. Sometimes it's your Pairing who needs you. In the next year or so, Eddie and I will get married. When that happens, I won't shift again for a couple years. Eddie will need me too much. And when I have a kid, then, for the first year or two, my child will need me most. After that, I'll shift again, seeing them occasionally as Eddie raises our child."

"That's horrible," I whisper.

She doesn't meet my eyes. "It's the way things are."

"Don't you want to stay with Eddie?" I take a step closer.

"Sure. But I also know how important shifting is. Eddie knows that too. We both understand the roles we play."

A canary of hope sings in my soul. If what Lark's saying is true, then I don't need to worry about my mother any longer. The hints dropped about her can't be true. What I believe has always been right. "That's how I know she's dead."

"Your mom?"

"Yeah, I mean, that's the only thing that makes sense. If she was still alive, she would have come home. My dad needs her."

Lark rises, turns her back on me. "Maybe."

The rigid set of her shoulders kills my little canary instantly. "Wh-what do you know about my mother?"

"Gabby, it's late. I have to be up early." Still with her back to me, Lark moves toward the door.

"Please. I've seen pictures of her my whole life, but I know nothing about her. She's like this ghost I can't shake. If I just knew something—anything. You don't know how lucky you are. You might not agree with your dad, but at least you have a relationship," my voice is low, but it stops her.

She lets loose a long sigh. "I honestly don't know much. People don't tell me things because of my dad's position. I've been sheltered from most things here."

"But you know something?"

"Just whispers." She rubs her hands over her arms as if she's cold. "But it's not good stuff. You'd be better off not hearing it. Sometimes ignorance is better."

"Did she die?"

"I'm not sure. But I do know she disgraced the Shifters, and they're afraid you will too. That's why people are wary of you. It's wrong. I understand that more than anyone. A person shouldn't be judged by their parent's mistakes."

That's all she's been told. It's clear in her eyes. She's done, spent.

After Lark leaves, I shut off the lights and lie on top of my bed sheets. Heavy fog descends upon my brain. I want to lie here and never get back up. I want an old dog-eared book to read, a warm blanket, and someone to rub circles over my back. My stomach aches like I swallowed ten pounds of lead.

In the almost dark, I stare vacantly at the ceiling fan, trying to single out a blade to follow. But nothing chases my thoughts away. *Disgrace.* The word will haunt me. Howl and accuse me when I'm all alone. My throat feels itchy.

Was my mom a traitor?

Or was she—like me—just trying to get home?

CHAPTER ELEVEN

Green? Yellow? Or orange?

I press my lips together. Loud ticks sound from the timer on the metal device. Letting me know another second of my life is gone. Like sand through my hands—wasted. Makes me think about the things I'll change if I get the chance. Hug Dad more often. Find more opportunities to laugh with my friends. Not freak out about little things.

The pointy wire cutters tremble in my hand. Lark's shadow looms behind me and her foot taps out a steady beat of annoyance. Why doesn't she just take over? Save the day and all that. The tyrant gene must run too strongly through her veins. Watch the little guy squirm for entertainment. Oh, joy.

Focus. Don't be bested by a machine. Okay, this has to be logical. I examine the three tense wires again. Let's get all symbolical. Green is the color of life, plants, and vitality. Yellow makes me think about long summer days spent basking by the lake and happiness. Then there's the orange. Nothing is orange besides construction cones, fire, and, well, oranges.

Red digital numbers tell me I have less than a minute. A bead of sweat trickles down my neck.

"All your people are going to die," Lark snaps.

I work my bottom lip between my teeth. Life, happiness, or construction? Yikes, the world has come to this.

A heartbeat later, I snip the orange. The timer stops. I shove damp bangs from my forehead and smirk at the evil contraption. Then there's a hissing sound and the one-foot metal box explodes. The force lands me on my back. I close my eyes. Tossing my arms over my head, I wait for the sear of pain.

The room falls quiet.

Well, if you don't count the snort Lark lets loose. "Great. You know you have to clean all this up before lunch."

I open my eyes. Tiny paper pieces float all around me like a ticker tape parade. They carpet me and the floor. I take my first real breath. "It's just confetti."

"Did you really think we'd use a *real* bomb for training?" She offers her hand.

I take it and she helps me gain my feet. "I'm learning not to assume too much around here."

Brushing confetti from her shoulders, Lark rolls her eyes. "Well, you can assume I'm not going to help you clean. They're serving Stromboli in the cafeteria today and I don't want to be late. The broom and dust pan are in the closet." She points. Call me slow, I thought she was kidding, but Lark leaves me alone.

"Dumb bombs." I kick the stupid metal box across the room on my way to grab the broom. It takes a ridiculous amount of time to sweep every little bit of confetti out of all the corners. Hello, static electricity! The stuff keeps sticking to the broom bristles, my pants, my hair.

It's more than a half hour later when I make my way to the cafeteria, toward an inevitable fate. People who show up late for meals get leftovers if they're lucky. Cereal if they're not. Believe me, the cereal in Keleusma is not the type with cartoon rabbits dancing on the box or loaded with marshmallow stars. Birds would refuse to touch the stuff they offer here.

Loud conversations and the smell of stewed tomatoes filter from the dining room. I push through the doors and scan the seating area for someone I know. Michael's at my side in an instant. I don't know where he came from. His soft brown eyes make me forget about terrible food. The edges of his mouth tilt up. I freeze as he gently reaches to remove something from my bangs.

"I take it training with Lark didn't go well today." There's a chuckle behind his voice. He flings the wayward piece of confetti to the ground. Guess I missed one.

"What can I say? Looks like bombs are not my thing."

"Don't worry about it. I'm terrible with them too. Well, you saw on Wall Street. When I'm near a bomb, I just try to get people to safety. It's not a big deal. Not one of us is good at everything. We each have different talents." He takes my elbow and we weave through the tables.

"Except it looks like I'm good at nothing," I say this under my breath because we've reached our destination.

Darnell gives me a chin-up form of greeting. Eugene waves his fork while he munches on an enormous bite of salad. Lark smiles, and I immediately forgive her for leaving me. It was silly to think she should help pay for any of my mistakes. Michael pats the seat beside him.

"I have to go scrounge up something to eat." Maybe they have some of Eugene's salad left.

But Michael snags my hand before I can move. "I saved some for you." With flourish, he yanks a napkin off of a plate sitting in front of him. On it rests a huge portion of Stromboli. More than I could eat in two meals. Meat and cheese ooze out the side. My mouth starts to water.

I drop down onto the bench. "Thank you." I want to hug him but rein that desire in. It hits me that it's been a few days since I've seen him. Well, other than in passing. We've sat at the same table at meals, but always separated by other people. I've missed him. But there's the Pairing to think of, after all. Would Porter save me food? Not likely. He'd eat both our shares and then raze me for coming too late. Poke me in the ribs while I choke down stale cereal.

Michael nudges a small bowl full of pasta sauce closer to me. "It's probably not warm still, but it has to taste better cold than the other options up there."

Slicing off a chunk, I dip it into the sauce and take a bite. Other than making me wish for Chicago deep dish pizza, the stuff is amazing.

I'm still chewing when Michael leans in. "For the record, I think there's a lot of things you're good at," he says quietly. Our friends don't notice.

I start to choke on my food. Eugene slaps my back as if that might help. Clearly, he didn't ever take a first aid class. Michael shoves a glass of water into my hands when I seize a gulp of air. My eyes capture his as I take a sip. *There's a lot of things you're good at.* I want to ask him what he means, but not in front of everyone else.

Eugene bumps my side. "You okay?"

"Yeah, fine. Wrong tube."

Darnell inspects me with a mixture of curiosity and humor. My gaze flits away, examining the table. His deep-set stare always seems to penetrate right to my soul. But it's Michael he addresses. "Have your meetings produced anything?"

Michael rests his arms on the table. "No. The travel specialists can't figure out how to send me back. It was probably dumb to even ask."

What's he talking about? "Slow down. Back where?"

"To Pinkerton. To the mission that you—"

"Messed up," I offer.

"I was going to say *joined.*" He sneaks a piece of my Stromboli and pops it into his mouth. The quick wink that accompanies his thievery keeps me from protesting.

Darnell castles his hands. "Think. Do you really wish to go back?"

"Pinkerton's one of my favorite people in history. I always wanted to get pulled to work with him."

Well, that's just great. Not only did I give Michael a mammoth scar for the rest of his life, but I robbed him of his dream mission. Why is this guy still my friend?

Eugene tries to spin his cup like a top. Instead, he topples it, spilling milk over the surface. He grabs a wad of napkins and tosses them over the mess. Shoving his glasses up his nose, he inclines his head toward Michael. "I think I can get you back to the exact moment you left."

Michael raises his eyebrows. "I've been told it's not possible."

Eugene's eyes dart back and forth over the room as he speaks. "That's because I haven't told anyone. See, it's all just theories. But my preliminary tests did well." He fishes a small memo notebook from his back pocket. Flipping it open, he taps a crudely drawn picture. Complete with stick figures and lots of swirls that look like tornadoes. Okay, so the computer whiz can't draw well. "I think I found a way to manipulate the portals. Use their unspent energy."

Lark cocks her head. "Even if it's possible, would that be wise? I mean, if Nicholas wanted him to go back to that mission, he'd send him there."

That makes Eugene shrug. "Shifters built the portals and no one sees anything wrong with that. If Nicholas gives us the knowledge to do things like this, then shouldn't we? Wouldn't it be negligent on our part to waste that?" He faces Michael again. "I can't send someone just anywhere. It won't work like that. The only reason I can try is because you went to that time, but never started the mission. It's like I've discovered this pocket of grace.

A chance for a second try. At least that's how I like to think about it." He tucks the notebook back into his pocket. "If you had attempted the mission and failed, I couldn't send you back."

Michael smacks his palm on the table. "I'm in."

Lark's eyes bug out. "It's way too dangerous. You can't do this, Michael."

I lay down my fork. "I'm going too."

Darnell buries his face in his hands. Michael and Lark answer me in unison.

"Absolutely not."

"No way."

My hands ball into fists and warmth rushes up my neck. "In case you forgot, I was part of that mission. I got pulled there instead of here. Doesn't that count for something?"

Lark shakes her head. "You're not ready. There's so much more to learn."

Under the table, Michael places his hand on top of my clenched fingers. "She's right, Gabby. It's not safe for you to leave Keleusma yet. Out of these walls, you'll be like a deer painted hot pink during hunting season."

I jerk away from his touch. "But you said—"

"Hey, I do believe you're really talented. But look at Eugene and Darnell." He gestures to each as he names them. "They're far more gifted than I am but neither of them shift much."

I search each of their faces. My supposed friends. So none of them think I'm capable. For all their kind words, not one believes in me.

Who cares? They don't know me. Not really. "You know what? I don't need people telling me what I can and can't do." I shove back from the table. "Forget it! Forget all of you." People at other tables are gawking as I storm out of the dining room. Well, forget them too.

Taking off at a jog, I bite back tears. They need to stay in my eyes until I'm safely confined to my room. Like a pinball, I smack off an older gentleman, which tosses me off course for a moment. I stumble, throw out a "sorry," and start running again. In front of my bedroom, I fumble to get my keycard out of my pocket. It flutters to the ground. With a growl, I snatch it back up and swipe the card through the reader.

My door swooshes open. I hate it. If only it was old fashioned, like the one on my bedroom at home. You can't slam any of these stupid automatic doors.

The tears start to fall immediately. I strip out of my clothing and stomp into the bathroom. My hand trembles as I jam the card into the slot. When the touch screen illuminates I choose hot, pulsing water. I let it drum into my back, making me numb. Salty tears slick down my face, onto my lips. The skin on my fingers starts to prune.

My mind floods with thoughts of home. Faded sheets on my old twin mattress and thin rugs over old wooden floors sound like a fantasy now. Can't they just set me free already?

Why waste time on all this training if they are never going to let me help? Have they been babysitting me this whole time? Keeping me occupied while something bigger is going on? Either that—or I've disappointed them. I don't know which option is worse.

Both mean the same thing in the end. They've all decided I'm useless.

Later, I sit in bed with the lights on, absently tracing my finger back and forth over the black spot on my shifting bracelet. The blemish. No matter how many times I try to rub it away, it stays. One more thing mocking me, reminding me I don't belong.

Someone knocks on my door and I glare at it, hoping they can feel my stink eye through the inch of metal. "Go away!"

"Gabby? It's Eugene. Please let me in."

Ugh. I jump off my bed and cross to the door, slamming my hand on the open button. It will take too much energy to be mean to Eugene. Besides, he brought me food in jail. We have a special bond. Anyway, I don't think he'll be difficult to get rid of. Let him say how sorry he is that I can't go. I can roll my eyes. Then call it a night.

Eugene has his hands looped in his pockets. He only steps about a foot into my room, enough space for the door to shut. Then he stays rooted right there.

I clear my throat. "If you're here to give me some pep talk, don't bother."

"I'll sneak you in. Tomorrow. When Michael shifts. I'll send you too."

My head snaps up. "Why would you do that? Everyone else said—"

He steps closer, clenching his hands together. "Everyone else is *wrong*. They don't understand. They've turned a blind eye."

I back up. "You're freaking me out a little bit."

"In the past few years, the Shades have grown too powerful. The Elders have ignored the signs. Shades aren't following the old rules. And us? If action's not taken, I'm afraid of what that'll mean. Keleusma's been waiting for someone like you—someone who didn't grow up knowing the ins and outs of how our world should be." He makes quotation marks with his hands for the last two words. "You can see things more clearly. Discern things the other Shifters can't. We need you. You might be the only one who can save us."

Hearing him mention the Shades makes heebie jeebies crawl down my back. And, wait, *save us*? I can't even snip the right cord on a fake bomb.

"You know, you're not helping me freak out any less."

Eugene crosses his arms. "Will you go, or not?"

I stare at the palms of my hands. Study the lines. "They all said I'm not ready."

"You understand what's right without being told." His voice is soft. "That's what makes you so special, Gabby."

"You don't think I need more sword training and debate lessons?"

"I think it'll come to you when you need it." He uncrosses his arms. "Honestly, I think your heart is all you need. You'll know what to do."

His words seep into me. Cutting bindings I didn't even know were fastened tightly around my heart, choking me. "Then I'll go."

A triumphant glow lights his smile as he tells me Darnell will come for me early in the morning. He instructs me not to tell anyone. Which proves almost impossible later when Michael comes knocking on my door.

I stride across the room and press the lock button. It clicks loudly, so he knows I'm right here listening. But I don't want him to be able to get in. If I see him face-to-face—sincerity written on his features—I won't be able to lie. To anyone else, sure. But not to Michael.

"Gabby." He knocks again. "I know you're upset with me, and you have a right to be."

I lay my forehead and hand against the door, closing my eyes. His voice is rich. It's become like a favorite song. I know he'll be on a warpath when I join the experiment tomorrow. For now, I just want to enjoy hearing him.

He stops knocking, but he's still there. "I wanted to say goodbye, and that I'll miss you. And if something ... goes wrong, know that I think you're really special and that I'm glad I met you. It might sound weird because we just met, but you've already changed me. The way I think about things. What's important. So I wanted to thank you." He sighs. "I guess that's it."

If something goes wrong? My eyes fly open. I don't know why, but I hadn't considered that. Lark suddenly sounds like the height of rationality. Eugene's idea is far too dangerous.

Every muscle in my body burns to fling open the door and throw my arms around his neck. To breath in that mixture of pine and peppermint. Beg him not to go at all. But I keep my word to Eugene. I fist my hands and shove them into my armpits and drag myself back to bed. That night sleep comes in snatches, and when it does I wake up screaming.

Shades. All I see are Shades.

In the morning, I shower and dress long before Darnell shows up at my door. We walk together in silence down abandoned hallways to a section of the complex I didn't know existed. Every inch bursts with computers and cubicles. Perhaps Keleusma has as much paperwork to fill out as the rest of the world.

He stops. "Are you afraid?"

"Should I be?"

We're shoulder to shoulder, but he doesn't turn his head at all to face me. "You're stronger than you think you are."

I force a laugh. "Well great. Looks like all that time on the bench press paid off."

Poor Darnell, he's always so serious. He probably doesn't know what to do with me.

He turns now and rests a heavy hand on my shoulder. The action makes me meet his eyes. "Inside. Where it counts. You are strong."

We don't talk again. He leads me through a labyrinth of dark rooms until we reach what I dub Eugene's Mad Scientist Lab. Eugene bends over a keyboard, furiously typing. He's oblivious to the fact that we've entered. There's a large circle platform in the middle of the room surrounded by five poles. The rounded tops of the poles sizzle with something that looks like green electricity. Or lightning.

If Eugene starts to chant *it's alive,* I swear I'll bolt.

Darnell points to a counter piled with electronic equipment. "Duck back there." I nod and do as I'm told, pulling my knees to my chest. Then Darnell steps in front of me like a body-guard. I can't see around him, and no one will be able to see me. The door creaks and Michael and Lark stroll in together. I can hear their voices, but they're speaking so quietly, I can't make out the words.

"Are you truly ready for this?" Darnell's tone rumbles like thunder before a strong storm. I feel like the question is meant as a last out for me.

Michael's voice is closer now. "As ready as I can be."

"Great." Eugene finally acknowledges that other people are in the room. "Go on up and stand in the very center." A pause. "Just a few inches to the left. One more step over. Perfect. Now whatever you do, don't move."

"Will it hurt?" Michael asks.

Lark's voice overtakes whatever Eugene was going to say. "I still don't think this is wise."

Eugene must flip a switch, because the poles begin to hum at a level that would make dogs whimper and opera singers cringe. A flash of light fills the room, zapping from the top of one poll to another. Energy surges through the room. I brace my hands on the floor.

"Here we go." Eugene sounds excited.

The words serve as a code to Darnell. In a quick movement, he turns and grabs my arm. Hauling me to my feet, he flings me into the center of the circle with Michael.

Taken by surprise, I crash into Michael, and he turns to catch me. "Gabby! No. What are you—? Why are you—?" The expression on his face cuts to my core. Confusion. Anger. Betrayal.

"Now!" Eugene yells.

I toss my arms around Michael's middle, snaking them underneath the backpack he wears. Press my ear into his warm chest. Hear his racing heart. He tries to push me away, but I hold fast. A sliver of light slices through us, shooting pain into every nerve. We both shriek, clinging to each other for support. My nails bite his back. His fingers dig into my shoulders. A bright flash blinds me.

Then the room disappears.

CHAPTER TWELVE

Darkness cloaks us, momentarily blocking out sound, smells, everything. My muscles shake. We hit hard-packed ground and roll together. Spots dance in my vision. As we come to a stop, I land on top of Michael. Air whooshes from his lungs, and he shoves me off him. I scramble to get on my hands and knees, coughing. I press my palm to my chest, where a deep burning sensation intensifies.

Michael slowly sits up, but then he hunches over, grabbing at his stomach. He dry heaves for a minute. The sound rips through me, propelling me forward. Ignoring the pain hitching in my side, I crawl over and rub his shoulder. "Hey, it's okay."

Without turning around, he pushes me away. "Don't touch me."

"But—"

He tries to stand, to pace away from me, but he trips over a log. Barely catching himself, he comes down hard on his elbows, his head drooping.

"Michael." My voice comes out soft, like I'm speaking to a scared, snarling dog. One hand extended, I step toward him. Twigs snap under my feet, crackling in the night air. The noise sets off a round of hooting from unseen owls. Where are we? Did Eugene work his machine correctly? Are we back on the original mission, or did he send us somewhere else? A shiver works its way up my spine.

Michael rises before I can reach him—help him. He turns on me, fists clenched and nostrils flaring. "I'm serious, Gabby. Leave me alone."

I lift my hands but let them fall back to my sides. "I'm sorry."

He adjusts the straps to his backpack, strides ten feet away from me, then circles back, finger pointing. "Know what? You're not sorry. If you were sorry, you wouldn't have done it."

Nausea prickles my throat, and the backs of my eyes burn. "Michael—"

"No. You forfeited your right to speak when you lied to me." He stalks closer, but stops a few feet away. Then he turns to the side and rubs the back of his neck. It's like he can't stay still.

My head spins. Lie? I would never lie to him. "I didn't—"

"You stood there last night. You *heard* when I came to your room. Heard what I said." There's a growl in his voice that I've never heard before. "Well, didn't you?"

It feels like there's a fist in my throat. I try to swallow, to speak. But I know my voice will waver. Instead I nod, slowly.

"So either you listened, basically laughing at me, because you *knew* you were going to come. Or you heard all that and still came. Knowing I didn't want you to." His hands move in jerks as he speaks. "Which is it?"

My mouth goes dry. "Don't be like this."

"Why not? Oh, sure, you'd love it if someone double crossed you."

I should be compassionate. He's clearly upset. But I'm not about to let him accuse me of betraying him. Not when I just want to be with him.

Dad always warns me that my Spanish temper gets me into trouble. Grinding my teeth, I square my shoulders. "Double crossed? Are you kidding me?"

Michael sighs and I see his stance relax. The fight's draining from him. "We were supposed to be friends."

"Oh, and that's why you wanted to leave me behind."

"Never mind. I was better off alone. I shouldn't have allowed myself..." He just laughs, once, clipped.

"We are friends," I whisper and try to catch his gaze. But he avoids me.

Fingers to his lips, he shakes his head. "If we were, you would have told me the truth last night. We could have talked it out. Come to some sort of compromise. But go behind my back?" He works his jaw back and forth. "No. We're not friends."

His words make me flinch. I want to argue. Fall on my knees and plead with him. But the dead look in his eyes tells me the conversation is over. He trudges away from me and lumbers through a grove of trees, alerting every creature in a half-mile radius to our presence.

Right before he disappears from my vision, he clears his throat. “Well, are you coming? Or are you going it alone on this one? Pretty sure there are a lot of wild animals in these parts.”

Why does he have to be so touchy? I growl. Then I storm after him.

We walk side by side for a while. Pine needles muffle our footsteps. The sound of water churns in the distance. My vision bounces to Michael’s face. I can’t help it. But his stays trained right ahead. As if I’m not even there. He keeps taking deep breaths.

It hits me then. I’ve ruined everything. The winks and the way he’d find me across a crowded room. His constant teasing and that ready laugh. It’s all gone. I killed it.

Maybe Michael was right about Eugene. Perhaps he is crazy. Why did I listen to him? Why did I allow him to say things to me as if they meant anything? Was I that starved for someone to see something important about me? Something worthwhile? I cringe. I’m stupid. Rash and dangerous, just like Lark and Donovan said.

My eyes dart to Michael’s profile. I’ve lost the one good thing about this whole shifting mess. His good opinion. No, I’ve lost more than that—*him*.

If justice existed, Nicholas would shift me right now. I don’t even care where to. The ideas are endless. For a start, how about he tosses me into the midst of a mine field? The belly of some giant whale might be nice. Or Mars. Honestly, he can have his pick.

Adrift in my thoughts, I'm not paying attention. My toe catches on a rock, and I pitch forward. Michael's firm hand grabs my upper arm, jerking me back so I don't fall. Just as quickly, he lets go.

I run my fingers over the warm spot on my arm. "Thanks."

"Be more careful."

We come to a clearing, and Michael makes his way to a grassy knoll overlooking a large river. Yanking off his backpack, he drops it to the ground. Next, he lowers himself to the grass. Slowly, as if his joints hurt. "Well, at least we know Eugene brought us to the right spot." He juts his chin to indicate the body of water. "The mighty Mississippi. Welcome to Tennessee."

Besides the dirt embankments littered with soldiers on either side, the Mississippi River looks like Chicago during rush hour—a flurry of stilled activity. Riverboats churn past each other in the black water, a steady slap ... slap ... slap. The lanterns onboard radiate light so brightly that they look like slow-moving behemoths, swimming through the water with their backs on fire. Some heave loads that cause them to list. Others seem determined to reach their destination first at any cost. Their chimneys puff up coal-laden smoke. Covering my mouth, I cough. The air tastes of cigarettes and fish.

I sit a few inches away from Michael. "So this is Memphis, huh?"

He scrutinizes the bustling harbor. "Yeah, not quite the same as in our time, but it's a pretty significant place during the Civil War." The light from the river traffic illuminates his serious expression.

One smile, would that be so hard? I nudge him with my shoulder. "Hey, you don't need to look so grim. I might not be amazing at history, but I do know the North wins."

Releasing a long burst of air, Michael shoves at his backpack. "That's just it. If you—if *we* mess up. If Shifters fail on our missions, then the South could win. Nothing has to end up how it was when you left." He runs his hand through his hair, and strands scatter across his forehead. "You could die out here, Gabby. I'm not kidding. Don't you understand that?"

His voice is so panicked, and his eyes wide and roving. He looks like he's been up for nights on end, pulling his hair out. My muscles burn to hug him—to take some of the tension from his shoulders. I'd reach out for his hand if I knew he wouldn't pull away.

I settle on speaking in a calm voice. "I'm not concerned about that."

Finally facing me, his lips curl into a sneer. "Not afraid of dying?"

"No, I'm terrified of that." Might as well risk everything. I lay my hand on his knee. "But I'm not nervous because I'm with you. You promised you'd protect me on our first mission together, didn't you?"

Uprooting wads of grass from the earth, he bunches the pieces in his hand and lets them sail upon the breeze. At least he doesn't jerk away from my touch. "I shouldn't have said that. I can't protect you. I can't protect anyone."

"I don't believe that. Not for a second."

"Well, you should." Now he moves his knee. My hand drops to the cold ground. He rises, crosses his arms. Watches the river like it's the most fascinating thing in the world. "People die around me."

What do I say to that? Really, beyond the last week or so, I don't know him. Well, his history at least. If I think about it, he hasn't shared much. Not that I have either, so no blame there. You don't shake someone's hand and ask for their life story. Still, I may not know *about* Michael, but I do know what *kind* of person he is. Maybe people have been killed on his watch, but in this line of work, I can't image that not happening. The Michael I know did everything in his power to save them. I feel that truth to the core of me.

Didn't he warn me once not to consider him a hero? Impossible.

Moving his weight from one foot to the other, he pivots to look at me. "The first real mission I went on was with my father. He was the Shifter out of my parents. A great one. We were dropped on this battleship." His eyes snap shut.

"You don't have to tell me."

"I do if you're going to understand." Crouching beside me, he raises his eyebrows. "It was the Battle of the Komandorski Islands. There was fog everywhere. We couldn't even make out the enemy ship. He didn't want me to leave his side. I was a scrawny kid. Every hit the ship took threw me to the floor. The firestorm came. Cannons tore the sky apart. If I hadn't been there ... if he hadn't been so worried about keeping an eye on me—he would have been paying attention. But he wasn't. And now he's gone."

Watched his father die in front of him? Blown to bits? My stomach churns. An apology burns in my throat, but it tastes hollow. I didn't know his father or what he meant to Michael. Tears swim in my eyes. "You were just a kid. It's wasn't your fault."

He snatches a rock from the ground and turns it over in his hand. "Believe me, it was."

I refuse to take in his words. "Just because you were there?" That's what he's worried about. "So don't worry about me. Okay? Let whatever happens, happen. I don't want you distracted like that. Not because of me."

He shakes his head. "Do you really think I could do that? Just let you die right in front of me when I could do something to prevent it? Come on, Gabby."

"Why does Nicholas allow stuff like that to happen? Why does he even put us into situations where we could die or lose people we love?"

He sends the rock sailing toward the Mississippi. It lands with a giant *thunk*. "Because he never promised us a painless existence. Nothing like that. Only that he will be watching out for us during those times."

"But—"

He drops down again. "Let's just change the subject."

Water laps against the shoreline and raucous laughter from a passing boat drifts up the bank. I wish all the noise would stop. That I was alone—unable to hurt the people I care about.

Why did I ruin another one of Michael's missions? As if botching the first one wasn't enough. Now here I am, adding more stress. Putting him in further danger because he thinks he has to watch out for me above everything. I have no doubt he'd throw his body between me and a speeding train. Foolishly sacrificing his life, even if mine couldn't be saved. Has anyone ever cared enough about me to consider doing something like that? But here's Michael, he's known me such a short amount of time and is ready.

Warmth spears my chest. I rub my palm back and forth over the pain. The weight of what I've done to him rocks through me. I'm so selfish.

He's been watching me for the last few minutes. "Is Eugene's time traveling getting to you too? It feels like insane heartburn, right?" He pounds his fist against his chest three times.

I bite my bottom lip. Nod my head.

He unzips his bag, digs through the contents and fishes out a sleeve of crackers. "I didn't bring much food. Not enough for two...." He shrugs. "No knowing how long we'll be here, so we'll have to ration what I have." He offers me a couple crackers.

I try to push them away. "Really, I'm fine."

"Eat them. It might take the feeling away."

I break each cracker in two and jam them into my mouth. They suck the moisture out of my cheeks. I lick around my teeth, trying to find all the crumbs. He's wrong about the food helping. The ache inside still throbs.

Michael hands over a water bottle. After a few sips, I give it back to him and he takes a long swig. He wipes his mouth with the back of his wrist. "If we're going to make it to town while there are still rooms available, we better get a move on it."

"Memphis is huge though, isn't it? How will we ever find Pinkerton?"

"Last time we were here, he mentioned something about Hunt House." He slips the bag over his shoulders and offers me his hand.

"Wow. Good memory."

"Comes with practice."

By the time we turn onto a street labeled Beale, my feet are sore and blistering. But the outline of houses up the bend breathes hope into my steps.

Michael keeps his voice low. "Hunt House gets fought over in the war. It has to belong to the Confederates right now if Pinkerton steered them there. I saw blueprints for it once. There's an escape tunnel that might come in handy. At least, if they haven't sealed it off. When we go inside, whatever you do, don't talk. During this time period guys spoke for women. Just go with it for me."

"Don't we need to ditch your backpack somewhere?"

"They see what they want. Remember?"

What I assume is Hunt House comes into view. Four white pillars gleam in the moonlight. They support a two story, brick mansion. The grounds might have once been beautiful, but it's all a bunch of mud ruts now. Too many soldiers and horses have trod here. Michael goes up to the door, and walks right in.

I grab his hand, silently asking him what he's doing.

"Relax," he whispers. "It's a hotel for Confederate sympathizers right now."

As we enter, the rich smells of cherry wood and tobacco greet us. Oriental rugs cover polished wooden floors. Ornate vases and sculptures decorate some shelves that line the walls.

A man with an impressive, curling mustache hurries over to us. "Might I help you two?"

Michael extends his hand. "I believe so. On this fine evening, my sister and I happen to find ourselves in search of lodging. We've had the pleasure of listening to such wonderful reports about your establishment. Might you have two rooms?"

My mouth drops open before I can stop it. How does Michael do that? Start speaking just like they do?

The hotel clerk pulls on the bottom of his vest. If he was a rat, he'd preen himself right now. "You're in luck. I happen to have two rooms situated beside each other available to let. I assume you want to be next door to your sister?" The man looks me up and down. What does he see? A girl in a giant hoop dress—they wear those now, right? Scarlett O'Hara type of stuff?

Before I can glance around further, Michael snags my arm and leads me up the stairs. "It's late. So there's no use for us to do anything but sleep right now. Try and get in as much as you can." He tugs a key from his pocket and opens the first door we come to. "Go on, you take this one."

Upon entering, I see it's like a bedroom from a period film. A high canopied bed and dark wood furniture. It even has a porcelain pitcher on the side table. When I turn back to the door, Michael's still there.

I work my bottom lip between my teeth. "How did you pay for this?"

He leans against the doorframe. "I knew what time I was going to. I brought some money. Although, had I known..."

"That I was coming, you could have brought more?"

A sad smile plays over his face. "Good night, Gabby. I'm next door if you need me." He grabs the handle and shuts the door.

I dip my hands into the pitcher of water and splash some onto my face. At the bedside I remove my shoes and massage my feet. I can't stop thinking of Michael and how angry he is. I should try to sleep, like he told me. Instead I find myself stepping out into the hallway, knocking on his door.

It opens a heartbeat later. Michael's shoulders sag. The front of his shirt is wet. His brows scrunch. "Is something wrong?"

I knit my fingers together. Stare down at my bare feet. "I made a mess of things. I'm sorry."

He braces his hand on the door jam. "I know you are."

Our eyes meet. "I should have listened to you. I know it's asking a lot, but can you forgive me?"

"I forgive you."

"Just like that?"

"Look, I'm still angry with you, but I'll get over it. What's done is done. You're forgiven."

"I promise I'll talk to you next time. I'll never keep something from you again."

"Never is a hard promise to keep." He smiles, but it doesn't meet his eyes. "Hey, wait a second." He leaves me in the hallway and rummages through his backpack. Pulling out a t-shirt, he crosses back and hands it to me. "Take it. Looks like yours got dirty when we landed."

I look down at the front of my shirt. It's streaked with caked-on mud. Lovely.

He taps his chin. "It'll be way too big on you, but...." He shrugs.

"Is this your only extra?" I try to hand it back to him, but he won't take it.

"I'll live. I might smell, but I'll live." He closes my hands around the shirt. "Do me one favor."

"Anything."

"Lock your door. I don't like the way the clerk eyed you."

Back in my room, I turn both bolts on my door. Making my way around the room, I blow out all the candles. Too tired to even take off my dirty shirt, I crawl under the blankets. Michael's shirt is still clutched in my hands. Closing my eyes, I press the fabric to my nose, willing it to smell like him.

No matter what happens on the mission, I must make him trust me again.

CHAPTER THIRTEEN

Pink hues pool in my bedroom, the blush from the first kiss of the morning sun. Situations always look different in the light of a new day. This goes double if your bedroom lacks twenty-first-century blinds.

With a groan, I yank the down pillow over my head. I have every intention of staying right here. Pretending Michael's not mad at me, and that I don't have to rescue some short, bearded man today. That is until I remember that people back in the day had bad hygiene and carried bedbugs. There isn't some sort of hotel inspection board that sets rules for cleanliness. I bolt out of the bed, and dance around the room, shaking my arms, hopefully flinging away any plague I might have picked up.

The water in the basin is now frigid. I splash my face with a yelp. My shirt's still dirty, completely crusted over now that the mud is dry. Why didn't I at least soak it in water last night? I could have gotten the worst of the mess off. Sure, it wouldn't have been dry by morning, but maybe I could have given Michael his shirt tomorrow. Instead, he'll have to go without the spare. But who knows, maybe we'll be back in Keleusma laughing tonight.

A girl can dream.

His shirt swims on me, but there's not much I can do about that. Grouping the extra fabric on the bottom, I tie a knot. I look every bit like an Eighties hair band groupie. Oh well. I yank the binding out of my braid and comb my fingers through my hair. Would it kill the people in this time to have mirrors in their rooms? Only Michael will be able to see what I really look like. Maybe he packed a brush in his backpack of wonders.

Doubtful. Michael's more of the focus-on-necessities type of guy. Besides, he rattled off most of the contents yesterday. Water bottle, iodine, crackers, beef jerky, a knife, and a wool blanket. Nothing that screams makeover.

There's a soft knock on my door. It's Michael. Complete with bags under his eyes and impressive bedhead.

He rests his hand on the hallway wall, leaning into, but not entering my room. "Ready?"

I want to tell him no. Offer him a chance to play hooky for once in his life. But he was so upset with me last night. That thought melts the words on my tongue. I need to be here for him in this mission. Not get in the way. More than that, I need to become an essential part. Prove to him that my being here isn't a mistake. Dare I hope he'll think we make a good team?

So instead of what I want, I say, "yup." Not my most eloquent moment, but it's early. I join him in the hall and we head downstairs.

The clerk from last night is in the lobby straightening a stack of papers. He beams when he spots us. "Breakfast is on the veranda this morning." Following us outside, he points in the direction of a metal table and chairs. A group of men mill around on the barren front yard, and one of them spits a long stream of tobacco.

Michael pulls out a chair for me. The clerk sets two full plates on the table along with cups of steaming tea. When he leaves, I poke the food with my fork.

Under the table, Michael's knees knock into mine. "It's just sausage and apples."

"Doesn't really sound like the best combination." I take a bite anyway. Not bad. Actually, it's five times tastier than the frozen sausages that I usually nuke in the microwave. The tea's good too. Blackberry.

"See." Michael drops a napkin into his lap. "It's passable. Just be happy it's not sheep's head stew or hardtack."

I gag on the chunk of apple in my mouth. "Sheep's head? Are you kidding me?"

A grim headshake, with something on his lips that looks like it wants to be a smile when it grows up. "The stew's not that bad. But the hardtack." He pretends to throw up. "I once lived on the stuff for a month. Hoping to never do that again."

Lowering my voice, I incline my head closer to him. "What's the plan for today? I was thinking we should just grab Pinkerton and get out of here."

He shakes his head. “Believe me, that man doesn’t need our help. Well, at least not like that. I think it’s more important to figure out what these soldiers are up to and pass that information on to Pinkerton. I’m going to focus on scoping out the Confederates he was with the other night.”

I set down my silverware. “Where does that leave me?”

“I need you to stay under the radar. Be around, but not in the way.”

I cross my legs, my arms, and lean back in the chair. “In the way?”

Michael rakes his hand through his hair. “Not like that. Listen, there are two ways those soldiers can view you. One, as either not capable because you’re a woman. Or two—as a potential spy. Let’s hope they see you as the first.”

My eyebrow arches. “A spy? I like the sound of that.”

He sets down his tea. Hard. “This isn’t a game, Gabby. You get that, right? War isn’t something to joke about. If those men think you’re a spy it could turn bad for us really quickly.”

My eyes dart to the Confederates on the front lawn. “If they figure us out ... what will happen?”

“Unless Nicholas chooses to shift us,” he works his jaw back and forth, “they’ll probably kill us.”

I continue watching the soldiers. Would they harm me—a woman? I’m certain they’d hurt Michael if they got their hands on him. More than hurt him. Above all, I can’t let that happen. “So they’re all evil? I’m glad the North wins if the Confederates are that heartless.”

Michael shakes his head. "The Confederates aren't all bad, just like the Union isn't all good. There's no such thing as a right side in war. They're just people, and they're hurting. All of them are sick of fighting and want to be done."

He leans closer. "Some of those men have babies at home that they want to see grow up. Some of them have a sweetheart and the only thing on their mind is to make it home alive to start a life with her. You have to think of them as individuals, each with worth and a story. When you start to think of people as groups or causes, you take away their humanity. If that's the case, why are we wasting our time doing what we're doing?"

"But, Michael ... kill us?" I really should have stayed back in Keleusma.

He traces his fingers over the curves on the top of the iron table. "Back in our time, my neighborhood was surrounded by a forest preserve. The main street to get there had ponds lining each side. People used to fly down that street. I'm talking seventy, eighty miles an hour. But there were all these ducks that lived there. They'd sun themselves a few feet from the road." He pauses.

I lock my gaze with his now. Let him know I'm listening, even though I have no clue why he's telling me this right now.

"Even as a kid I remember thinking, wow, those stupid ducks. You know? They have wings. Can go anywhere in the world they want, but they pick to live by that road." He shakes his head. "Each day, right there on the edge of death." His gaze rakes over the group of soldiers.

I stack my plate on top of his. "Did any of them ever get hit?"

"Every summer, you'd see two or three smashed on the road each month." He taps the table, then whispers, "Stupid ducks."

His words transform the breakfast in my stomach to a twenty-pound knot.

He rises from the table. "I'm going to try and talk to the officers. Wish me luck."

I'm left alone, drumming my fingers on the tabletop and staring at the sunrise. My eyes keep wandering back to Michael, expecting the other men in the group to pounce on him any second. If they did, what would I do? I can't take them. Not in a million years. They're all two or three times my size. Not to mention the gun each of them carries. And there's no one who would come to our rescue if I yell.

Please keep us safe. The words are there, but I don't know who they're for.

The hotel clerk smiles down at me as he collects our dirty dishes. He waggles his eyebrows. I shift my gaze away from him. Gross. He's probably twice my age. That would be like Eugene or Darnell hitting on me. Although, in this time period, I don't think they cared much about age. Note to self—do not look weird men in the eye. Wait, how about, only look Michael in the eye.

Okay, that's not the safest thing for me either. He makes my stomach flip-flop too. But that's different.

Without encouragement, Creep-o-Clerk ambles back inside Hunt House. He leaves the front door standing open. No doubt an invitation for me to join him. I'm about to get up and saunter away when I recognize a voice. Every muscle in my body freezes. I only heard it once before, but Pinkerton's—well, he goes by E. J. Allen here—tone is distinct. Michael said he's not our concern as much as finding out secrets, but I can't help listening.

"What say you, Mr. Allen? Will you join us in traveling as far as the encampment of troops at Camp Beauregard?"

Pinkerton says, "Gents, as I both lack an engagement and enjoy your company, that sounds like a marvelous plan. I may even join to do my part in the cause like you've all been encouraging me to do." There's a scuffling of shoes and grunts of agreement, then nothing. The stable is around back so if they're leaving right away, they'll exit the other end of the house.

Latched onto the armrest of my chair, my fingers go white. Weren't we originally sent here to help the Union spy? Michael sensed a leading to save Pinkerton the first time. Now the man's leaving Hunt House to go who knows where. I'm on my feet now, pacing the veranda. Oh, and biting my nails. I make myself stop.

Michael's in the circle of men, swapping stories. Hitting each other on the back and laughing. Is it proper in this time to walk over there and snag him? Can I holler out his name to get his attention?

My friend Emma once forced me to watch *Pride and Prejudice*. Thankfully, it was just the two-hour one and not the eight-hour saga that requires an entire day devoted to watching. What did the mean-headed sister call her brother in the movie? I press my fingers to my temples. She referred to him by his last name. Not that this is the same time period. Actually, that story takes place in a different country all together.

I work my bracelet around my wrist. Taking action is better than thinking about movies. I start across the lawn. "Mr. Pace?"

Michael raises his eyebrows toward me, and then turns back to the men, bowing slightly. "Excuse me, friends. My sister is prone to lightheadedness when left in the sunshine over long." He comes over and puts his arm around me, steering me away from both the house and the soldiers.

I dig my elbow into his ribs. "Lightheadedness?"

He squeezes my shoulder. "It was the best I could come up with. What's up?"

"Pinkerton is leaving."

He stops walking. "You saw him?"

"I heard him."

"When?"

I shrug. "Two minutes ago."

"Did he say where he was headed?"

"Not just him. I think he's with some of the soldiers."

"The clerk will know. He's been feeding information to them this whole time. I asked him how to give money and pretended to be from a wealthy family that wants to help the cause. He'll tell me where they went." Grabbing my arm, Michael tows me into Hunt House and flags down the clerk who gives him the information about the Confederates. "Do you have carriages to let?"

Creep-o polishes the table without looking up. "No, sir. The last one left moments ago. I have a horse." Then he glances at me. "Only one. If you need to travel somewhere, there are rooms open this evening. Should you pay in advance, your sister can stay here under my care for the duration of the day."

I dig my nails into Michael's hand.

He grits through it with a smile. "What a thoughtful offer." He pays for the horse while I panic. If Michael leaves me here, I'll take off into the woods and live like a hobbit until he returns. I will not stay at Hunt House alone.

Without wasting time, Michael ushers me out of the house and we're tramping to the barn. He tosses me the backpack, and I sling it over my shoulder.

While he pulls a chestnut-colored horse out of a stall, I stalk back and forth, fists bunched at my sides. "You're really going to just leave me here. I can't believe this."

He swings up onto the horse and trots it over to me.

I leap back. "Okay, you know how I feel about those animals."

Maneuvering his shoe from the holder, he reaches out his hand. "Put your foot in the stirrup and climb up behind me."

I'm lifted onto the back of the horse by more of Michael's strength than my own.

He peeks at me over his shoulder. "Hang on tight. This isn't going to be a little stroll."

"I thought you were going to leave me behind." I lace my arms around him. Perhaps hanging on too tightly.

Clucking his tongue, he gets the horse to jog out of the barn. Michael turns his head slightly. "I'll never leave you behind. That's a promise."

Michael lands a swift kick to the horse's side, sending it into a full run. I pull closer to him, bury the side of my face against his back and close my eyes. Sway against him as the horse tears across a field.

Instead of thinking about falling off the horse, I focus on Michael. He's warm and carries the mixed scents of the outdoors and hard work. When I was younger and spent all day playing outside with friends, I used to come home smelling like that. My dad would pick me up, twirl me in a circle, and say I smelled like the sun. What a great way to say it. So much better than saying someone reminds you of sweat and dirt.

We're at the train depot quicker than I expected. Michael's easing me off the back of the horse before I get a chance to open my eyes. He loops the reins over a hitching post and strides to the front doors, then pauses. "I'm going inside to do some surveying. Wait for me out here, okay?"

Once he's inside, I skirt around the horse and decide to check out the other side of the station. Where the horse is hitched faces the road, but I want to see the side with the rail. Someone has planted a few flowers to trim the building, but they're in horrible need of watering. Stuff like that must fall to the wayside during a war. One wayward bee searches each wilted blossom for nectar. Bad luck, buddy.

I turn the corner and stop dead in my tracks. The three men I saw the first night I shifted are there on the platform, waiting beside a monstrous black train as it belches smoke. I have to do what I can to find out about Pinkerton. The sooner we finish this mission, the better.

Raising my chin, I try to act the way a lady in this time would, although I don't really know how that is. I saunter toward the train, pretending to be dazzled by the contraption. My ploy works. The men talk as if I'm not even there.

"Why the pretense about showing him the fort?"

"If he's the spy I think he is, capturing him will get us promotions and loads of money. We could also be granted positions off the battlefield for a capture this grand. Isn't that what we all want—to be done fighting once and for all? This could be our ticket, but I'm being careful until we have him surrounded by a thousand soldiers."

"You did send a telegram? They're aware we're coming with him?"

"From the second we step off the train, he won't stand a chance."

I'm inching my way down the platform when I spot Pinkerton. He's seated inside the train, reading a newspaper as if all is right in the world. Without thinking, I scale the three large steps into the train and hurry down the aisle.

I slide into the seat next to Pinkerton. "I know you don't know who I am, but I just heard those men you are traveling with. They know you're a Union spy and they have people ready to jump you at the next stop."

Pinkerton's eyes narrow. "Jump me?"

Okay, so not the best word choice for the 1800's. "Abduct you."

He glances out the window, then stands. "I'm indebted to you, Miss."

My heart is pounding so hard I'm afraid he can hear it. "Exit on the other side of the train. You can make your way off the platform on that side before they realize you're gone. I'll keep an eye on them for you."

Pinkerton follows my instructions. Once off the train, he ducks behind carriages until I can't see him any longer. Who knew I could complete a mission that easily? I take a long breath. Bite my cheeks to hold back a smug smile. Wait, I need to get off this train before it decides to go somewhere.

Just as I turn, a hand clamps around my mouth and another wraps around my middle. Strong body odor makes me gag. It happens so fast, I don't have time to fight. I'm jerked backward and dragged off the train.

The long-haired Confederate soldier slams me against the outside wall of the station and smiles at me like the Cheshire cat. Except there's black ooze dribbling down his lip. "Do you realize you just cost me a trip home to see my family? You're either the greatest fool in history or another spy. Either way, you're coming with us."

I try to wiggle free. Shift! *Nicholas, if you're real. Shifting now would be nice.* "Please. I don't know what this is about. Let go."

"I think you know exactly what this is about. Anyone who warns a Northern spy has either picked the wrong side—or is a spy herself. My gut says—I got a spy. If I'm correct, Commander Bragg may give me a promotion yet." His giant hand locks my neck to the wall. I gasp for breath and claw at his skin. He spits tobacco juice all over my shoes.

As my brain starts to go fuzzy from lack of air, only one discernible thought pounds over and over in my head.

Stupid duck.

CHAPTER FOURTEEN

The world snaps back into view as I gain consciousness, and it smells like a Dumpster. They've hauled me around the corner of the train depot, near a small shed. Two men bind my arms, my feet. I try to struggle, but my limbs feel so heavy. I half close my eyes against the stinging sunlight.

It's impossible to scream with a sweaty handkerchief in your mouth. Try it if you don't believe me. My brain commands me to shriek, but each attempt ends in a cough, which leads to eye watering and gagging. Why do I even bother? There's no one to ride in on a white horse and rescue me. Any other Confederate sympathizer will slap these men on the back for a job well done if they see me. Of course there's Michael, but the thought of him in danger makes my gut clench.

These men aren't really going to injure me, are they? A woman can't be hanged for spying. Or were they? I wish I paid better attention in history class. My mind trips down a bunny trail to flannel-clad men who kill women in the woods, or worse, lock them up somewhere for twenty years while they waste away. Maybe I've watched one too many true crime shows on cable.

The soldier with the long hair hoists me onto his shoulder. "Round up the rest of the men. Tell them we won't be taking the train today. Not with this little bit of cargo. We'll have to keep the horses from Hunt House and be late delivering the medical supplies, but I don't see a way around it."

"Sure thing, Sterling."

When the others leave, I pound on the man's—Sterling's—back, and try to land solid kicks to his stomach. With a growl, he secures my legs and gives me a shake. "Don't mess with me, girl. Promotion or not, I've a mind to shoot you right here if you don't quit."

He's right. Now's not the time to make an escape. Because if he set me down—then what? I'm tied, and he has a horse. Not really a fair match for a getaway.

Grunting, he tosses me over the front of his saddle. The horn jabs my spleen. Sterling mounts, and his knees dig against me. I hear a group of men joining us. It's more than the two who were here a moment ago.

Sterling circles his horse while the others unhitch theirs. My head's no more than three or four feet from the ground. I bob with every move the animal makes. Each muscle twitch could pitch me face-first to a death by trampling. Stiffening only makes me totter more. I swallow hard. Relax. Just relax. Easier said than done.

"I thought I made it clear, we're not bringing anyone else with us." Sterling does not sound pleased. In fact, he snarls whenever he talks. As hard as I try, I can't lift my head enough to see the others.

Different voices filter my way.

"The boy checks out. He wants to join the army, but they told him he was too young."

"He doesn't look too young."

I hear Michael's soft laugh. "People always tell me that. I'd like to join, if you'd allow me."

No, no, no. Michael is not supposed to be here risking his neck for me. His words from last night pierce through me with the power of a breaking dam. *"Do you really think I could do that? Just let you die right in front of me when I could do something to prevent it? Come on, Gabby."*

I should never have come. When I see Eugene, I'm going to call him every foul name I can think of. How quickly I broke my promise to help Michael. I'll never gain his trust again now. The backs of my eyes sting with gathering tears.

Sterling rests his hand on my back. "You can join as long as you don't slow us down. Understood?"

Without another word from the men, the horse I'm on takes off. As we bump along, I shut my eyes, and try to keep this morning's sausage and apples from making a reappearance.

If some great and powerful Oz really does control when we shift, now would be an excellent time. Besides, Pinkerton's safe, so at least Michael should have shifted. Unless this is punishment for bending the rules.

We ride for what feels like a few hours. Summer sun scorches my neck and arms. Horse sweat lathers along the straps of the saddle, which are near my head. I find some relief as we enter a wooded area, and the horses slow to a walk. As we weave between trees and tramp over shallow rivers, I lose track of time. Before long, we stop.

Sterling dismounts and lifts me, only to drop me onto the ground. I land hip first. Pain shoots into my spine, and I have to bite the nasty cloth to keep from crying.

Another man carries over a large rope and fastens me to a tree. The thick hemp cuts into my wrists. I slump there and watch them set up camp for the night. Most of all, I follow Michael's movements. He gathers dry branches and sets up tents—jokes around with the other men as if I'm not even here. Which is probably his plan. Showing interest in the captive girl will toss unwanted attention his way. Still, a quick wink or a chin-up couldn't hurt.

A short guy plops down a few feet from me. "We're going to be fried as a floured chicken by the time we reach the fort."

Sterling spits a long stream of tobacco. It explodes against the hard-packed dirt, flinging some onto my pants. "We'll ride by night from here on out. Sleep and hunt by day. That way, we avoid crossing paths with other troops—both kinds of troops."

"And avoid getting yelled at for taking so long on our errand." A man near the horses yawns long and loud.

"Don't tell me you wanted to get back straight away to the fighting?" Sterling smirks.

Since being captured, I've avoided looking at them, but I do now. Even if they end up hurting me, I want to see the men as individuals like Michael said I should. Where once they might have been handsome, their cheeks have sunken in from lack of food. They all sport matching bags under their eyes. No wonder they've taken their time heading back to their post.

The soldiers are worn down—bitter from war. Who can blame them? In my time when people are separated from their loved ones for long durations of time there are ways to stay in constant touch. Email, texts, and video chats keep spirits high. But in this time? They probably can't even get a note delivered since they travel from battle to battle.

Evening swathes the sky in a thick, purple cloth. While some leave to hunt, a few soldiers start a fire. The flames are high enough to make a cub scout squeal. Fingers of smoke tickle the canopy's underbelly. Heat bathes the area. I press my tongue against the inside of my cheeks—my mouth is dry, and my lips cracking. Even my eyes burn, as if all their moisture has disappeared. No one offers me water. If they did, I'd gulp it right through the handkerchief. I shut my eyes, but my head still throbs.

Shuffling as best as I can, I try to work my way to the other side of the tree they tied me to, but the rope snags halfway. I'm stuck at an angle, but if I look to my left, I can pretend they're not there. My eyes rove over the underbrush, trying to remember what Indiana Jones does in moments like this. The snap of a twig nearby announces men returning, and the end of my escape plans.

They've bagged a few squirrels and four fish. I watch dinner roast over the fire, knowing they aren't planning on sharing any with me. I'm right. The men pick the carcasses clean, piling the bones nice and nearby. A barrel is pushed to the end of a supply cart and tapped. The men line up. Each waits to fill their tin mugs with the brew.

Sterling toes off his boots, stretching out near the fire. "With a spy in our midst, let's keep our wits about us tonight. Only one drink a piece then water or tea."

A couple of the men grumble.

Michael downs his glass. "No worries, men. I'm famed in my town for making the best tea in a twenty mile radius."

"Only ladies make tea." The shortest of the soldiers mutters, but as he talks he pulls a bashed up kettle from a pack on the supply cart.

Michael rubs his hands together. "Just wait, you'll see."

"That sounds intriguing."

Nodding, Michael turns his back to the group of men and sets to work going through the sacks on the cart. I hope he thinks to bring me a drink. He starts to make rounds, filling mugs with his concoction from the kettle and skips me. Great. Don't mind me, I'll just sit here and die of dehydration. No big deal.

Sterling takes a swig and starts to cough. "That's the bitterest tea I've ever tasted. What'd you put in there, son?"

Michael grins. "It's my ma's secret recipe—I promise it gets better after the second cup."

Which seems to be true because they all ask for seconds ... and thirds.

Some of them play a game with marbles. I press my elbows into my middle when my stomach grumbles. But for the most part, everyone's forgotten I'm here. By now a group of the men have already dozed off.

Michael jiggles the kettle. "There's still more." Men wave their cups in lazy arches in the air. He works his way around the group, providing more refills.

Someone to my left yawns. "Know any songs, boy?"

Michael clears his throat. "There is a land where cotton grows, a land where milk and honey flows. I'm going home to Dixie. Yes, I am going home." Who knew he could sing so well? His baritone lulls a few more men to sleep. Others join him for all seven verses, but their words slur a bit.

By the fourth song, Michael sings alone again. "For Southerners never yield. And when we think of those who are away, we'll look above for joy that Bobby is a Southern soldier boy."

He falls silent then. My eyes meet his in the dying light of the fire. He raises one hand, palm toward me, asking me to wait. A symphony of crickets back up a chorus of piping toads. It would be pretty, except half the men are snoring too.

After what feels like an hour but is probably five minutes, Michael reaches for his backpack. He picks his way over the men toward me. I don't dare move or say a word. From his bag he pulls a knife and flicks it open. Squatting over me, he presses a finger to his lips, and then starts to saw the binding from my hands. Next he releases my feet, and finally he cuts the rope securing me to the tree trunk.

Hand under my elbow, he helps me rise. My knees start to cave, but he steadies me. "Careful, don't make any noise," he whispers.

I latch onto his arm. The muscles in my legs are cramping from not moving all day.

His eyebrows lower and he leans closer. "Can you walk? Do I need to carry you?"

I shake my head. Pulling strength from deep inside, I take a few steps. He points out a path that has the least amount of branches and crunching leaves on the ground.

Michael's mouth is close to my ear. His breath warms my cheek. "We have to go slow for the first bit here, but when I say to, we'll run."

I glance back over my shoulder. "We won't be able to put enough space between us and them before they realize we're gone. Someone's bound to wake up."

"We'll be fine."

"But if they—"

"Gabby, relax. I drugged them."

I stop walking and meet his eyes. "They aren't dead ... are they?"

"No, just sleeping." He winks. "Heavily."

"What kind of crazy herbs did you put in their drinks?"

He chuckles softly. "They were transporting medical supplies. I helped myself to some of their Laudanum."

Laudanum? Somehow, the word unlocks a part of my brain that actually must have listened in class. Civil War. High injury rate. Soldiers with opium addictions.

Of course, the pain meds of the day are potent.

"Thank you."

He places his hand on the small of my back and guides me deeper into the forest. "Don't thank me until we've put some distance between us and them."

But we are free. Even if those men wake and see I'm not there, their minds will be far too clouded to track our movements, let alone catch us. Still, I don't argue with Michael. Having him beside me again is enough to calm the tightness wedged inside my ribcage. Every muscle screams, and my legs tremble, but none of this matters. We're safe. Michael's safe! I trip, and when he rights me, I throw my arms around him, hugging tight.

I expect him to push me away. Tell me we need to press on further. Instead, his hands rest on my back, and we stand there leaning against one another.

His jaw presses against my temple. "I've got you. Everything's going to be okay."

Since I don't have to make eye contact, words I don't want to voice find their way to my lips. "I was so scared."

Keeping his arms around me, he sets me back from him so our eyes lock. "I promised I'd never leave you behind."

A strange surge of warmth floods my body. In his rich, chocolate eyes I see everything I've ever wished for—home, safety—someone who cares. My first thought is to lean in and kiss him, but I shake that away. Besides, he wouldn't welcome something like that, even if I wanted to. I lick my lips and break eye contact.

He squeezes my shoulder and we start to walk again. Feeling more awake now, I take the lead on the narrow path.

"What I can't figure out is how you got into that mess, anyway? I mean, what would they gain by taking you captive? It doesn't make sense." Michael's making far too much noise as he walks behind me. The boy needs to learn to lift his feet.

"Oh, you'll love this." I launch into the story about overhearing the soldiers and saving Pinkerton.

Before I can finish, Michael hooks my arm and wrenches me backwards. He uses so much force it whirls me in his direction. In the silver light of the moon that slices through the forest's ceiling, his brows are drawn low, and his eyes blaze.

"Don't ever do that again!" He shakes me. "Do you hear me? Don't ever put yourself in danger like that without letting someone else know. You're not allowed."

I'm tired and hungry, and emotion wins the battle of my strung-out nerves. Slamming my palms into his chest, I shove Michael hard. "How dare you! Not allowed? Oh, I'm sorry. No one told me that you were the only one allowed to have a hero complex around here."

"Forget you." He steps around me, crashing his shoulder into mine as he stalks off.

Staggering without the use of him as a crutch, I trail him. Today's been too long. My stress level is off the charts. I don't know why I'm suddenly so riled up. But I know we're far enough away from the soldiers to yell, so I do. "You don't just get to walk away from me whenever you're upset!"

Fists clenched and arms pumping, he keeps walking. "I can do whatever I want."

"Why? Oh, right. I forgot. You're Michael the great and wonderful. Everyone adores you. Funny, everyone in Keleusma thinks you're so capable as a Shifter, but when I ask them, no one knows anything about *who you are*. Or is that your angle? Be all mysterious?" He doesn't answer so I continue to bait him. "Michael—the man who works alone and saves the world. Don't pretend you can't hear me." I'm only a foot behind him now. "I *know* there's something special about you. Lark told me."

He stops abruptly, and I crash into his back. But he doesn't turn around. "I'm not special." He pushes the words out through gritted teeth.

I hate the set of his shoulders. And I'm the cause of them. What's wrong with me? Why did I provoke him after he just risked his life for me? I'm such a jerk sometimes.

Biting my lip, I lay my hand on his shoulder. "But you are. Lark told me you're the youngest person to ever shift. That's a big deal."

"Yeah, but she doesn't know why I shifted early." As he turns to face me, I keep my hand on him.

The contact grounds me again. "Right—just that you were pulled when you were eleven."

He rests his forehead in his hand. "None of them know. If they knew, they'd look at me differently. Might force me out."

I run my fingers down his arm and take his free hand in mine. "Why?" I squeeze his hand. "Tell me."

He turns away. "It doesn't matter. We need to keep going."

I force myself to keep up with his fast pace. "It matters to me."

His eyes dart to my face. "That's what I'm afraid of."

Enough. Snagging his arm, I bring him up short. "What happened? Michael, please."

A mocking smile pulls his lips to an odd angle. "I'm not the saint you pegged me for. Nicholas pulled me before I could cause any more damage."

Great. Another ambiguous non-answer. Clearly he'll never trust me.

Releasing my hold, now I'm the one to march off without him. "Fine. I thought we were friends, but I guess I was wrong. Way wrong."

"Don't be like that." He hurdles a bush to catch up.

I face him, my hands balled at my sides. "*Then tell me*."

For a moment I don't think he's going to answer. He looks up at the sky, and works his jaw back and forth. But then he leans toward me, into my space. "I killed my Pairing. Is that what you wanted to hear?"

I take a step back, bumping into a tree trunk. Uneven bark scratches my skin.

Any warmth I felt earlier becomes ice lodged in my veins.

CHAPTER FIFTEEN

Killed her?

Sweat slicks my palms. My first impulse is to scamper away from Michael. Put as much space between us as possible. But all I can do is stare at him. I'm sure my mouth hangs open. His chocolate eyes hold mine, but not like a predator. No, they are soft—pleading—like a doe about to be shot.

I wait for him to tell the story. To explain what drove him to do something so horrible. *Ask him what he means.* He just stands there, a few feet away, watching me. Then again, do I really want to hear all the sordid details? Yes. Of course I do. Not to judge him, but to find an out clause, because it can't be true. This is Michael, after all. Quick to laugh, takes a kick to the stomach and still likes me. Michael.

Then why doesn't he explain? Or slap me on the back and tell me he's joking?

He's most likely waiting for me to say something—anything—but what can I say? If it's true and I tell him I don't believe him, that won't go over well. If he's kidding and I act horrified then I'll lose my friend. He's asked me to trust him so many times. Can I?

Michael hooks a hand on his neck. I flinch at his movement, and it's like I've failed a test. His eyes flicker to the ground, and he shakes his head. "We might as well finish this mission so we can both get out of here."

So we don't have to be together anymore.

Somehow I've disappointed him acutely, and he's ready to be done with me. To pull back into the world where he works alone.

He tugs the bag off his back, drops to his knees, and riffles through the contents. I slump to the ground in a heap at the base of the tree. Waiting to see what he's doing.

"Here." He hands over a small bundle wrapped in white cloth.

I unwrap his offering, and my mouth instantly starts to water. It's a chunk of meat that he must have saved for me from the Confederates' dinner. My eyes mist over. He's thought of my needs before I even remembered I'm hungry. Starving, actually.

"You haven't eaten all day." He dives again into his pack, fishing out the water bottle, crackers, and beef jerky.

One bite in, and I start devouring the meat. I have no clue what it is, and my world is better that way. The chunk is gone in a flash and I'm licking the flavor from my fingers when Michael hands over the water. Without a second's pause, I bring the bottle to my lips and chug. I used to avoid drinking water at home. Pop and juice always sounded so much better, but this water tastes magical. As if it's the best drink of my life. I forget that maybe Michael wants some and finish every drop. He doesn't say anything as he tucks the empty bottle back away, just hands me a couple crackers and a strip of the jerky. After I swallow the crackers, I wish I hadn't drunk all the water just yet. It would have been nice to wash the crumbs down.

Adjusting the straps on his backpack, Michael stands. With his impromptu picnic, I figured we were going to rest here for a little bit before continuing on. Clearly I was wrong about that. The moment I gain my feet, he pivots away from me, setting off through the forest. Okay, we're still not talking. I scrub my hand down my face, then follow after him.

The air around us is humid, and the sweet smell of moss mixes with something heavy and wet on the wind. Perhaps there's water nearby? There is. If I cock my head I can hear a stream.

What is Michael's plan, anyway? Where is he leading us? I don't dare ask him. Now is a time for silence. The pace he sets speaks volumes. He wants to focus on doing something, not thinking. And definitely not talking.

I'll respect his wishes for now. At some point, he will have to give me answers, though. This ceasefire way he ends uncomfortable conversations isn't acceptable. Not when we're trying to accomplish something together. And not when I still want to be his friend.

It all makes me want to pick something up and throw it at him, just to force him to stop for a bit. Let me regroup. But then it hits me. Have I ever been a friend like I'm expecting him to be? Seriously, have I ever really opened up to Porter or Emma?

Lost in my thoughts and masked by darkness, I bash into a fallen tree on the ground before I see it. It happens too fast to catch myself. I tumble over. My hands splay out to break my fall, and something pierces my left hand. Searing pain shoots up my arm. I roll over and land a solid kick to the offending tree. I instinctively bring my sliced palm to my lips, and it tastes metallic. Blood.

Michael's at my side in an instant. He eases my injured hand away from my face. "Does anything else hurt?" His eyes rove down the length of my body.

I extend both my legs, making sure nothing else is wrong. A dull throb on my shins, but otherwise I'm fine. "Just my pride." I offer a weak smile.

He doesn't smile back, doesn't even look at me—just the cut on my hand. Both of his hands cradle mine. He tilts it, trying to find the best light through the canopy to examine my wound. His thumbs trace over the sides of my palm, sending the sensation of a thousand marching ants up my arms.

"You're lucky. It doesn't look too deep." Releasing my hand, he fishes the iodine from his bag. "This will hurt."

With my bottom lip between my teeth, I nod. He tips the bottle. A screech escapes from my lips. I can't help it. The iodine sears into my cut. It's deeper than I think we both first imagined. Michael gently tugs my hand closer when I try to snatch it away from him. He leans over, blowing on the cut. This cools the burn at once. Next he finds my shirt in his bag and tears a line of fabric from the bottom. So much for being able to return his spare. He wraps the makeshift bandage around my hand, tying it off at the end.

I'm about to thank him when a sound makes us both freeze. Boots clomping over the ground mingle with the pound of horses' hooves. All those noises are followed by a voice that raises the hair on the back of my neck—Sterling's. "Did anyone else hear a scream? They're near. Find them." He swears.

I dig my nails into Michael's arm. He touches a finger to his lips, and then slings his bag back over his shoulder. We're still crouched together next to the rotting log. Basically out in the open. Surely the soldier will be able to spot us.

A large bug scurries over my exposed ankle and I fight the desire to shoo it off. Any second now, a gun will be leveled at us or someone will toss a burlap bag over our heads. Taking us to who knows where. If the Confederates were angry with me before, they must be livid now. And not just at me, but at Michael too. They must have realized by now that he freed me.

Less than fifty feet away, twigs snap, and there's a smattering of low conversation.

Michael squeezes my good hand. "Now."

He doesn't wait for me to figure out what he means. He hauls me to my feet, and we take off at a sprint. Without breaking our handhold, he leads me in a zigzag pattern through the woods. We skirt trees, hurdle logs, pound over shrubs. Hopefully, our movement is masked by the Confederates' own footfalls. But they have horses, and there are far more of them than us. They can fan out over a great distance. It's only a matter of time before they catch up.

Somehow, while I'm mentally spazing out, Michael formulates a plan. Or gets lucky. He whirls me around and shoves me toward a large tree. I see right away what he wants. The trunk has a narrow opening. The tree is dead, so inside is probably hollow. Just like when I hid in Keleusma, I suck in and squeeze through the hole. Please don't let there be any animals inside. At least not a mean badger, angry bats, or anything along those lines.

There isn't much room. When I try to stand to make space for Michael to enter, I bash my head along the jagged ceiling. Rotten tree chunks shower down onto my shoulders. I have no clue how, but Michael shimmies in. He leaves the bag outside, probably stashed in a bush if I know him at all. But there's hardly room for him. We both try to move, but have to squat at odd angles. His elbow digs into my side and my knee is pinning his ankle. My leg starts to spasm.

As usual, Michael thinks faster than I do. He crumples to the ground, hooks my waist and pulls me into his lap. With my feet resting on his leg, I have to perch like a bird, but we both fit. He wraps his arms around me. The action steadies both my body and my thundering heart.

I'm safe with Michael. That is a truth I can never doubt again. He will always take care of me first. In fact, I'm certain he's beyond uncomfortable for my sake. With his back against the decaying inside of the tree, and holding all of my weight, he can't be enjoying this moment. Who knows what bugs are racing over his back, yet he doesn't twitch or move.

I loop an arm around his shoulder and rest the side of my head against his. Adrenaline surges through my body, but I try to even my breathing nonetheless. It sounds like he's doing the same until his muscles tighten beneath my hand.

Sure enough, the troops draw near. At first I thought maybe we lost them, but no chance. The sound of a dozen men crashing through the woods is unmistakable. No longer just murmurs, they're close enough for me to make out what they're saying.

"Maybe you only heard a pack of coyotes."

"No, it was them. They're around here somewhere."

Why didn't the Laudanum hit them harder?

Moonlight glistens off a polished boot just outside the hole in the tree. The term *sitting ducks* finally has meaning for me. Michael tightens his arms around me, pulling my side flush against his chest. I lay my free hand—the injured one that he fixed—over his heart. Feel the constant, racing beat beneath my fingertips. It makes me set my jaw. We can't get caught. I won't allow it. I'll claw at those soldiers tooth and nail if I have to. Whatever it takes. As long as I can be assured that his heart will keep pounding like this.

My stomach twists when I look at his face, though. Even in the dim light, the thought churning in his mind is easy to guess. His eyes are narrowed, his forehead wrinkled. He's thinking the same thing I am, only about me.

Save us. Hide us. It's the same two phrases I begged when I was hiding in the dining room at Keleusma. Although this time, I know who I'm voicing my plea to. Nicholas. He has to be real. At least, I want to believe that he's real and that we're not stuck on our own. It helps to have an image in my mind of being watched over. Even if it's not true.

Besides, there's no way shifting came about on its own. It's too intricate. There are too many details. Someone has to be the mastermind behind our missions. And like Michael's said before, there is a sense of being led, even though I don't hear guidance like Michael says he does. When I stepped onto the train and warned Pinkerton, I knew I had to do it, even if it put me in danger.

A voice breaks my thoughts. The soldiers are still right outside. "Why are we wasting our time on these two, Sterling? We don't need them when we still have Pinkerton cornered."

No. I helped Pinkerton get away. They must be bluffing to draw us out.

"I take it you enjoy being bested by a pretty-faced lady and a conniving boy? I say get all three of them—imagine the welcome that'll be waiting for us if we succeed."

"It would be nice for the rest of the encampment to think highly of our group, for once."

It feels like hours before the Confederates move on, and even then, I wonder if they're just outside the tree. Waiting to ambush us the second we crawl out. Every muscle in my legs burns. Itching to be stretched, or rested. But we stay, barely breathing as the night ekes onward. I rest my forehead against the side of Michael's head. Close my eyes.

Once sufficient time passes, Michael finally nudges me. I move to crawl out of the tree trunk, but he catches my arm and eases his way in front of me. Of course he'll go out first. When he flags for me to follow, I squeeze back through the hole. My hip makes a loud cracking noise as I stand.

As Michael finds his backpack, I tread a few feet away, craning my neck to locate the direction of the stream I heard earlier. I'm not paying attention as I wander farther from Michael. I turn past a group of trees and someone smacks into me. Toppling me off my feet, the person lands right on top, and the back of my head smacks the ground. Air is suctioned from my lungs and I wheeze.

I'm at the edge of a small field. Long grasses whisper around us. How did I get so far in the open without realizing it? I'm so stupid. Why did I leave Michael's side? Or have they captured him this quickly too?

But this isn't an irate soldier come for my doom. This person is smaller. It's a woman, and she's crying. No, not just crying. She's sobbing. Should I shush her? The Confederates are bound to hear and circle back.

Grabbing her shoulders, I slide to my knees, bringing her up with me. "Has someone hurt you?" I whisper. "You need to be quiet."

This brings even more flood works, and a long, loud moan. "He's gone." In her hand is a piece of rumpled paper. She presses it to her face as she rocks back and forth. Breath shudders from her lips. "I don't want to live without him."

Even though I don't know who she's talking about, my insides tear in two. I want to hug her and rub her back until her pain ebbs. How many times have I witnessed my father in this state over my mother? I know enough about grief to know the ache never truly leaves.

Michael's firm hand clamps over my shoulder. "Gabby, we've got to get out of here. Now."

I tip my head back to see him. "Something's wrong with her. We have to help."

"No. Stand up." He's not looking at me anymore. His gaze is fastened on the far side of the clearing.

Expecting to see Confederates, my eyes follow his. I stifle a scream. It's not a soldier that makes his way across the field.

It's a Shade.

They feed off despair. No wonder he's drawing closer.

"Ma'am." I grab the woman's hand, enclosing it in both of mine. "I don't know what happened to you, but you have to think about something else right now. Something hopeful."

She shakes her head. "They killed my husband. He's dead. He's not coming home from the war. Not ever." Pressing the letter to her eyes, she whimpers.

Michael doesn't wait for my consent before jerking me away from her. His arm around my middle, he tugs me backward until we're draped in the darkness of the trees again. I try to break away, but he draws my back against his chest, both arms snagging me in an effective vise.

I arch in an attempt to gain freedom. "That woman needs us. That Shade is going to get her if we don't do something."

"Sorry, Gabby. I'm not risking it seeing you."

"I thought you could only see them in photographs. How did you know—"

His chin moves on my head. "We can identify them, it just usually takes a while to pick them out in a group of Norms. I may not be able to see his face melting, but only one creature walks that slow and drags his feet that much."

"Why are we afraid of them?" I push at his arms.

His muscles flex. "We're not, usually. But remember the first time, when they caught you ... do you really want to go through that again?"

No, of course I don't, but I also don't want to stand by while this thing harms a desperate woman. Like watching a train wreck, my vision is glued to the clearing. The Shade shuffles toward her, mummy-like. The woman hunches on the ground where I left her.

When the Shade reaches her, he clutches her chin. He bends her head back and starts sucking at the air above her mouth, like I saw them do at the Wall Street bombing. Except this time it's different. The woman's body starts to tremble, and she claws at her throat like she's choking.

I jostle in Michael's arms. "He's killing her!"

Michael twists me around, and brushes the hair from my forehead. One of his hands is still locked around my upper arm, in case I try to run. "Don't worry. They can't do that. They don't. They have the power to cause hopelessness, depression even, but not death."

I look back over my shoulder just in time to see the last ounce of life fade from her face. Then her body goes limp. The Shade lets go of her chin, and she hits the ground with a hollow thud. When the Shade stands, he stretches to his full height. If it's possible, he looks stronger now, more muscled and sure footed.

Breaking away from Michael, I stumble forward. "She's dead."

Michael steps beside me, his cheeks draining of color. "It's not possible."

That's when the Shade notices us. Eyes snapping in our direction, he squints right at me. The Shade's head tilts to the side. "Rosa?"

My mother's name shatters through me with the force of a hail storm.

CHAPTER SIXTEEN

The Shade steps over the woman's body and advances toward me, not stumbling or walking stiffly like I've seen them move before. No, he strolls forward as easily as I can. I should try to get away, but it's like I'm in a trance. I can't move.

Good thing Michael's there to help me. He spins me around, breaking whatever hold the Shade seems to have on me. "Run!"

That's a simple enough command to follow. As if I'm back in the State Championship race, I take off at a fast clip. This time, there's no marked path. Then again, this time, an evil creature hunts me. Tree branches slash at my skin. My pants snag on a thorn bush. I keep running, but I feel a few bristles burrow into my leg. We pound over the stream I've been listening to all night, startling a large buck who takes off crashing in the other direction. My shoes are waterlogged now, squishing with every impact. So heavy.

What time is it? This night has been the longest of my life, and I don't think we've hit midnight yet. As we skirt trees, I hear

Michael's bag pounding against his back and his breath coming out hard. He starts to lag behind me, even though I'm slowing down too. The night's events wear on me. Why won't the Shades just leave me alone? I'm tired of running away, so sick of hiding. But I don't want to fight either.

I want to go home.

Just shift us already! I warned Pinkerton, what else can there be left to do? Why does Nicholas make everything so difficult? Why can't he just tell us things plain and simple? I have a novel idea. Why doesn't he show his face once in a while? Take on a mission himself instead of sending us to do everything?

When I judge that we've run almost a mile, I stop. With my hands on my knees, I suck in long breaths of chilly air and listen for signs of being followed. Nearby, Michael collapses on the ground. He paws through his bag for the water bottle, but then realizes it's still empty. Poor guy, I forgot that while running is the one thing I'm really good at, it might not be in his top five. And he's had to run a lot so far tonight. Hopefully that's all done with now.

A rabbit skitters from an adjacent bush, but that's the only movement I sense. The Shade hasn't tracked us. I relax the muscles in my shoulders. We can breathe now.

I'm about to sit beside Michael, but remembering the Shade makes me halt. Now that the terror is behind us, rational thought crowds in. He seemed to know the Shade would come after me. There's something he's not telling me.

I glower down at him. "Do you happen to know why that Shade said my mother's name?"

He pulls the bottle out again, rising to his feet. "We need to fill this and treat it, or we'll both be cramping from dehydration by morning."

When he turns to leave, I act faster. Slamming my palms against his chest, I block his path. "Answer me."

"Here's an answer. Stay here while I go get us water, and try to keep out of trouble."

Not likely. Growling, I fist the fabric of his shirt in both my hands and give him a firm shake. The water bottle clatters to the ground. "How did that *thing* know my mother's name?"

He studies the leaves above him. Then he shrugs me off. "Will you let go? I don't know what you're talking about."

My teeth ground together. I back him into a tree. "Don't lie to me, Michael Pace. Don't you dare lie. You heard him say Rosa. I know you did."

"Sure. But throughout all of history, want to take a guess at how many Rosas there are? Out of all of them, how do you know he meant your mom?"

Oh! I want to curse. "Because I'm not dumb. I've seen pictures of her my entire life. I look just like her!"

He reaches out to me, but I evade his touch. His hand falls to his side. "Gabby, keep your voice down. I think you need a minute. Grab a seat and cool down. Take some deep breaths. Let me just go get—"

I square my shoulders. "Are we friends?"

"What?"

"Easy question. Yes or no. Are we friends?" There's a hitch in my voice. I hate it.

He looks up at the sky before taking a long, deep breath. "If tonight doesn't prove how I feel about you, I don't think you're ever going to pick up on it."

I cross my arms over my chest. "Then for once, don't dodge out of a hard conversation. Tell me what's going on. Trust me."

He treks a few feet away from me then walks back, hands shoved in his pockets. "You know how everyone keeps telling you that you're special?"

I nod, once, tightly.

"Well, you are."

"Continue." I stare down at my palms. Fiddle with my shifting bracelet as if it holds the answers.

"There's a reason half of Keleusma stares at you when you walk by. Some of them are afraid of you."

"Yeah. Eugene already told me that," I snap.

"So you know?" His eyebrows dart upwards, and relief washes over his features.

"No. Nothing to do with my mom. He only said what you just said, about some people being afraid of me, but it didn't make sense."

"Oh." Michael sighs. "Your mom was a Shifter, just like you and me. Rumor has it she didn't love doing it like most people do. She wanted to find a way out."

My mouth goes dry. I shuffle my feet. She sounds a lot like me.

"She didn't talk to the other Shifters much. Sure, she would go on missions. Do what was asked of her, but she got pulled home often. Your dad needed her more than most Pairings do."

Makes sense, he still does.

Michael presses his hand over his forehead. "We've told you about the Shades. How they'll try to convince you that the way they live is better. Well, I don't know how else to say it other than, they got to her."

I close my eyes. Not sure if I can process this information. "Is she ... she's a Shade."

He presses his lips together. "You know how we follow Nicholas? The Shades have a leader too. His name is Erik, and if you ever happen to meet him, run."

Erik? Donovan mentioned him when we first met. What did he ask me? He wanted to know if I spoke with Erik. Why does he think I want anything to do with the leader of the Shades?

"What does he have to do with my mom?" I realize I've been rubbing the skin under my bracelet the whole time he's been speaking, back and forth over the white scars on my wrist. I stop.

"No one knows the specifics, but we do know Rosa started meeting with him. Made some sort of a deal. See, when most Shifters decide to become Shades, they drink a cup of this stuff the Shades call the Elixir. That or they can choose to have it injected into their bloodstream. I guess it doesn't taste too good going down at first. At least, that's what we've heard."

"So she ch-chose to be injected?"

"Yes, but there's a catch—Erik gave her the Elixir while she was pregnant ... with you."

I gasp. A sharp pain registers at the back of my throat. I try to swallow it away, but it stays. "Go on."

"Usually when someone drinks the Elixir, their transformation is almost instantaneous. At the most, it takes a few days. But, he gave your mom the injection and she didn't change until a few months *after* you were born."

I splay my hand over my stomach. Rub my fingers down my arm. My whole body feels like there are snakes slithering over me. "Then it's in me too. Some of it has to be or else she would have switched right away."

He nods. "The Elders think that's why it took her a couple months to change. Because she didn't get the full dose of Elixir."

"Is that why I can see their faces melting and you can't?"

"Honestly, I don't know. People were afraid you'd be the first Shade ever born. Like Erik had discovered a loop hole."

No wonder Donovan tossed me into jail. Michael's words explain all the silence and strange looks in Keleusma. Were they all waiting for me to unlock the door and let in a hoard of Shades?

"Welcome home," they said the first time they saw me.

"Wait. Do they *want* me?"

Castling his hands together, he presses his fingers to his chin. "I think so."

My whole body is shaking. I want to clap my hands over the pounding in my ears. Block everything out.

"That's half the reason I didn't want you to come on a mission. I don't want them have a chance to get near you. Hurt you." Michael's eyes soften. "Hey, it's going to be okay—"

He moves to cup the side of my face, but I slap his hand away.

"You knew, this whole time. You knew and you didn't tell me?" I break a branch off a nearby tree and point the jagged edge at him. "It never crossed your mind that I should know?"

Taking a step back, he puts his hands up in surrender. "Gabby..."

"Shut up. I've wondered about my mother my whole life. You had to realize I'd want to know something like this. You can't tell me you're really that dense."

He snatches the branch from my hand and tosses it to the ground, voice rising. "Come on. Seriously, does knowing make anything better?"

His words make me flinch. "No. But it sure helps explain a lot of things about myself."

"Like what? What could your mother's mistakes have to do with you?"

I tap the blemish on my shifting bracelet. Forever tarnished, just like me. "I don't fit anywhere."

He growls. "Don't talk like that. There's nothing wrong with you."

"There is! Don't you get it? This explains why I never feel like I belong. Because I don't. Not at home. Not in Keleusma. And not on these missions." I toss my hands in the air. No wonder I can't hear Nicholas. He probably doesn't want a brain connection with someone who has a high chance of turn-coating on him.

But would I?

"Do you think you fit with them?" Michael voices the question I am too afraid to form in my mind.

"No. Absolutely not." Blood rushes warm through my chest, and I'm able to relax my shoulders.

Michael doesn't say anything for a minute. Just lets me digest everything. Bless him for that, at least.

I don't really know what to say next. I mean, my mom's a traitor. She didn't even love me enough to wait until after I was born. To give our family a chance to change her opinion. She just abandoned us. She didn't want me. Not only that, she tainted my future. Then again, if she changed, it means there's a chance she's alive.

"Is my mom still with them?"

"As far as I know, she's a Shade. But listen—"

I hold up my palm. Whatever more he is going to say, I don't want to hear. "Please. No more."

"Whatever you want." Dropping to his hands and knees, he searches for the empty water bottle. "We should probably find somewhere to sleep. And get some water for morning."

Usually his voice sounds like a favorite melody to me, but right now, every time he opens his mouth, it's like nails on a chalkboard. I can't deal with him, with anyone. I need to get away. Swinging around, I'm planning to stride off all purposeful-like, but my legs feel like they're made of whipped cream. I stagger and almost fall. Why does my head feel so fuzzy?

"Maybe you should sit down." Michael moves to help me, but I brush him away.

"I'm fine. Just moved too fast."

"Okay."

"I'm going to take off for a few minutes."

He reaches for his bag. "How about I come with you?"

"No. I want to be alone." I rub again at the ache in my chest. "Leave me alone."

Michael sighs. There's no way he's okay with me wandering off alone, but perhaps our bickering over the past two days wore him down because he says, "All right, Gabby. I'll stay right here until you're ready. Don't go far, though, okay?" His voice drops, like he's talking to a cowering dog that's been abused its whole life. I don't blame him. Just like that animal, if Michael says the wrong thing, I'm sure I'm bound to bite.

Without another word, I shuffle away. I try to follow a straight line so that I can find my way back to him later. Well, if I decide to go back, that is. Maybe we're both better off alone.

After a few minutes, I'm at the bank of the stream we crashed through earlier. Was that only just tonight? I feel years older than I did this morning.

Sagging to the ground, I crawl to the water and cup some into my hands. It's cool, fresh, but I know better than to trust drinking it. Organisms that can kill me or make me sick are microscopic. Clear water doesn't equal clean water.

Instead, I splash some over my face and wash my arms. Unwind my bandage and plunge my hands into the coolness. Next, I toe off my shoes and dip my feet in the trickling stream. I should have brought the water bottle and filled it. How long has it been since Michael had water? At the Confederates' camp?

Before then? He's always thinking of me first and I fail to do the same. It's probably the Shade part of me. I grimace.

Don't think like that.

Yanking my feet from the water, I towel them off with my socks and tug my shoes back on. I forgot they were waterlogged. So much for drying off my feet. After that, I examine both my legs. Dig out the burs and thorns from all the bushes I ran through. Removing my bandage and exposing my wound is probably a stupid move. But I don't care. I wrap the fabric back around my hand. Without Michael there, I can't tie it off, so I just tuck the ends in. See. I don't need him.

Why didn't he tell me sooner? Did he think I'd go running to the Shades right away? That makes me clench my hands so hard my nails bite at my palms. My fists itch to collide with something, or someone. How could Michael keep that from me?

Well, because he'd do anything to protect me—like shield me from the worst sort of news. Because Michael cares about me. Although I can't imagine why. I mean, being friends with the half-Shade girl hasn't really scored him any points in Keleusma. Since he met me, it's not like I've made his life any easier. No, just heaped worlds of grief on top of him. And still he stays.

Running my fingers over the cuts on my arms, I assess the damage caused by our sprint through the trees. Only skin deep. I'll be fine.

If only I could probe inside. See what damage my mother inflicted with The Elixir. Is there some dark part lurking within me? Am I connected to Erik like the Shifters are connected to Nicholas? Can he talk to me too? That makes me shudder.

I pull my knees to my chest and circle my arms around them. Rock a bit. Allow my mind to go numb. Too bad I can't shut it off.

A squirrel launches himself off a branch above me. I jump at the sound, then watch him sail through the night air, landing on the next tree over.

Something else clatters in the jumble of thoughts inside my brain. What if I see my mother? What should I do? Would I even recognize her? Maybe I should save my fists for her. Everything in me wants to find her and shake her, good and hard. Demand to know what was so wrong with Dad and me. Ask why we weren't enough for her.

I palm at the tears tickling down my cheeks. Wipe my nose on the back side of my bandage. Maybe Michael was right. Ignorance would have been so much better than this turmoil.

As the water dries on my skin, I start to shiver. My teeth chatter. When did it get so cold? I try to massage heat back into my arms, but I'm still trembling. Besides that, I'm drained from being alone. I need an arm around me. I could use a kind word, or a joke to make me forget.

I crave Michael's company.

Besides, that Shade might still be prowling around.

On wobbly legs I lurch back to where Michael's waiting. Sitting on the ground, he leans against a wide tree, eyes closed.

But he opens them when I draw near. "You okay?"

I have to look up at the sky to keep more tears at bay.

He stretches his legs. "I do that all the time. Look at the stars when I feel lost. They're the only things that are the same no matter what time you're in. Maybe it's stupid, but for some reason that gives me hope."

Working my lip between my teeth, I nod.

Michael doesn't get up. He's watching my every move, like I might go to pieces at any moment. Which he's probably right about.

A tremor works its way through my body. I step closer. "I'm so cold. Is it all right if I sit by you for a bit, just until I warm up?"

"Always." Immediately he lifts his arm and shuffles to the side to make room for me.

I grab the seat beside him, and he lays a protective arm around my shoulders. Leaning my head back against him and the tree, I close my eyes. But I'm still shaking.

Without taking his arm away from me, he pulls the small wool blanket from the bag and drapes it over us. "Are you hungry at all?"

My eyes jolt open. "I should have gotten water. I was down by the river."

A soft laugh rumbles in his chest. "Didn't have to tell me that. You're all wet. Did you fall in or something?"

"No." I pull away. "Sorry."

He draws me back to his side. "Don't be stupid. Believe me, I don't care." His fingers find the end of my braid. "Listen, whether you believe me or not right now, I have to say this. You're going to be okay."

"I'm sorry about earlier."

"You have nothing to be sorry about."

I offer no reply. Instead, I curl up tighter against him, stealing all his warmth. My head finds a perfect pillow on his shoulder, and my eyelids droop. With him beside me, I'm okay. I'm not going to worry about the other stuff. Not tonight, anyway.

All I know is that for the first time in my life, it feels like I fit.

CHAPTER SEVENTEEN

Sleep doesn't come. Not that I expect it to. There's too much to think about.

I imagine my mother walking through the woods, laughing at me. The next time I see her, she's asking me to join her. Beckoning me. I shake my head, but then an army of Shades descend from behind her, telling me I have no choice. They reach for me, and I snap my eyes back open to make the nightmare stop.

Besides these hallucinations, there's the Shade I witnessed killing the woman earlier. Is he still in the forest? Could he be trying to locate me? Unless he shifted afterwards, but that's if they work like we do. I have no clue. Maybe I should. I need to be better prepared from here on out.

My eyes refuse to focus on anything. Not on the trees opposite us, not on my shoes. If a monster or the Confederates come for us now, I probably won't notice them until it's too late.

Stop thinking. What good will any of this do me? *Close your eyes.*

But I'm still awake. When I try to shut my mind off, another thought takes hold. Like the fact that Michael's right next to me. My head rests snug on his shoulder. In my dad's house, no guys are allowed in my bedroom. Ever. Not even Porter. When I'm downstairs watching a movie with Emma and Porter and someone starts nodding off, I can count on Dad to shoo Porter out the door in less than ten seconds flat. It's like he has radar for that sort of thing. I always considered Dad's antics a bit overboard.

Now it makes complete sense. Cozying up to Michael feels good too good. I'm cold, and I need to get warm. But we shouldn't make a habit of this, even though I kind of want to. I've missed human contact. How the presence of someone beside me can lift my spirits. Knowing another person is just there. If I'm honest, though, it's more than that. It's Michael. He makes me feel safe, like I belong.

Michael's distracted too. His chin will rest on my head for a few minutes. Then he'll lift it, scan the forest, lean it back against the tree and take a deep breath. Is he watching for Shades too? Or worse—does he not want to be beside me? For all he said, it is possible that he thinks I'll go over to the bad side now. That I'm too dangerous to keep around.

I run my hand back and forth over the tip of the blanket. "Are you afraid of me?"

He turns toward me, face scrunching. "What are you talking about?"

My chin trembles. "There's something *wrong* with me."

Shoving the blanket down, he removes his arm from where

it was wrapped around me. Drawing his legs in, he faces me. “Gabby, you’re ridiculous.”

So much for hashing things out with him. I cross my arms, look away. Blink rapidly.

When he squeezes my arm, I peek back over my shoulder at him.

He shakes his head slowly. “You’re something else, you know that, right? I tell you I killed someone, and you cuddle up next to me. Then you ask me if I’m scared of you?” One side of his mouth tilts upward, but there is no humor in his voice.

Does he think I’m stupid? I know Michael’s not a murderer. I shoot him a quick glare and turn my back on him again.

But he lays his hand on my neck, underneath my braid. “Sorry. It’s just—no one can determine who you are besides you. Do you get that? What your mother did doesn’t mean anything. At least not to me.” He rubs a warm circle on my shoulder. “You choose what type of person you’re going to become, and what path you go down. That’s set by your actions, no one else’s.”

His words open a deadbolt over my heart I didn’t even know was there. I am not my father’s mistakes. I am not my mother’s wrongdoing. I can be Gabby.

Now if only I could figure out who that is.

I spin around, enclosing Michael’s hand between both of mine. “I’m not afraid of you, either.” He tries to pull away, but I hold tight. “I know you, Michael. You didn’t hurt anyone. You couldn’t. It’s not in you.”

"You don't know enough about me to say that." He lets me keep his hand, but he scoots back against the tree. I do the same. There's about half a foot of space between us. We're not touching anymore, except for our hands.

Michael's quiet for a long time. Not quite the reaction I pictured.

Then the muscles in his arm tense, even his fingers as they lace with mine. He sucks in a quick breath. "Her name was Kayla. My Pairing. Scrawny little girl with this hair that couldn't decide if it wanted to be blonde or brown."

I rub my thumb over the top of his hand. Letting him know I'm here.

Lost in a memory, he chuckles. "We were just kids. Our favorite thing was to reenact cartoon movies we liked. I'd play the hero. Save her from the troll under the tree house. Stuff like that."

"Sounds like a good childhood."

He brings his free hand to his jaw and grasps it for a second. "We had a snow day from school. During one of those bad winters in Chicago." He presses his thumb and pointer fingers on the bridge of his nose. "Feet and feet of snow. Next to the roads, where they plowed, it was the highest. I spent all morning digging out a fort for us there."

His chest heaves. "Kayla wasn't adventurous. Not brave like you are. She didn't want to go into the cave I built. Never liked closed-in spaces much. But I convinced her. Told her I'd tell her a secret if she would just come in and see how cool I'd made it inside. Something dumb like that."

Silence blankets us for a minute. I don't jump to fill it. Whatever Michael wants to tell me, I'm going to give him the time he needs.

He stares out at the tree across the way from us. "Once she was in there, she told me she liked it. But I always wonder with the Pairings—do they actually have a mind of their own? Could they decide not to like us if they wanted to? That always bothered me."

My shoulders droop. Is it that way for Porter? Somehow is he stuck or forced to care about me? I've always kind of thought he and Emma would be good together. She's made goggle eyes at him since the third grade. Not that he's noticed. Perhaps it's because he didn't have a choice. "It doesn't seem fair that way."

Michael nods. "We were in there awhile and I finally went into my house to get hot chocolate for the both of us." As if he's shielding himself, he brings up his knees, and rests his head in his free hand. "The snow plow came. They didn't know she was in there."

The world seems to slow down. My gut clenches. I gasp without realizing it as I imagine a small girl being killed by the blade of a plow. Did the snow turn red? Did Michael have to see her like that? My arms burn to hug him. To take any amount of his pain away. But I don't know if he'd welcome my comfort. Does he miss her? Wish it was her here holding his hand instead of me?

His eyes are still closed.

What to say? Nothing. Keep my mouth shut. I just hold his hand. Make it warm. Let him know I'm still here, and will be, no matter what.

I rub my brow, blinking back tears for the boy who saw his friend die. Also for the guy who's carried around the unnecessary weight of an accident for so long. But I don't want to say something empty. Now's not the right time. He doesn't want to hear that it wasn't his fault. People never want to hear that. It steals their guilt, and sometimes that's all they have to cling to. If I take that away, he might drown. Besides, I can tell him that until I'm blue in the face, but it won't mean anything until he believes it for himself. Until he lets go.

He breaks our handhold. "Nicholas took me before I could make it worse. I didn't even get to the sidewalk before I shifted. It's ironic really." He pauses, looks away. "The one time Kayla actually needed a hero, I didn't save her."

I study him, but it's difficult to read his face in the shadows. "Were you in love with her?"

"I was eleven." A bird calls in the distance, long and low. When the song stops, I listen for another to return it. But the only other sounds are the churning creek, a few toads crooning, and bugs carousing during their evening journeys. No other bird. No answer.

I pick at a scratch near my elbow. "So that's why you never went back to your time?"

Standing abruptly, he shoves his fingers into his hair. "My mom could pull me back, if she wanted to. But that'll never happen."

"You can't be sure. She might still."

"No. After I left, she wrote me off. I ruined her life. There was a dead girl in her front yard and a missing son. When the cops arrived she had no way to explain it. They suspected her of wrongdoing. Don't ask me how. I only know because my dad went back without me once before he died. Right before he and I went on our first mission together. Our only mission together."

"It still could happen."

He snorts. "It's been seven years. I'm not exactly holding my breath." Plucking a leaf from a nearby bush, he weaves it through his fingers. "I don't blame her. Because of me, Dad's gone too." He balls up the leaf and tosses it to the ground.

With my chin in my hand, I watch him. Wonder what's going on in his mind. Does the past keep him up at night? Drive him to take on tougher missions? I don't understand how his own mother wouldn't want him. She has to understand that Michael was a kid, and the snow plow was a freak occurrence.

Okay, so maybe I'm not the best one to process this kind of stuff. I mean, my mom doesn't want me, so who am I to rationalize about Michael's mom? What I do know is, if I could, I'd travel to her time and make her sit down and listen to what an amazing son she has. Tell her all she's missing.

Leaves whisper as the breeze stirs around us. I trace my finger over my bracelet. Michael's arms are crossed. With his head tipped all the way back, he's looking through a break in the canopy at the night sky. Didn't he say that's what he does when he feels lost?

"They're the only things that are the same no matter what time you're in."

My heart feels like a giant gaping hole. It's a hollow ache, something that, while not particularly painful, is always there. Does he feel that way too? Do memories snare at his heart, tugging and ripping at him? I rub the heel of my hand on my chest, trying to make it all go away.

How is he able to encourage others and not walk around jaded? Well, now it's my turn to help him think about something else, although I don't have his gift of making people smile.

But his story has caused my own dark days to bubble to the surface. Times I would like to keep locked away in a trunk marked 'do not open.' Too bad I've never been able to hold my tongue.

"Once I tried to kill myself." I slap both my hands over my mouth. Way to lighten up a room. What on earth is wrong with me? That's not the right thing to say after someone spills their darkest hour with you.

Michael freezes. Slowly turns toward me. Even with only sparse moonlight, I see his eyes grow wide. His lips press together.

Okay, if calming Michael is my goal—that was definitely not the right thing to say.

He strides to where my feet rest, towers above me. "Are you messing with me?"

Why did I even say it? I focus all my attention on a cricket as it hops near my side.

Dropping to his knees, Michael takes my face in his hands. He tips my chin so he can read my expression. "Tell me you're kidding."

I push my shifting bracelet down my arm as far as it will go. Trace the white scars that glare underneath it.

He grabs my arm and brings my wrist a couple inches from his face. His eyes narrow. "You cut yourself?"

"Just one time. It's not like I make a habit of it." Snatching my hand back, I tuck it under the other. Press them both to my stomach.

He sits down fully. "Once is enough. Don't ever do that again."

"It's not like I planned it. Life with my dad got rough. I was lonely."

Leaning forward, his voice is hushed. "But you know your worth now ... don't you?"

I shrug. "Don't other people decide that?"

"No. You have worth because you're a Shifter. Because Nicholas cares about you. Because you breathe. Okay?" He snags the blanket from the ground, and tucks it back around me. "Besides, you're not alone anymore. I'm here with you, and when I'm not, remember Nicholas always is."

I fight an eye roll. "He's not all that comforting."

"You'll figure him out eventually." Michael yanks the book bag from beside the tree. "Here. Use this as a pillow. You need some shut-eye."

I take it and lay down.

He pulls the blanket to my chin. "Warm enough?"

No. I want him back next to me. "Yes."

Then he strides about twenty feet away—it feels like miles—where he leans against another large tree and slides to the ground. Hooks his ankles together, crosses his arms, and tips his head back.

Why did he leave me? Okay, we're still in the same clearing. But it's not the same.

A lone bird sings in the darkness again. His song sounds like five different bird calls mixed into one. I can't quite place it. Aren't birds supposed to be silent at night?

What if the bird is some Shade signal and he's leading them to us?

"Are you still awake?" I whisper.

"Yes."

"Do you hear that? The bird? It's eerie." Tucking my knees to my chest, I try to stay fully covered by the small blanket.

Michael tilts his head to the side. "That's a mockingbird."

"Do they ever knock it off?"

"It's a male. He hasn't found a mate yet. They're not unlike us in that way. He's lost or alone, so he'll stay out late. Making noise, no matter how long it takes until someone notices him."

Great. Now I'm sad for a bird's plight too. "I wish he'd find someone."

It takes a minute, but Michael stands up and claps a few times. A small bird takes flight from a shrub. It circles in the air, calling out, until it reaches the treetop where it begins its song all over again.

Michael takes a couple steps my way. From the way he shuffles, I can tell he's tired. "I better go get water so we have it in the morning."

The water bottle is still resting on the ground from when he dropped it. I sit up, grabbing Michael's hand as he walks past me. Stopping him. "Don't. Don't leave me here. I don't want to be alone right now."

He squats down to my level, cocks an eyebrow. "If I'm gone too long, you could sing for me, like the bird." Pointing up, he smiles deep enough to bring out his uneven dimple.

I swallow hard. "Would you answer me?"

"Always." It's just a whisper, but the single word thunders through me. Does he know what he's saying?

I count to a hundred in my head. He's still there. Smiling. "Michael?"

"Yes."

"I can't shut my eyes. What if that Shade comes back? What if he finds us while we're asleep?"

He tucks my bangs back behind my ear. "He won't."

"You can't be sure of that. If they catch me, what will they do?"

"You don't have to worry." His tone is soft, even.

"Please don't leave." I'm selfish. Completely. He needs water, but I can't stand the thought of being alone.

He sighs. "I won't go anywhere. I promise. Lay back down."

When I obey, he adjusts the blanket so it covers me.

I'm on my back, so I can gaze up above me. Keep an eye on the mockingbird.

Before I realize what's happening, Michael presses a kiss to the palm of the hand he holds, and tucks it under the blanket.

The place where his lips touched burns. I won't have to worry about being cold again tonight.

Even still, I sit back up and grab Michael's hand again. "Stay."

He rubs the back of his neck. "I just said I would."

"Not over there again. *Here.* I want you close by." I might regret being so bold tomorrow, but right now, I'm okay with it.

His hand closes around mine. "Are you sure?"

I answer by tugging on his arm, which throws him off balance. He chuckles, if only for a second, and then drops to his knees next to where I lay. Michael doesn't lie down next to me. Instead, he leans, sitting up, against a tree near where I am. His legs are inches from me.

The nearness isn't enough. I need contact.

I lift my head, scoot over, and use Michael's closest thigh as a pillow. I turn so I face him. "The backpack's too lumpy."

Michael doesn't say a word. But he relaxes, uncrosses his arm and rests a hand on top of my head. I reach up and lift his hand off my head.

Michael starts to pull it away, but I hold his hand tighter. Letting him know I didn't mean I don't want him touching me. I just want to hold it again. I lace my fingers with his and tuck our clasped hands in the hollow of my neck in between my chin and collar bone. I stare up at him. He's looking out at the clearing, his brow furrowed but his mouth relaxed. Is he angry? Annoyed? Pleased?

Just before I close my eyes, he looks my way and catches me watching him.

"Sleep, Gabby. No more fears. I'll watch over you."

CHAPTER EIGHTEEN

Birdsong wakes me, more than just the mockingbird. Sunlight pierces through the treetops like a dozen blazing javelins. Sweat already covers my forehead and my upper lip. I scrub a hand over my eyes, my mouth. I start to roll onto my back, but something blocks my way. Michael. I freeze. His hand rests on my hip. It's dead weight. He's still asleep.

I lift his hand and scoot out from under it so I can place it on the ground without waking him. Sitting up, I turn and look at him. His other hand rests on his chest. His head leans to one side, mouth open, breathing heavy. The sight charms a smile to my lips. Do all men look that cute when they're sleeping? I fight the urge to brush the hair from his forehead. He deserves rest. Clean water should be ready for him.

Yawning, I stretch and my spine makes a bunch of popping noises. My whole body is sore. Note to self, sleeping on the ground is not advisable. Those men on survival TV shows are certifiably nuts. Or they're paid an obscene amount of money to live like this.

I run through the last few days in my mind, taking stock. Confederate soldiers on our trail who want to kill us. *Check.* Shades intent on capturing me. *Check.* When we get back to Keleusma, we'll be in trouble for taking part in Eugene's science fair experiment. *Double check.*

Way to start off the day with excellent odds.

I push to my feet. How long did we sleep? Whatever, I'm awake now. I grab the water bottle resting near my feet, then search through Michael's bag and find the iodine. In this heat, we need water if we're going to accomplish anything. I stuff the blanket into the backpack and zip it carefully, not wanting to wake him.

In an effort to make the least amount of noise possible, I step heel to toe and head to the river. At least, I think I do. Last night, I stumbled to it right away. I'm walking in the same straight line I think I followed then, but I guess not. Closing my eyes, I hope to sharpen my senses. Where is the water? If those stupid birds would take a breath, I might be able to hear something. I tilt my head, turn in a slow circle. Then—right there—the distinct gargle of a stream. Odd, how things can seem different by night.

The river skips over a pile of boulders here. I sit on a dry outcrop. Plunging the bottle into the water, I try to remember how many drops of iodine Michael told me a container this big needed. The water has to be treated before we can drink it. He explained all about typhoid and dysentery and how people aren't clean in this time period. Really, it was a lovely conversation. Okay, I'm lying. I wish I hadn't been there. A spinal tap might have been more fun. Now I'm terrified of all water. Which I'm sure was his whole point.

I squint at the bottle of iodine. Directions on the label would be nice. More is always better. Right? I take the eyedropper from the iodine. Fill it up four separate times and dump the liquid into the water. Place the bottle on a nearby rock. Now just wait thirty minutes and I'm set.

It's hard to tell thirty minutes without a watch, though. If there are suggestion boxes at Keleusma, I'm going to fill out a comment card. Wardrobe needs to get on inventing a watch that'll work no matter where you are. Come on, they can make clothing, bags, and shoes that trick the Norms. How difficult can a watch really be?

I wrap my arms around my knees and gaze down at the ever changing stream. Watch a broken twig sail down the rapids. Basically zone out.

Last night, Michael asked me if I knew my worth, but the real question is—does he know his? His father dead before his eyes, carrying the weight of the accident that killed Kayla, then add his mother's abandonment. How does he smile so much? See good in the world? The truth is, Michael's far more special than I will ever be.

Even when it comes to me, he's more patient than anyone should be. His ready laugh alone leaves me feeling more positive about life than usual. I'm starting to grin even thinking about him.

Wait. Do I have feelings for Michael Pace?

I let go of my knees. Snap my eyes back into focus. No. It's not possible. I mean, we haven't known each other long. That's not how I work. I have to really know someone to feel such a strong attachment. Or do I? It's not like I've been in love before.

Maybe I'm just confused. Michael's always there for me. He sacrifices for me and thinks of me first. No one else has ever done that for me. He makes me smile and offers constant encouragement. His presence makes me feel safe without him even saying anything.

Okay, that's all fine and good. But we also fight like two hound dogs over the last scrap of meat. I've never had an urge to shake someone as many times as that thought hits me about Michael. Then again, I've also never felt the need to protect someone like I do Michael.

Oh. I cover my face with my hands.

He's my Obi-Wan. You don't fall for your trainer. Besides, I don't *know* him. There, that's settled. I cross my arms, but I can't help the smile that tickles its way over my lips again, or the light haze floating in my head.

Concentrate on something else already. Like hurting feet. We walked too much yesterday. I bet a wade into the stream will help sooth them. I tug off my shoes and peel off socks that have seen better days. Sigh as I dip my feet into the frigid water. This is why we treat the water. Because gross people like me dangle their nasty appendages in the stream. I close my eyes for a few minutes and tip my head back to catch the sun. The contrast of coolness on my feet and warmth baking my cheeks is perfect.

Finally I determine that thirty minutes must have passed. I take my feet out of the water, shaking off the droplets. I'm in the midst of dabbing off my damp skin when I see the two inch scar near my big toe. I outline the raised skin with my finger. That scar's from a time when Porter and I were both trying to ride one bike together. He peddled, and I held my feet to the side. My foot ended up tangled in the back wheel. Ripped through the skin clear to the bone. I screamed loud enough to make Porter jump off the bike. After letting it, and me, clatter to the ground, he ran home to get my dad. I stayed on the curb howling, my foot still stuck.

I hold my thumb over the scar. *Porter*.

I bite back a moan. It's not fair. Even if Michael doesn't have a Pairing anymore, I do. I can't care about Michael, at least, not in that way. That's how this all works, right? Does Porter feel for me the way Dad loves my mom? I swallow hard.

Besides, after all the insight Michael gave me about my mother last night, I need to follow the rules from here on out. Prove I'm nothing like her, and that the rest of the Shifters can trust me. Rejecting the Pairing won't go well for me. It can't happen.

No boat rocking whatsoever.

After a very deep breath, I lace my shoes and start back to Michael. But again, I can't remember the way. Why do trees have to look the same? Can't one be crooked or weepy? A simple landmark, really, I'm not asking for much. I march up the stream a ways. This looks like the spot I came through last night. But I can't be certain.

A moment later, I hear talking. Michael doesn't talk to himself, so ... who is it?

Curiosity takes control of my movements. I wade through the water and crawl up the opposite bank. There's a narrow dirt road on the other side which looks like it leads to a clearing. I skirt a pile of horse manure. A horde of flies buzz around it. Fresh.

Lowering my center of gravity, I follow the sound of a few men laughing. There's a large copse of berry shrubs right in front of me. Inch by inch, I work my way into them. Their thorny security systems prick me, but I bite my lip and duck further in.

Six feet away, several Confederate soldiers lounge near a spent fire. My hands shudder a little. Adrenaline. One man leans back on his elbows, adjacent to where I hide. His boots are off, and his toes peek through the holes in his worn socks. Hopefully, even if he spots me, I can get a good lead.

Sterling's long hair is unmistakable. Unfortunately, his boots are still on. Rats. Now if I'm spotted, I'm in for trouble.

Afraid the colored water bottle will be easy to spot, I hug it to my chest. They were *this* close to finding us last night. Correction. They are still a stone's throw to discovering where we are. One more careless minute at the river and they might have stumbled upon me.

I have to get back to Michael. Warn him. Get us out of here.

"No need to feed him." Sterling's voice rattles through me. I brace myself with a palm to the ground.

I adjust to get a better view. A soldier stands near a type of carriage I've never seen before. Not that I'm a carriage expert, but it looks like a jail cell on wheels. Okay, what I imagine a jail cell looks like. It's a black box attached to a horse. The back door has a padlock and bars. A man's pale hands hang out of them. Well, that or a woman with baseball mitts for hands.

"If you say so." The soldier near the caged carriage tosses a pan of food to the ground and stomps away. That's when I see him. Pinkerton. They've captured him.

"Soldiers on his side burned my whole village to the ground and slaughtered every pig from my barn so my family wouldn't have food to eat. He can go a day without food."

Creeping backwards, I hold my breath. Berry juice and bristles slash across my upper arms.

One of the soldiers stands up. "Did anyone else hear something?"

"Sounded like a raccoon in the bushes. Go check it out."

The man tugs on his shoes.

I back away as quickly as possible. Once I'm by the stream, I jump the three feet of water. Almost going right back to our camp, but I stop. What if they spotted me? If I'm being followed, I can't lead them directly to Michael. Not that I know the right way, but I know for sure our camp isn't further up the river. Turning in the opposite direction, I stick to the curves and bends the water has carved in the earth. I walk for a good ten minutes and then stop. If someone followed me, I'd know by now.

Any mist from this morning has dissipated in the heat of the risen sun. It's going to be another stifling day. If Michael's awake, he's more than likely thirsty. Beyond that, he'll wonder where I am. Rather than let him go searching for me, I'd better make my way to our camp now.

Leaving the stream's trail, I circle back through the woods. A heartbeat later, I come close to falling into a jagged ravine, wobbling on the edge for a minute, arms and water bottle flailing. Breathe. Wow, glad we didn't run across one of those last night. There wasn't a slope or anything to hint of danger. Keeping an eye out for more, I press on. It is Tennessee, after all.

It takes me a few minutes to reach a narrow space in the ravine. I hop to the other side. Where's that idiot mockingbird when I need him to sing me back? Our camp must be this way. It has to be near. Sure enough, as if I suddenly have some inner compass, I'm there. Michael stands a few feet away, his back to me.

"Michael!" I almost plow into him.

He twists around, smiling like he's five and it's Christmas morning. "You're here." He catches me in a hug. He crushes me to his chest, and his lips are right under my ear. "I thought you freaked out. After that talk last night. I thought you just took off on me."

He's squeezing hard enough to steal the air from my lungs. I squirm from his hold. Thrust the water bottle between us. "Drink up. You have to be dying of thirst."

"Thanks." He tips the canteen in a salute, takes a sip. Nose wrinkling, and eyes scrunching, he looks like he smells a skunk.

Oh, no. I lace my fingers together, feigning innocence. "Too much iodine?"

Hitting himself in the chest, he coughs twice. "You could say that."

"Sorry, guess I'm not perfect." I try to snatch the bottle from him, but he lifts it out of reach.

"I know." He winks. "I heard you snoring last night."

My hands pop to my hips. "I do not snore."

"You do." He takes another swig of the water and wipes his lips with the back of his hand. "But don't worry. It's real soft. Cute."

No one is cute when they snore. I'm about to argue, until I remember my pact not to engage with him. Remember the Pairing.

When he kneels to shove the canteen in his bag, he's right at eye level with my arms. He hand hovers above the bag, not zipping it. First his eyebrows lower. Then he reaches for my closest wrist. "Why do you have—"

I slip both arms behind my back.

Standing, he puts his hands on my shoulders. Keeping eye contact the whole time, he tip-toes his fingers down my arms until he can grasp my hands, which he tugs from their hiding spot. "You're all scratched up."

"I fought some bear for his share of berries." I smirk.

He rolls his eyes.

Right. I did have something to tell him, but once again, his easy banter has thrown me off course. "We need to get out of here. The Confederates are right across the river." I point in the general direction.

The smile on his face melts. His hands tighten around mine for a second. "They're right there? Did they see you?"

"I don't think so."

"Then let's put some distance between them and us." He jerks the bag off the ground, slings it over his shoulder, and holds his hand out to me.

"We can't. They have Pinkerton."

His eyes widen. I probably should have started our whole conversation with that little piece of information. If he hadn't gone and hugged me, I would have remembered to.

"I don't know." He hesitates, which makes no sense at all. This is the guy who ran down Wall Street knowing a bomb would deploy any moment. At Keleusma he begged to come back on this mission.

I toss my hands into the air. "Come on. There isn't anything to think about. We were sent to rescue Pinkerton. So we're going to go over there and rescue him."

Rubbing his temples, his jaw twitches. "There's always a choice. We can pick not to do it. To walk away from this right now. A shift will happen eventually."

"What's the matter with you?"

"All right." Taking off his bag, he tries to hand it to me. "I'll go over there. You wait here. No matter how long I take. Stay hidden until I come back."

I push the backpack away. "No way. We're in this together."

"Gabby, please."

"Maybe I should go without you." It's a bluff, but I spin on my heels anyway.

He snags my elbow before I can take a step. "Not going to happen."

"Fine." I brush his hand off my arm. Blow my bangs out of my eyes. "Then we go together."

His gaze ping-pongs from tree to tree as he brushes his thumb back and forth across his bottom lip. "It's dangerous."

"We're Shifters. Doesn't that basically come with the territory?" Okay, now he's bugging me. If he wastes one more minute considering our options, I'm going to sprint away. He'll never catch me.

"I guess. But I never thought about it—the danger." His gaze locks on me, caressing over my face. From this short distance I see his Adam's apple bob. "Not until now."

I skirt my eyes from his. "Well. You picked an awful time to go soft." I grab his hand and tow him as I weave my way to the stream. This time I get there right away. We jump to the other side. I swivel toward Michael and press my finger to my lips.

Side by side, we sneak up to the bush again. Peek through the thinner places. The Confederates all seem to be dozing. Didn't Sterling say that was their plan? Sleep during the day and travel by night? It's smart actually. No one should travel in this heat.

Michael lays his hand over mine. I look at him and he raises his eyebrows. Moving closer, he leans his head so his mouth is near my ear. "Stay here."

I flip my hand over, clutching his so he can't move. Make my eyes big. Silently ask him what he's doing.

He mouths the word 'horse,' and points to the horse from Hunt House. The animal stands on the edge of the camp. Tethered to a tree maybe six yards from where we crouch.

"You're going to steal from them?" I keep my voice low.

"Technically, they stole from me first. To have any hope of success, we need a horse. We might as well leave if I can't get him back." He rocks on his heels. "If anything happens, hide. I don't want them to see you."

"You're the pro, nothing will happen." I try to smile at him, but I know it wavers.

Before he leaves, he hands over the backpack. A few feet away, he looks back at me, a glint of excitement in his eyes. I shake my head. Adrenaline junky. He lives for this stuff. No telling why he tried to back out when we were at camp.

I'm biting my nails as he slinks over to the horse. He's so low to the ground that I can hardly see him. Michael's reaching to unloop the reins when the guns cock.

Three men materialize from the forest. Each with a rifle aimed at Michael's chest, back, head.

My heart stops beating and works its way into my throat. I can hardly breathe. I debate screaming. The sound might startle the gunmen and give Michael a couple seconds to dart away. But he'll need more than seconds to avoid a bullet.

The man with his gun leveled at Michael's heart takes a half step closer. "Hands up. Nice and slow now."

I hold my breath. Dig my nails into the dirt. *Do something, Michael.*

When Michael raises his hands, the soldier behind him waggles his gun back and forth. “Drop to your knees.”

Michael glances over his shoulder. Then he obeys. I wait for him to bust out some special move. Attack them. He always has a plan.

Instead, their guns follow him. All three pointed at his head.

CHAPTER NINETEEN

My muscles turn to concrete, and my lungs refuse to fill. They wasted time at Keleusma teaching me about horses and bombs. They failed to prepare me for a situation like this.

There's a small knife in Michael's backpack. What? Jump out of hiding and wave the four-inch blade at his captors? A whole lot of good that'll do—probably get us both shot. Besides, unzipping the bag alone would draw the gunmen's notice. Basic self-defense is no match for a rifle.

If only I could find a rock. That's what they do in the movies, right? Throw something in the other direction and send the buffoons chasing after the sound. Maybe two of them would run off and Michael and I could take down the last one without waking up the six men snoozing around the campsite. Okay. There's no chance of that happening. Even if there was, I'm not risking one of those men putting a bullet through Michael or myself.

I inch away from a prickler in the berry bush that's pinching my arm. Why doesn't Michael do something? Not sure what exactly, given his situation. But like I told him before, he's a pro. He should know what to do, even if I don't.

The soldier in front jams the point of his rifle into Michael's throat. "Sterling! I think you'll want to come see what we've got cooking over here."

Half dozing, Sterling curses as he flips over. "This better be good, Bryant. My heads still aching from that drink last night."

"You're in luck, because we found our tea-maker." The rifleman standing behind Michael smirks.

Sterling stomps over and lets loose a hoot. "Well now! You found our dirty rat."

Making a huge show of his actions, Sterling scratches his chin as he walks a circle around Michael. But Michael keeps his eyes trained forward, as if Sterling doesn't exist. In front of Michael again, Sterling squares his shoulders and draws a smaller gun from his belt. It looks like one from an old Western.

Now there are four guns pointed at Michael. My stomach drops to the ground.

He waves the gun. "Customarily, I don't take kindly to people who put medicine in my tea unless I call them doc. First things first, someone needs to tie him up so he can't try any more tricks on us."

The soldier who's been standing to Michael's side trots back to the campsite and pulls a length of rope from a nearby wagon bed. He hops over a few of the sleeping Confederates on his way back, waking them. Now there are ten men to me and Michael. And I thought our odds were bad this morning.

While most of the soldiers are paying attention to the ones rising to their feet at camp, Michael tilts his head ever so slightly in my direction. His eyes rush to find mine for a split second. Then he closes them and shakes his head just once. The message is obvious. He doesn't want me to help. I'm not to put myself in danger at any cost. No matter what happens to him.

Cold creeps down my spine.

Two men wrap the cord around Michael's wrists. When they tighten the knot, he winces. Grabbing hold of the rope, one man yanks Michael to a standing position. The action wrenches his arms into a weird angle. Heat races across my chest, down into my fists. I have to bite the side of my cheek before I yell at them to stop.

Sterling spits out a wad of tobacco, and it lands near Michael's feet. "Who else is with you?"

Michael stares at the base of a nearby tree.

"Talk, boy." The man behind Michael shakes him so hard I'm sure his teeth rattle.

Clearly agitated, Sterling works his jaw back and forth. "Speak up now. Who do you work for?" When Michael offers no answer, Sterling growls and lunges toward him, grabbing Michael's shirt in his fists. "I'll kill you. Hear me? You're no use to me unless you talk."

Even though Sterling has him hauled up on his tip-toes, Michael doesn't flinch. Just looks the man dead in his eyes.

With a long huff, Sterling releases Michael. "Jake, turn out his lights. Maybe some down time will loosen his tongue."

Jake—the soldier standing behind Michael—turns his rifle around and slams the butt of the weapon into the pressure point on Michael's shoulder. Michael drops immediately to his knees. The other men stand back as Jake strides around to face Michael.

"Nighty-night."

As if it's a baseball bat, Jake swings his rifle. It connects with the side of Michael's face with a loud crack. A bloody gash erupts across his temple. I jam my hand into my mouth to keep from crying out. Michael doesn't even have time to groan or yelp. He crumples to the ground. Hopefully, he's unconscious.

Two of the men lift him while another unlocks the caged carriage. A few drops of his blood splatter on the ground while they wait for the door to open. With a heave, they toss him inside and slam the door closed again.

I scoot back as quietly as possible. But my whole body is trembling. How bad is Michael hurt? Will the bleeding stop? What if he doesn't wake up?

This is my fault. In the end, there's no other way to dice this situation. I'm not supposed to be here. If Michael had come alone, then he never would have had to join up with these men and betray them to save me. He'd probably be sipping coffee with Pinkerton right now, laughing about some daring escape as they travel to meet up with President Lincoln. Instead, once again, I'm to blame for a world of pain falling upon Michael.

"What now?" The one named Jake straps his gun back to his belt.

"Plan doesn't change." Sterling kicks at the pile of ashes in the fire ring. "He'll be out for a good while. We'll start moving when the sun goes down and continue to head toward Camp Beauregard. Now we'll have two spies to toss at the Commander's feet."

A soldier only a few yards from me snorts. "Who knows? Maybe he'll talk and we'll knick ourselves a couple more."

"Yup." Sterling adjusts his coat. "I sure would like to get my hands on that gal again."

His voice alone makes me shiver. With great care, I crawl backwards out of my hiding spot and slink down until I'm near the river. I run about fifty paces toward the river's source and then cut back through the forest on the same side as the Confederate troops. The road they've been traveling on must be this way. I have to find the path and follow it.

In my haste, I'm stumbling through the underbrush, making altogether too much noise. I stop, glance around and gain my bearings. The river still trickles behind me, but I don't hear conversation from the Confederate camp, so hopefully I'm far enough away to avoid capture. After a deep breath and a sip of iodine-laden water, I press on. More slowly now, picking my way through the down branches and years of rotting leaves.

Back in my normal life, if I found myself in a situation like this, I'd run. Okay, let's be honest, that's all I've done since finding out I'm a Shifter. Ran away from Michael when we first met, pushed him aside in Keleusma took off on him when I found out about my mom. Something inside begs me to flee now too. But I can't. Abandoning Michael is not an option.

The day is fading to evening when I decide to rest for a minute. Finding a log that's only half rotted, I test a portion to see if it's safe to sit on. It seems sound enough. I dig into the backpack and stuff down a couple crackers, which make me thirsty. The water is truly terrible, and almost gone now. I'll need to refill soon. If by some stroke of luck I do rescue Michael, he's going to need something to drink and I'm going to need clean water to doctor that cut on his head. Hopefully I can get him back to Keleusma before he gets a big scar there too.

Beef jerky doesn't sound too tempting, but I'm still hungry, and any protein would be helpful right now. I rip off a hunk and chew on it, forcing myself to swallow. The guys at school tote this junk around with them everywhere. Beats me.

Rescue Michael? Yeah, I'm not going to be able to handle this on my own. Tipping my head back, I study the sky through a break in the canopy. I don't know if that's the direction I should point when addressing Nicholas. But *up* sounds right. Above is pretty—the sky, rain, the sun. At my level is discouragement, people living beside each other and not really caring about anyone but themselves. And people hurting each other. Below me? Dirt, worms, moles, and dead bodies in coffins. All considered, up is my best option.

I sigh. "Okay. Not quite sure how to do this. But could you help us out? I'm not good at any of this stuff. I don't really think you have the right girl, but I guess that doesn't matter because Michael needs someone and I'm what's here. So, please work something out so that he can be saved. If I have to give up going home so he can be safe, I will—I do. Just protect Michael."

Without realizing it, I closed my eyes. I open them now. The world seems the same, my situation hasn't changed, but the knot in my chest feels a little looser.

More of the day has passed than I realized. Hints of darkness begin to stretch across the sky. I have an hour, maybe two before the Confederate soldiers are on the move. The muffled sound of people talking makes me freeze. Boots crunch on the ground. I duck behind a tree with branches that grow all the way to the ground. The glossy leaves hold a pungent smell, and I wrinkle my nose.

After waiting a few minutes, I don't hear anyone talking, so I crawl out from my hiding spot. On the other side of the tree is a dirt road about ten feet wide. Deep ruts carved by wagon wheels and coated with horse droppings tell me this is a commonly used path. I just need to find out if it's the road the Confederates plan to use to reach Camp Beauregard.

Sticking to the heavy growth on the edge of the road, I stay on my hands and knees. I'm ready to drop to my stomach and shroud myself in the branches again at any moment. Each sound, even birdcalls and hopping squirrels, sends me glancing over my shoulder. I'm well concealed, but those soldiers know this area better than I do. What if Michael cracked and told them about me? I banish that thought right away.

He'd never.

Still, I peek over my shoulder again. My hand moves forward and lands on something that doesn't feel like ground at all. No.

It's slick, leathery, and warm. I pivot my head back to looking forward and gasp. A shoe. Not just one, but two, only six inches from my face. My heart rockets. I lick my lips.

They've found me.

But then, those don't look like the boots the Confederates were wearing. Actually, they look pretty similar to the ones I have on. My eyes travel to the person's knees. The pants look like mine too. My gaze bounces up the person's tiny frame. A set of wide blue eyes look down at me. Blonde hair falls over her shoulder as her lips twitch in an effort not to smile.

Bursting to my feet, I toss my arms around her, hugging tight. "Lark! You have no idea how glad I am to see you."

She laughs. "And you have no idea how bad you smell."

Same old Lark. Shaking my head, I grab her arm and lead her a few feet off the road. "How did you know to come? Did Eugene send you?"

"No. He couldn't have. I wasn't part of the original mission."

"But then how—"

"Looks like Nicholas just thought you needed a little Lark Power." She pushes up her sleeve, making a muscle.

"We sure could." I want to ask her how long she's been here. Did she get pulled because of my plea to Nicholas or is this a coincidence? But now's not the time to hash that out.

"Speaking of 'we.'" Lark makes a show of standing on her toes to glance behind me. "Where have you hidden Michael?"

I clamp down on her arm again. "They have him."

Her eyes grow bigger. "Who has him?"

I spend the next ten minutes filling her in on everything. Tell her about my mistakes and about Pinkerton and getting caught. The only bits I leave out are the parts about my mom and Michael's past.

Hands on her hips, she waits for a pause. "Well, you're in luck. When I shifted here, I spent a couple hours canvassing the area. This is the main road leading from Memphis to Nashville, so the soldiers will be using it to get to the camp you mentioned. About a half mile back, I saw a good tree that you can climb. The troops while have to pass under it tonight and there is a wide limb that grows across the road. We'll have you wait there."

"Then what?"

She shrugs. "We'll have to improvise from there. I'll stall them or something, and you'll have to jump down onto the carriage and free Michael and Pinkerton. That's all I've got."

Pouncing out of a tree in the midst of a band of armed men is crazy. It's also better than any plan I have. We start down the path. After a couple minutes, I'm pretty certain that Lark misjudged her half mile. She stops and uses the heel of her boot to kick out the dirt around a protruding stone. When it's loose, she picks the rock up and tosses it to me. "Here."

"What's this for?"

Her brows arch. "You'll need something to break the padlock with. At least, I'm assuming the carriage is padlocked."

"Awesome. Bust the lock and fend off a group of gunmen. Sounds fun."

"Do you want to save Michael or not?"

I cradle the large rock in my arms. "Sorry. I sass when I'm nervous. I'll be quiet."

"You'll have to be. We're here." Lark points upward. Just like she explained, an ancient-looking tree with a huge trunk juts into two, and one large limb reaches in an arc over the road.

"So, I'm going to climb it." I tilt my head from side to side, cracking my neck.

"Sounds about right."

I approach the tree. Large nodules and knobs along the trunk are perfect for climbing. It won't be difficult to scale, but I'm worried about the whole dangling from the branch and dropping down at the precise moment. What if I miss the carriage and end up with a broken leg?

Lark snaps her fingers. "Hand me the bag."

I slip the straps off and pass the pack to her. It feels good to get rid of the weight. I'll balance better without it. Although I don't like letting go of my last physical link to Michael.

My vision has adjusted to the waning sunlight. When I reach the tree, something catches my attention. Two pairs of eyes watch me from a few feet away. My legs go stiff. The people in the woods freeze too.

Lark's beside me. "Who's there?" she calls out.

No answer.

She stalks into the forest. "Are you runaways?"

Everything registers now. Civil War. People hiding. "They're slaves," I whisper. I can see them now—a man and a woman clasping hands.

Lark looks back at me and huffs. "Of course they are." She turns back to them. "Well, go ahead and take off."

They start to back away, but halt at the sound of hounds baying.

I step closer. "Wait. Is that...?"

Lark nods. "Trackers." She taps the side of the tree. "Well, climb, Gabby. Time's a-wasting."

"No. Not until we help them."

Lark's hands pop to her hips. "Absolutely not. They're on their own. We're here to save Pinkerton and Michael. End of story."

Dropping the rock near the base of the tree, I cross my arms. "That's where you and the Elders are wrong. See, I think we're here to help anyone who needs us."

A pounding rattles the ground. Dogs surge through an opening on the other side of the road, followed closely by three men carrying guns.

Lark shoots me a glare and tosses the bag back to me. "If Michael dies, that's on your head." She calls to the couple behind us. "Step onto the street. I promise to protect you."

As the trackers loom forward, I hide my shaking hands behind my back. Some have missing teeth. All have dirt and grime caking their pants.

Lark waves the slaves even closer to her. They line up behind us, heads lowered, like men waiting on death row. She squares her shoulders, and somehow looks like she's grown three inches taller in the last few seconds. Her chin held high, she struts toward the trackers. "Evening, gentlemen."

Like they're in the presence of a queen, they remove their hats and hold them to their hearts. "Good evening, Miss. What has you out at such a late time?"

Lark sweeps closer to them. "I could ask you men the same question." I imagine they see her in some impressive gown, something fitting for a spoiled plantation debutante.

The two dogs are circling me and the slaves, baring their teeth. I fight the urge to kick the animals away.

"Hunting runaways. After them slaves, I wager." The man wags his gun to indicate the slaves behind me. My breath catches as the barrel of the gun points in my direction. I can only guess what must be racing through the slaves' minds.

"Those slaves?" Lark's voice goes into soprano. "Surely not. On whose order?"

"Old Mister Hanz. They're his property."

She fans her face. "Oh. I see now. This is a misunderstanding. For those are not Mister Hanz's slaves. They can't be." A tinkering laugh follows.

"Why not, Miss?"

"Because, they are my slaves. How can they be both his and mine at the same time?"

"Are you certain they're yours?"

"Of course I'm sure. Someone doesn't mistake their own property, now do they?" She's a foot away from the ring leader, batting her eyes.

He yanks on his collar. "Makes no sense. Why would you be out with them so late? A lady like you don't usually go about alone."

Lark lays her hand on the man's arm. "You are right, sir. I'm on my way to surprise my sweetheart. I've heard he's been moved to Camp Beauregard. With this awful war, I haven't been able to see my Edward in so long." She pulls a handkerchief from her pocket and dabs at her eyes. "Do you men have wives or sweethearts?"

"Yes, Miss. All of us."

"Then you understand the pain of separation. I know I shouldn't be out so late. I should have obeyed my Papa, but I had to see the man I love."

"Pulls at the heart, Miss. But it don't explain the slaves."

"Oh, but it does." She balls the handkerchief in her fist. "I couldn't possibly go alone. So I brought the strongest slave from our farm to accompany me, but I couldn't possibly be alone with him—so I had to bring my housemaid as well—for safety of course. They are very loyal. And so I wouldn't be alone with them, I invited my impoverished cousin." She points at me.

Thanks, Lark.

The man slaps his hat back on his head and whistles to call off his dogs. "I advise you run on home then. The camp's a far way off yet and there are no stopping places fit for ladies in between."

She squeezes his offered hand between both of hers. "Yes. My feet are tired. I believe I'll heed your kind advice."

Just like that, the trackers leave. We stand in the middle of the road in silence. I can't gauge when it's safe to move.

Lark can. "Well, that's that. Now shimmy up that tree."

The male slave steps forward. "We thank you, Miz. You saved our lives."

She nods, a smile tugging at the corner of her lips. "You best carry on."

They back away, disappearing into the darkness.

I grip the tree's lowest branches but look over at Lark. "You were great. I could never have pulled that off."

She yanks the backpack off the ground, looping it over one shoulder. "You better hope we shift before they realize their mistake, because once they catch on, they'll kill us on the spot."

CHAPTER TWENTY

I'm trying to work out how I'm going to scramble up this tree while carrying a rock when Lark's words sink in. I look back at her. "You really think the trackers will come back?"

"Most definitely." She's a few paces away from me now, her face draped in half shadows. Her hair glows like new snow in the few rays of moonlight that reach her.

"Will you be in trouble with Donovan because you helped those slaves?"

She shuffles her feet. "You know, my father's not as bad as you think he is."

"No offense, but you could have fooled me."

Lark takes a step back that covers her in darkness. "The Elders come by their positions because they've experienced great hardship. My dad is no exception."

Sure, but growing up without a mother in the care of an alcoholic father, I'm no exception, either. I cross my arms. "What could have possibly happened to make him so rough around the edges?"

Lark rests a hand on the side of her neck. "My mom loved him so much, and the same goes for him. I can't explain it. They were more devoted than any movie or story."

My shoulders relax. "I think I understand."

"You don't, though. When I got old enough not to need him the most, he shifted and it crushed her after so many happy years together. Then when I shifted—I guess it was too hard on her and she's ... not alive anymore."

Did her mom commit suicide? I can't bring myself to ask her. But the pain in her voice is evident. I rub the scar on my wrist. Michael was right, no matter how bad life gets, I can never take it out on myself again.

I let go of my wrist. "Is it the same for the others?"

She purses her lips. "Have you heard of the Salem witch trials? The Shades convinced the people of the town that the twins were witches. They were tied and burned at the stake. Only shifted seconds before passing out from pain. There was too much damage to their skin. It couldn't be repaired when they got to Keleusma. They have no hope of Pairing and refuse to shift anymore."

The story makes me grimace. "Understandable."

"And I don't know Beatrix's story. My dad said it's the saddest of them all, but he won't tell me, and no one talks about it." She starts to turn, to leave.

"Where are you going?"

"To find a horse. I'll be back soon. Get in position."

I'm left with no choice but to scale this tree. Wedging the rock under my armpit, I climb slowly. When I arrive at the fork,

I shimmy inch by inch out onto the limb until I'm over the road. Lark was right about this branch. It's almost wide enough to hide me, but each time I move, the whole thing wobbles. Bracing my elbows against the scratchy bark, I lay against the surface, the rock between my hands. My only options now are to wait, and think.

Nicholas has to be real. Lark's appearance proved that for me. I may not understand him and how he works, but at least I know he's there. Whatever that means, I hope he has the power to keep Michael alive. Because if something happens to Michael ... what if this morning was the last time I'll ever see him?

My throat tightens with tears. I miss the weight of his backpack on my back. At least I'm wearing his shirt, though it doesn't carry any scent of him. The piece of fabric once belonged to him, however paltry that may be. And on my hand, I still have the jagged cut he mended.

"Miz? Miz, are you up there?"

I almost lose my grip and tumble to the ground. Using a smaller branch as an anchor, I latch on with one hand and bob my head over the edge. I recognize the man as the slave from earlier.

He waves at me. "I'm here to help you."

"That's really nice, but you need to go. The trackers will be back." The branch is biting into my cut palm. I wince.

"No, ma'am. You saved my sister's life, so I'll repay you now."

"But if you get caught—"

"My sister is all I have in the world and she's safe at the next stop on the rail tonight because of you. I'm stronger than those men. So don't you worry about me." I don't doubt that. His muscles are clear through his thin shirt.

"I'm waiting for a group of Confederates. They'll have a jail wagon with them. My friend is inside."

"How about, I wait on down the road a spell and when I spot them I'll do this." He cups his hands around his mouth a releases a long coyote howl. "After I warn you, we're square."

I nod. "Completely."

Just as silently as he arrived, he wanders away. I'm left alone again.

A few minutes later, footfalls and conversations announce people are traveling on the road. I lean to look down, but it can't be the soldiers I'm watching for. This group is approaching from the wrong direction. I'll just wait for them to pass. But they don't. They hear someone in the woods and stop right below me. I cross my fingers. Lark's too smart to go tromping around like that, right? Abel too. That's when I hear the dogs barking. A second later, the two hounds from earlier crash through the underbrush and bay again. Trackers.

They're back.

The ringleader explodes out of the woods, his gun drawn. "Did you see them?" He surges toward the men on the road.

Both men put their hands up in surrender. "See who?—and put that thing down."

The tracker spits. "Some slaves and two ladies hiding them. One blonde and one mousy one."

Wait. That makes me the mousy one. Even though he can't see me, I shoot him my best glare.

Something small crawls up my leg. The bug must have made its way under the fabric of my pants, right onto my skin. I bite my tongue, but I can't help wiggling my foot. Leaves rustle as the branch sways. Some sort of large seedling near my hand breaks free and plummets into the air.

Someone bellows, "Ouch!"

Like a little kid hoping to become invisible, I close my eyes.

But I'm still here because I hear an angry voice say, "Now. What in the world? Who tossed this at me?" Boots move against the road. I think I'm safe, and then I hear the loud bang. A bullet whistles in my direction, slicing into the tree limb. Bark splinters near my hand. My heart beats a triple-time march. Can they see me? Are they trying to shoot me out of the tree?

In the commotion, they've startled a squirrel. It scampers across a limb a few feet from my head.

"You're being bested by a tree rat." The comment is followed by a round of laughter.

This time I hear the gun cock. I hold my breath. Ignore the bug creeping further up my knee. The shot cracks the air like a whip in the night. I watch the squirrel stop in the middle of his run, teeter, and fall out of view. A second later, there is a distinct, small thud. The men talk for a moment more. I can't tell what they're saying because their voices are too low. Whatever it is, they all leave.

Has an hour passed? Or mere minutes? As the moon carves its way across the deep purple sky, my eyelids start to feel heavy. So heavy. Maybe a minute with them closed might help. I'll be more energized.

A loud yawn escapes before I can stop it. Where is Lark, anyway? Why do the other Shifters always have to leave to find horses? She should be here. Help me. She's better at this sort of thing and knows what to expect. At the very least, I should have asked a few more questions. Like, after breaking open the lock, how, exactly, am I supposed to fend off ten soldiers?

A sick feeling rocks through my gut. What if she's been captured? Maybe the Confederates won't even come this way now. I could sit up here for days and not know what to do next.

I'm contemplating scrambling down from my perch when I hear a long, mournful howl that makes the hair on the back of my neck stand on end.

I blink a few times. Willing myself to be alert and focus. "Thank you," I whisper.

Sure enough, horse hooves beat like a war drum against the ground. The wagon carrying Michael and Pinkerton creeks forward on squeaky wheels.

I scan the edge of the forest and can't find Lark. What on earth am I going to accomplish without her? Maybe she'd want me to abandon the plan and start fresh tomorrow. No chance.

I have to try. Michael's in there. I owe him. No. It's more than that. I care about him. Maybe more than I care about anyone else in the world.

The carriage moves closer, and sways back and forth. No one is riding behind it, most likely because nobody wants their view blocked by a jail wagon for hours on end. I study the roof. It's flat. If I hold on to a branch and dangle, I'll only drop a foot or two before I land on top of it.

I can do this.

Purpose surges through me. I wait for the very last moment before clutching the rock in one hand and swinging down on the branch with the other. Bark rips at my skin, but I don't feel the pain. I drop down onto the top of the jail wagon. The troops ride on. They haven't noticed me. Gripping the edge for balance, I worm to the back end. Blessedly, there is a handrail across the top of the door. My guess is it's for extra guards to hang onto while the thing is moving. I grab the bar and lower myself down the back.

My hands are sweaty and my grasp starts to slip. Feet spinning like a cartoon character, I find a three-inch ledge near the bottom of the door to steady myself. Readjusting my hold, I wait for the men's song to crescendo. When they do, I smack the top of the lock with the rock as hard as I can. I have to strike it again before the metal breaks clean off.

The door flings open, sending me tumbling head over feet on the ground. I'm dazed for a second, but with it enough to see Pinkerton hop down and tear past me. Someone whistles. Lark stands twenty feet back, a horse next to her as she motions for me to run to safety.

But Michael hasn't come out of the carriage yet. Jumping to my feet, I take off at a sprint. The swaying movement of the carriage makes the door start to close. I push myself harder and lunge toward the wagon, sticking my hand between the door and where it will close again. Pain shoots up my arm. I can handle it, though. My actions have kept the door from clattering shut and giving us all away. With strength I didn't know I possessed, I yank myself into the carriage and find Michael tied to a bench.

He tries to shove me away with his feet. "Get out of here. They'll catch you too."

I grab his arm and squeeze hard enough to make him flinch. "Knock it off. I'm not leaving you."

Even in the half-dark inside this box, his condition makes my heart constrict. The entire side of his face is one big bruise. A deep gash carves its way around his eye, and dried blood cakes his hair. The knot holding him in place is easy enough to work free. Once it falls to the ground, I pull him to his feet, wrap my arm around his waist, and we jump to the ground. Fall to our knees. For a heartbeat I think we're free. Then I realize the carriage isn't moving anymore, and no one is singing.

"Get up, Michael. Now!"

He must have some energy left, because he's on his feet before I am. Michael grabs my waist, shoving me in front of him as we run. His body is a shield protecting me from any attack the soldiers might launch.

The troops holler something I can't make out, and my lungs burn for air. Hooves pound behind us. We can't outrun horses. Four gunshots break the stillness of nighttime. Then five, six, I lose count. Bullets hiss around us and pelt into the dirt and into nearby trees. Too close.

I spot Lark and veer toward her. But Pinkerton and the horse are gone.

"Hurry!" Lark waves her hand. "There's a portal just over this bend." She points into the forest.

I'm a foot away when I see her stumble. I leap forward, catching her by the elbow. She gasps and coughs. Her eyes trail down her front, and I follow them to the bullet hole in her chest.

Michael's beside me now, his breath coming out hard and fast. He throws his arm over my head, making me stoop as more bullets rip through the fabric of night above us.

I shove his arm away. "She's been hit."

The horses are off the road and charging through the bushes now. In seconds they'll descend upon us. Probably crush us.

Lark totters. Her eyes droop shut.

Michael takes her from me, hoisting her into his arms. At a fast clip, we head in the direction Lark pointed. As we turn a small bend, I see the bright rippling light. The portal's ready for us. I could weep. I glance back over my shoulder and gasp at the coming troops. Why did I stop running?

Michael's more than twenty feet ahead of me, stumbling into the light with Lark limp in his arms. Everything around him starts to glow. He's headed back to Keleusma.

Michael looks back just in time to see a Confederate soldier round his horse in front of me, cutting me off from Michael and Lark. The portal goes dark. They're gone. Safe.

Two more horses close me in. Three guns cock.

I fling my arms over my head, as if that'll save me from a bullet. Heat coils around my wrist, and at first I think they shot me, but then comes a familiar bolt of light, wrapping me in a wave of charged air.

The soldiers unload their guns, but the bullets pass through me. Their choice words sound far away.

My feet aren't touching the ground anymore, and my body feels bigger than the space around me, stilting my breath. Wind rushes past my ears. Darkness comes like a heavy shroud. I hear whispers and screams from a distance—other Shifters passing through time. They're unable to control their own future.

Just like me.

CHAPTER TWENTY-ONE

Maybe I'm getting better at this, because I land on my feet. Then again, maybe not because I feel like I'm going to puke. Hands and knees still trembling, I try to concentrate on my surroundings, but I can't shake the time travel induced haze. My ears register sound, but nothing in particular. It's like listening to the hum of conversation in the middle of a packed cafeteria and not actually hearing anything. As if there's a blindfold over my face, my eyes refuse to focus.

"Out of my way, lady!"

My vision clears just in time to see a huge team of horses hooked to a carriage clip-clopping toward me. The driver yanks on his reins. Luggage attached to the roof of the carriage wobbles like crazy. The people inside probably bang into one another. Both horses thrash their heads to the side, but their progress barely slows. Just in the nick of time, I dive out of the way, toppling onto the road. Crawling quickly in the other direction, I miss being crushed under their pounding hooves by a couple paces. A twister of dust coats me as they thunder away.

Near death experience number four. Or more? I don't know. It's only been a few weeks and I've already lost count. *Breathe.*

On my hands and knees, I take equal turns gasping and coughing up dirt. I spit once to clear the taste from my mouth. It doesn't work. Dirt clings gritty and bitter to my tongue. What I wouldn't give for beef jerky right now. But the bag with provisions is gone, left in Pinkerton's time somewhere in the middle of the woods of Tennessee. Will the Norms find it? Or does it become camouflaged? At least Michael and Lark are safe back in Keleusma. *Please let Lark be alive.*

More hoof beats. I swivel my head only to discover that I'm in the middle of a large road. Night cloaks the area, but I'm in a city of some sort. Despite the late hour, pedestrians clog the street, weaving in and out of people on horseback. Intricate glass and iron lampposts line the road, casting circles of light and painting shadows in between.

I scramble to the edge of the road, pulling myself out of traffic. A small boy with blazing red hair watches me from a few feet away.

He tilts his head. "Are you all right, lady?"

I tap my chest and rise to my feet. "Me?" I brush off the dirt clinging to the back of my legs. "I think so."

His eyebrows furrow. "You don't look too well."

"Thanks, kid."

Large green fields stretch out on either side of the road. There are more trees in the area than I would have thought. I'm used to cities from my time where we tear down every hint of wilderness. Throw up concrete and steel monstrosities and paste every inch of the land with urbanization. Only to add a square block of park with shabby grass, toss some greenery on a building's roof, and plant a couple saplings along the road. All because we want to be tricked into thinking we're still around nature.

The city I'm in now seems to be constructed around large trees. Maybe they lack the ability to yank them down. Or maybe they appreciate the beauty. Who knows?

"You like my outfit?"

I jump. Totally forgot that kid was nearby. I glance his way. Capri type pants meet long socks. Wearing a coat that cuts a few inches above his waist and a funny hat, he looks a bit like a character from a movie.

I shrug. "Sure."

Not the right thing to say. His gaze bounces to the ground. Okay, I'm not getting better at this shifting stuff. What would be time appropriate? Think like Michael or Lark. Become these people. I glance around. Who are these people? I don't know where or when I am. I shouldn't even be wasting time with this kid right now. That is, unless he's a part of my mission.

Why did Nicholas send me here? I bite my lower lip and ball up my hands. Why can't Nicholas just speak to me plain and simple instead of turning everything into a colossal game of pin the tail on the donkey? There's no one here to spin me around and direct me the right way to go. Fine. He can sit somewhere with his feet up while I do all the dirty work. I unfurl my fists, letting the blood flow back into my fingers. I can do this without his help.

I put my hands on my knees, bringing myself to the kid's eye level. "Your outfit is very handsome."

A blush masks his freckles. "Ma said I had to wear my new duds for service today."

Perhaps it's a clue. "What kind of service?"

"For church tonight. Good Friday. Sometimes the President comes to our night service."

"So the President is in town?"

"Of course, Miss." His lips pull, like I've said something very wrong.

I force my smile bigger. "I apologize. I'm new here. Can you tell me why the President is in town?"

"Why, he lives right there." The child points behind us. Bathed by lamplight, a house glows in the distance across the large field. I have to squint to make it out. It's two stories and has a circle driveway. The white house doesn't look that impressive.

Wait. "The White House. We're in Washington, D.C.?"

The kid hides a chuckle behind his hand. "You sure are a strange lady. I don't know what you mean by D and C. This is Washington City and Georgetown's yonder that-a-way."

If that's the White House, then—I look across the street. Dad and I went to D.C. once when I was younger. I remember more from photos than the actual trip. But I recall enough to know that the Washington Monument should pierce the sky just across the street from here. I crane my neck. Sure enough, the start of the monument gleams white against the curtain of night. It's only about a third of the way built.

"So he—the President, is at your church right now? Maybe you should show me where that is." Anyway, a child like this shouldn't be wandering the streets of a big city alone. Where are his parents?

"Naw. He didn't come to service tonight. Caused a stir among the parishioners. Ma and Pa are back talking it over with all the adults. I could bring you there." He motions me to follow, but I don't.

For some reason, a tug in my gut tells me I need to locate the President. "Where did he go instead?"

"To the theatre. Can you believe it? On a Christian day?"

My mind races over any bit of information I might have retained from history class. Anything to do with a president and a theatre, but I come up void. "That does sound odd. Why would the President ... I'm sorry, who is the President again?"

"Are you certain you didn't hit your head on the road? My pa is a physician if you need help."

"I just need you to tell me who the president is." A bell tower somewhere across town rings out half after the hour. But what hour? What time is it?

He backs away from me a few steps. As if he's afraid to catch my crazy. "Mr. Lincoln, ma'am."

Mr. Lincoln. "Can you show me where the theatre is?"

"No, Miss. I don't know the way."

I take off running without thanking the boy. Without knowing the direction to go, I stay on the street where I landed.

What I wouldn't give for a cell phone with Google Earth. Surely Nicholas wouldn't put me far from the target, would he? I don't even know. Nicholas is still ambiguous to me. Is he all good? Worth following? I can't answer either of those questions. All I know is that people I care about—Michael, Lark, Eugene, and Darnell—all trust him. So for now, my best option is to imitate what I've seen them do.

Something else wiggles its way into my brain. People like Donovan also follow Nicholas and do his bidding. I shake that thought from my head. Confusing myself now will only lead to despair. And I don't have time for that, at least not now.

I'm sprinting down the side of the street. A large crowd parts for me. Women gasp as I pass. Amidst complaints, I shove through a group headed in the opposite direction. Like lightening bugs, candlelight winks out of windows as I pass. There are buildings on either side of the road now. Two, three stories at most, they stack side by side. No alleys in between like we have in Chicago. The air reeks of animals and trash and mud. Every intake of air sears my lungs, making a cough tickle my throat. How long have I been running? A stitch pulls at my side and I stop. I cup my waist as I drag in deep breaths.

My eyes burn and I blink them a couple times. Is Lark alive? She has to be. I have to believe that Michael got her back in time. Will the Shifters in the medical center be able to fix Michael's face? I relive the gun hitting him, and my stomach coils into a tight knot. If only he never had to shift again. He'd be out of danger forever. Although, I don't think he'd agree with that plan.

Something inside of him lives for helping people, and putting himself at risk to rescue them. At this point, I just hope I get to see him again someday. *Don't even consider that.*

A shiver races through me, drawing a crop of goose bumps to my arms. I trail my fingertips back and forth over the raised skin, trying to warm myself. Good Friday means the beginning of spring. Where I grew up, this translates into cold evenings.

I don't recognize anything on this corner. Fewer people travel here. A sandwich board plaque is propped near the intersection. Hopefully it lists the cross roads. I shuffle forward to read it. No luck. The sign announces that tonight is the last evening to see actress Laura Keene in a play called *Our American Cousin*. The play will show at the Ford's Theatre on Tenth Street.

I'm halfway across the street when my muscles freeze.

Information rushes into my mind. President Lincoln. Ford's Theatre. The name John Wilkes Booth. Booth killed him. Right after the Civil War ended, President Lincoln was assassinated.

I finish crossing the street. Touch the spot on the back of my neck. It's ridiculous that I remember the assassination only because of the time when Emma, Porter, and I went paintballing and Emma came up behind me and shot me at pointblank range in the back of the neck. She called it getting Abe Lincolned. It hurt bad enough that I gave up paintballing from that day on. With no clue what she was talking about, I laughed, but looked it up on Wikipedia later.

I can picture the internet page. There was a cartoon drawing of Abraham Lincoln, his mouth open, and his arms thrust forward as a man with a dark mustache shoots him from less than a foot behind.

I'm supposed to save him.

Impossible.

My skin feels feverish. Who am I to fend off a madman with a vendetta and a gun? Oh sure, I'll just wrestle the weapon from his hand and do a couple fist pumps with the president. Come on. I pinch the bridge of my nose. Close my eyes. I don't have to do this. It's my choice, right? I can spend the evening touring Washington City. Go dip my feet in the river and let Lincoln get shot. It's happened before and the world carried on fine.

Someone needs help. And I'm going to ignore it? My dad taught me better than that.

What transpires tonight is completely up to me. The knowledge feels like a fifty-pound weight around my neck.

I snap my eyes open, and my vision lands on a castle across the street. From where I stand, it appears to be made of stones. Tall towers flank either end. It belongs somewhere in Europe, not here. The building is beautiful and somehow familiar. Using both my pointer fingers and my thumbs, I make a frame, looking at the tall spires. I have a photo like this at home. It's me in front of that building. I'm ten and wearing frayed, cut-off jeans shorts and an oversized pink T-shirt. The Smithsonian. In my old picture, you can see the street signs. Constitution and Tenth Street.

A bell tower rings out, closer now than before. I count the loud dings. Eight ... nine ... ten. I search the sky for the tower.

Maybe it'll lead me to Lincoln. My palms sweat. Have I already failed my first solo mission? Do I care?

I start running again.

Yes. I do care. I do want to save Lincoln.

I *will* save him.

Not because I have to. Not because Nicholas wants it or even because that's what Michael would do if he was here. I'll complete this mission because I am a Shifter. This is what I was born to do. I am not my mother.

I have to stop focusing on getting home. I mean, what if I never figure out how? My life needs to count for more than just existing. My shoes pound the ground harder, faster. I can do this. My good record will wipe away my mother's in Keleusma. Then they'll want me there.

I never fit in my time. Porter and Emma were kind and Dad needed me, but I always felt like a fish stuck in an aquarium when I wanted the ocean.

Maybe, if I follow the rules and complete my missions, I can belong in Keleusma. With Lark and Michael and the others. As long as I can convince people to see me for me instead of for my mom's mistakes, they'll accept me. I just have to do this. Acceptance will be based on my success. If I can't change their minds, I don't know what I'll do, because then I'll belong nowhere.

That's a future I refuse to face.

I keep running.

CHAPTER TWENTY-TWO

Like a beacon leading the way, the bell tower I heard earlier comes into view. Churchgoers clad in their finest spill out the front of the building. I stare at the bell tower for a moment. What time was Lincoln shot? Why aren't history teachers more interesting? If they were, I might have actually listened in class. The notes Emma and I passed back and forth were hilarious, complete with cartoon scribbles of our teacher, but they're definitely not coming in handy on these missions.

Am I too late? No. If Lincoln was dead already, I'd have shifted. Right? I should have asked Michael about that. I have no money and no place to sleep tonight. Unless I go the homeless route, but that seemed like a better idea when Michael was nearby.

Up the street twenty or more carriages are hitched along the front of a building. Sticking to the drier parts of the road, I squint at all the signs I pass. Right above the line of carriages, a plaque reads *Ford's Theatre*. I dart across the street and push through some coachmen standing together in conversation.

"Watch where you're going!" one man snarls.

I trip on the lip of the raised boardwalk and thrust my hands in front of me. The uneven wood rips into my palms when I land, blasting pain into the cut from earlier. In less than a second, I'm back on my feet. My heart pounds into my ribcage like a battering ram against a castle gate. With a grunt, I shove the heavy front door open and stumble inside. Rich red carpeting covers the floor and marches up a wide set of stairs with a polished wood railing. Spotless white walls are decorated with framed paintings and yellow details.

I catch my breath. Lincoln is upstairs. They'd have him seated somewhere alone, probably in a private booth. I try to recall the picture from Wikipedia—which side of the theatre?

A young man approaches me at a quick clip. He wears a coat the color of the carpeting with large shiny buttons that catch the glare of electric lights hanging above us. I hold up my chin like I saw Lark do. Hopefully he'll see me as a refined woman, late for the play.

He extends his hand, palm up. The smell of cigar and cinnamon clings to him like an overcoat. "Ticket?" His voice has a squeak to it and he's fighting a losing battle with acne.

I make a show of patting my sides, which makes his eyes pop. "Oh, dear. I must have misplaced mine." I move to walk around him and he sidesteps to stop me.

"You can't enter without a ticket."

"I don't have one on me, that doesn't mean I'm not supposed to be in there." I gesture toward the theatre. A twitter of laugher echoes from behind the closed doors. The audience must be enjoying the play. If they knew....

"I have to ask you to leave."

Another usher paces over and stands next to the younger one as if they're some intimidating ticket taker gang. "Please exit the theatre or else we'll have to assist you out."

I cross my arms. Glare at them. "You'll have to make me."

Each man grabs one of my upper arms and hauls me back out onto the street. They weren't kidding. I drag my feet. Make them rumble over the ground.

I latch onto their shoulders, steadying myself. "Listen. The President is in danger. You have to let me see him."

The young usher narrows his eyes at me. "You stay out of here."

They both brush me away.

I stagger. "You have to believe me."

The front door slams hard. I rush forward and grab the handle. Locked. I slam the heel of my hand against the door. "Let me in. You don't know what you're doing. This is a huge mistake."

The coachmen have all stopped talking.

Heat rises to my cheeks and tears threaten to tumble from my eyes. Lincoln is going to die. I'm so stupid.

I kick the door, then spin around. All the coachmen are watching me. They part without a noise as I stalk into the street.

The building is sandwiched between others. There isn't a side alley with an escape ladder that I can climb. And the bricks wall looks too high even to attempt to scale. Yeah right, like I would have even tried.

I doubt the ushers will unlock the door anytime soon. So I'm left with the back of the building as my only option. I just have to hope that none of the coachmen grow curious and follow me.

With careful steps, I fade into the shadowed area that lamplight doesn't reach. I back away slowly, then pick up my speed when I'm a good distance away from the theatre. Because of the way these blocks are built, I have to make it to the very end of the block first. When I do, I swing around the corner and slink against the side of the end building. The smell of alcohol and the twang of rowdy music pour from a tavern just across the street. It makes me think about my dad. Is he okay? What has he eaten for dinner all these nights? I halt my thoughts. None of that will help me right now.

Finally I locate the back alley. I spread my hand along the brick wall and hope I'll be able to recognize the theatre from behind. Lamplight doesn't reach into the alley, and the buildings are angled so close together that not much moonlight slips down here either. The alley is only six or seven feet wide. The stench blisters my nostrils, worse than a full garbage truck on a one-hundred-degree day. Breathing through my mouth doesn't help at all. In fact, that just makes it feel like I'm tasting trash. I pull up my shirt, and breathing through the fabric helps. Not much, though. It looks like people heap all the waste from their businesses right back here, but who cleans all this up?

A strange feeling washes down my spine, raising goose bumps on the back of my neck. As if someone or something is watching me. Shades? I imagine one tip-toeing less than a foot behind me but am too afraid to check. *Stop, Gabby!* Keep walking.

I slip on a pile of garbage and have to fling my body against the wall to stay upright. Something large scurries across my foot. I can feel the pressure of its claws through my boot. I have to slap my hand over my mouth to hold in my scream.

With a rattling breath, I shuffle forward. Must keep my eyes open. My vision adjusts to the lack of light, at least enough to tell that a horse is tethered less than ten feet from where I am. Nearby there is a door with *Ford's Theatre* painted across the frame. Bingo. I pat the horse as I walk past it and hold in a laugh. Michael and Lark would probably instruct me to steal him, but it's not like I can bring the animal into the theatre with me. Maybe it'll still be tied here when I'm done. There's something to be said for having a quick getaway planned.

There's no handle, so I press both hands to the door and give a push, and it opens. I inch inside and slowly close the door, hoping not to draw attention. Somewhere in here is a guy with a gun, and the only weapons at my disposal are a hard elbow and a quick wit. Let's face it, my odds aren't great.

As far as I can tell, I'm in a room filled with props. Dust and mildew invade my senses. The voices of the actors on stage boom across this small back area.

I squeeze behind a giant ship on wheels, making sure not to get snagged on any of the handholds. At a muffled footstep to my right, I angle backward. My heart lurches into the back of my throat as a hand comes down on my shoulder. I want to scream, but I hold it in. Spin around. Just a mannequin. A creepy one dressed as a bullfighter complete with a swirly, painted mustache, but he's fake. A prop. Welcome to the club, buddy.

I weave deeper into the maze of props. Will there be any way up to Lincoln other than the main stairs at the front of the theatre? I can't risk seeing those ushers again.

Voices drift closer to me. A group of off-stage actors press together, their whispers too low to make out any actual words. I drop behind a fat wooden elephant, crouching until they all pass. Are they all in on the assassination? It takes a few more minutes, but I reach the edge of the curtain without anyone noticing me.

I spot Lincoln right away. Still alive. He's directly across the theatre from where I stand. Not that I've ever met him, but I've seen his likeness in enough President's Day mattress sale commercials to recognize the real man. He's seated in a booth on the second level at stage left. Bright red wallpaper behind him, yellow drapes framing where he and three other people sit. I imagine the one holding his hand is the First Lady. I have no clue who the other two are, but the man of the couple wears an army uniform. Four American flags hang near them. They might as well have painted a bull's eye right on Lincoln's forehead. Or neck.

The rest of the audience area is unremarkable. The same red carpeting covers the floor here as in the lobby, and the same white walls close us in. On the main floor and in the two balconies, most of the seats are filled. The people are dressed in their best, rich-colored fabrics splashing across the sea of the crowd.

Since I have no idea what John Wilkes Booth looks like, warning Lincoln is my only viable strategy. That means venturing out where the ushers might capture me again. Sweat has gathered in the creases of my palms, and I rub my hands on the thighs of my pants. Shake my shoulders. I can do this.

Working my way along the side of the backstage area, I find a door that leads to the main theatre hallway. I poke my head out first. The coast looks clear, but just as I step into the hall, an usher storms at me. Act fast. Using his momentum, I grab his arm and spin him toward the open door leading to the backstage area. He's flung off balance and topples over. I sweep his feet out of the way and shut the door as quietly as I can. Blessedly, there is a lock on my side of the door. I know I'm breaking every fire code known to man, but this is a national emergency. The usher will either have to rush out onto stage, or use the back door and run to the front of the building, which might still be locked as well. Either way, I need to move.

Right as I'm trying to make up my mind, I see a spindly man with a coat that falls to his knees. He has dark hair and a thick mustache. Just as he disappears into a side stairwell that I hadn't noticed before, I catch the glint of light flashing off a gun in his hand.

I spring into action, grabbing the door handle before it has time to click closed. Booth is at the top of the steps, almost out of sight.

I launch up the first set of stairs, using the banister for leverage. "Stop! Mr. Booth! Stop!"

He tosses one crazed look over the railing and vanishes.

I can catch him. I can stop all this.

Taking the stairs two at a time, I make it to the second level and fling open the door. From this direction, Lincoln's seating area must be to my right. A couple of the doors leading to the balcony are open. People glance back at me as I dart down the hallway, arms pumping. At the end of the hall is a final door. This has to lead to where Lincoln and his party are. Booth must already be in there. Jerking the door open, I waver between jumping on the assassin and kicking the gun so it unloads into the ceiling. I grit my teeth, prepared to do whatever it takes.

Behind the door is not what I expect. This is a small room, and there's still another door to get through until I'm in the booth. Just as my hand touches the doorknob, the audience breaks into a round of laughter, hooting louder than I've heard them all evening. I yank open the door, and the ring of a gun discharging echoes through my chest.

I'm too late.

CHAPTER TWENTY-THREE

Curtains hang in my way. I shove the billowing fabric to the side and rush forward. Blue smoke clouds the area, and it takes me a second to adjust. I cough twice as gunpowder stings my nose and throat. The play continues as if something horrible didn't just occur. Maybe they don't know yet. Lincoln's head is slumped, almost as if the play bores him and he's fallen to sleep. But I know better. Dead. My knees wobble.

As I clear the last sheet of fabric I see Booth. Teeth bared, he wrestles with the man in uniform who sat near Lincoln. Booth wrenches a large machete-type knife from under his coat and slashes at the man. He cuts two deep gashes across the man's chest and another slice across the soldier's head. A woman shrieks. My ears throb from the pitch.

Blood gushes from the soldier's wounds, covering his coat before he staggers back against the wall. Lincoln's wife rocks back and forth, her whole body taken over with tremors. The actors on stage stop talking and audience members swivel their heads in our direction.

Booth leaps a chair and runs to the edge of the balcony. Diving forward, I snag his foot before he can clear the ledge. His boot is polished and slips right from my hand. Not that I would have been able to hold the weight of a man dangling upside down, but I had to do something. At least I've done enough to pitch him off balance. When he lands on the stage there is a loud crack and he groans in pain. He limps badly. I hope his leg is broken.

I point at Booth. "Get that man! The President has been shot!"

Women in the audience screech and flap their hands. A few men rise to their feet. Others clutch their hearts. Collective gasps echo in the high-ceilinged chamber.

Booth hobbles across the stage, his bloody knife brandished high. "*Sic semper tyrannis!* The South is avenged."

I turn to the First Lady. She shakes Lincoln's limp arm and starts to sob. The other lady seated nearby is visibly shaking. Great. Neither will be of any help to me. What I wouldn't give for a little Lark Power right now.

I tug a shawl from the headrest of one of the chairs and press the thin fabric to the back of Lincoln's head. "Don't die. Don't die." I can still make this work. Think. Why did he die? Was it the bullet? Or because they took it out? Did he bleed to death?

Lincoln's head tips back, the wound cradled in my hand. His eyelids flutter and, for an instant, his eyes open and lock with mine. Brown, deep, soulful.

"I'm so sorry," I whisper.

Lincoln's eyes roll, sliding closed again. Unshed tears sting the back of my throat.

Someone brushes past me. "I'm a doctor."

The young man eases Lincoln out of my hold and lowers the President to the floor. He starts to strip Lincoln's coat from him, feeling his shoulder.

I look down at my trembling hands. They're covered in the President's blood. I try to wipe them on the shawl, but it's full of blood as well.

The doctor's on his knees, pressing all over Lincoln's torso. He looks back up at me. "I thought you said he was sh—" His words still as he stares at my hands.

One drip of blood falls from my finger, cascading to the ground. "His head."

There's a rumble of footsteps behind me as more people pile into the private booth.

The doctor stares at the blood dripping from my finger, then explodes to his feet. He reaches for me. "Who are you? What have you done to the President?" I jerk away from his outstretched hands. "Someone get her. She needs to be questioned."

Both of the ushers from earlier close in.

"She told us the President was in danger. Acting very peculiar just minutes ago. She's in cahoots with the shooter." The pimply usher lowers his eyebrows as he descends upon me.

I raise my hands to block them. "No. You're wrong. I was

trying to help." More people, seven now, are advancing toward me. My back hits the edge of the booth.

Save me!

Too much has been happening all at once. I didn't feel my bracelet searing my wrist. I didn't see the metal beginning to glow. Just as the ushers grasp at me, light floods around me, blocking them from my sight. Every hair on my body stands on end as I'm thrust into time again. As quickly as it came, the light evaporates, leaving wind and darkness and a tight, closed-in space. My lungs scream for a breath.

I land on my hands and knees in in a patch of long grass. Not just any grass—I scan the burning bush plants that line the lot, the rotting porch—this is my backyard. I claw across the ground, haul myself to my feet and creak over the uneven two-by-fours that make up our porch. The back door's unlocked. I grab the handle, leaving a smear of Lincoln's blood across the door's white paint.

If they had captured me, what would they have done? Burn me alive like the Elder twins?

I'm shaking so bad that I bash my hip into the kitchen counter when I shut the door. I wince, hobbling to the sink. "Dad? Daddy!"

He's not home. I know he'd come running if he were. With quaking hands, I turn on the hot water and let it scald my skin. I scrape my fingernails over my palms again and again until it hurts. But I still feel blood. Under my fingernails, seeped into my pores. I'll never rid myself of the President's blood.

I mean to go up to my bedroom, but as I stumble into our front room I know my legs won't carry me up the stairs. The howling starts before I realize that I'm crying. Correction. I'm all out bawling. Tears paint my face, dribble down the side of my neck. Crumbling to my knees, I yank on my hair.

I failed. I'm done for. No better than my mother.

I hug my arms around my stomach, around the hollow ache inside that will never be filled. Always throbbing, reminding me of all the wrong I've done. I want it gone. I don't want to be able to feel anything.

I ball up my hands. I never asked for this—the life of a Shifter. I don't want it.

One of my father's wrenches rests on the coffee table. I scramble across the room, pick up the heavy metal and stretch out my arm on the floor. With all the force I can muster, I slam the wrench into my bracelet. Pain lances through my bones, up my arm and down into my fingertips. I don't care. I bash the bracelet again, and again, and again. It has to break. I want out. After ten hits, the thing doesn't dent. The wrench clatters to the ground and I paw at my bracelet, trying to yank it over my hand.

"It won't work."

I still. *Michael.*

When I look up, the same calm washes over me that always does when I'm in his presence. I don't know how he got in here without me hearing him, but Michael can break and enter into my house anytime.

He's a few feet away, his head tilted to the side as he watches me. "I've tried to take mine off too. It's not possible." The corners of his lips lift in a sad smile.

"Michael," I whisper, and then I leap from the ground straight into his arms. I grab his face in my hands. Run my finger over the new scar near his temple. "I'm sorry for this."

"Shh. It's nothing." He catches my hand and kisses my palm.

I press my head against his heart. Close my eyes as I listen to the steady thump inside. My fingers twist into the back of his shirt, pulling him tighter. His scent, fresh and minty, rolls over me and I breathe deeply.

His arms come around me, pressing me protectively to his chest.

I start to cry all over again, my tears soaking his shirt.

Michael strokes my hair. "You're okay, Gabby. I've got you." His lips are near my ear. His breath rushes hot against my neck.

"You don't get it." I press back, but I'm only able to lean six inches from his face because he doesn't let go. "Lincoln's dead. It's my fault."

Michael shakes his head. "He was dead before and the world survived. It will again. The important thing is that you're safe."

"I was so scared. Alone."

"I know."

"Why does Nicholas set us up to fail?"

Michael works his hands up and down my arms, squeezing slightly, as if he's warming up a shock victim. "He doesn't. He gives us an opportunity to succeed, and even if we fail, he always gives us another chance. Nicholas isn't upset with you. Don't lose hope in him, okay? He hasn't given up on you after one failed mission. Neither have I."

"How are you even here? Did Eugene send you?"

"It doesn't work that way. You know that."

"But then how?" I latch onto one of his hands.

"I shifted." Using one finger, Michael brushes a chunk of hair back behind my ear. Where his fingertip trails, my skin burns with heat I can't explain.

"Maybe," he whispers. "Maybe you needed me the most in the world."

My eyes meet his gentle gaze. "I do."

He pulls me back into a hug.

"Stay with me." My head's near his shoulder. When I first met Michael, I considered him lean. Now I see him as strong. A rock.

"You know I can't." His words rumble in his chest, against my hands.

I study his face. Memorize the scars, the exact shade of chocolate in his eyes, the way his skin crinkles on his forehead, the quirk of his lips.

He swallows a couple times, like he's uncomfortable or holding back words. I can't tell. Maybe he doesn't want to hold me like this? He's doing it just because I threw myself at him and he feels like this is part of his mission. Wait. Am I a mission? Someone who needs an infusion of hope and encouragement?

Maybe that means Nicholas cares about me on some level, because he wouldn't have sent Michael to me if he didn't. But that could also mean Michael doesn't like me as much he seems to right now.

It's like a slap. I've known since that night lost in the woods of Tennessee that I have feelings for him. But maybe he doesn't enjoy holding me for even a few minutes. I shrug out from under his arms and pace away. "Is Lark...? Did she...?"

Michael hooks his hand around the back of his neck and sighs. "Lark's fine. Herself. Already prancing around Keleusma telling everyone how we couldn't have saved Pinkerton without her."

"We couldn't have. I'm glad she's fine."

"Eugene and Darnell say hi."

I chew the inside of my cheek. "Do you know why I'm here? In my time, I mean, instead of on another mission. Is it because...."

"No. It's not a punishment. Sometimes Shifters go home for a while to reenergize. It has nothing to do with success or failure. Think of it like a vacation."

"You've never had to do it, have you?"

"I don't count." Michael turns his back to me. He walks the length of the room, straightening knickknacks lined along the top of our piano. Dust dances in a trail behind him, illuminated by the splash of sunlight drifting through the open curtain of our large front window.

Michael picks up a framed picture and stares at it for a moment. I know which one is in his hands. Porter and I, arms around each other's shoulders, heads tossed back, laughing. We're in our track uniforms, both having just won our events that put us on course to go to the state finals. Before the meet started, we had made an ice cream bet about the results, and Dad snapped a picture of us teasing each other about coming out even. We ate through a whole pint together that night.

"Is this him? Your Pairing?" Michael turns and jiggles the picture.

I reach to snatch it out of his hands. "Yeah, that's—"

Michael shakes his head. "I don't want to know his name." He sets the photo back in its spot. "He looks nice. That's good, at least." Hands shoved deep in his pockets, he heads for the door. "I should go."

I cut him off. "Is there a portal? Take me with you. I want to go back."

Michael smiles finally, full out. His fingers graze my cheek again, and his touch lingers. "Believe me. I'd like to bring you with me, but I'm not supposed to. Don't worry. You'll be back eventually. Don't rush it though, okay? Promise me you'll have fun and enjoy whatever time you have with your dad and your friends. There'll be plenty of days left for saving the world after that."

"So this is goodbye. Just like that."

"We don't say goodbye. More like, see you ... in time." He gives my arm one last squeeze, and then strolls out my front door.

I glare at the closed door, feeling locked away from more than just my neighborhood. How could he do that—leave me with so many unanswered questions?

I only wait a breath before chasing him out the door. But Michael's already gone.

ACKNOWLEDGEMENTS

Don't ever let someone tell you that books are the sole work of one person. It's just not true. This book would not be in your hands today without the help of many people.

Thanks and endless cupcakes to Charity Tinnin and Amanda G. Stevens who pleaded with me to write faster so they could get the next chapter in their hands when I was in the writing stage. You both made this story so much better. Lisa Marie Winchell and Sadie Wunderlich, I'll probably always mention both of you in every book because each of you believed in me long before I ever believed in myself. Many thanks to Paloma King who was my first beta reader, your kind words gave me the courage to put this book out into the world.

Mary Virginia Munoz and Susan Kaye Quinn, thank you both for being so transparent in your writing journeys. I've watched you both fearlessly blaze new paths and encourage others to follow. You're both my heroes. Kristen Ethridge and Michelle Massaro—you both deserve copious amounts of coffee for putting up with all my wavering and listening to my more-than-occasional freak outs.

I'm going to mention Mary Weber, Kim Vandel, Melanie Dickerson, and Charity Tinnin (yes, again. She's pretty great that way) because all of them are dedicated to Young Adult Fiction Awesomeness and I'm excited to be a part of this genre with such amazing women. Look them up. Seriously.

The love of my friends in the BCGE and my NovelSisters pushes me on everyday—I love and cherish all of you. Thank you to my parents who have cheered on my writing efforts from the beginning and who offer to help with the baby while I'm working. And, as always, thank you to my amazing husband and sweet daughter who give me the time and love needed to pursue this crazy dream of writing.

ABOUT THE AUTHOR

Jess Evander is the pen name for author Jessica Keller's young adult fiction. A Starbucks drinker, avid reader, semi-professional fangirl and chocolate aficionado, Jessica spends way too much time on Tumblr and Twitter. She is multi-published and writes both Young Adult Fiction and Romance. When she's not writing, she can be found dancing in her car at stoplights.

She lives in the Chicagoland suburbs with her family.

Jessica loves connecting with readers. You can find her at:

Websites: www.JessicaKellerBooks.com & www.JessEvander.com
Twitter: @AuthorKeller & @EvanderJess
Facebook: www.facebook.com/JessicaKellerAuthor

If you enjoyed this book please consider doing the following:

1) Write a review for *Saving Yesterday* on Amazon and/or GoodReads.

2) Share a link to the book on all of your social media outlets (feel free to tag me!).

3)Tell your friends (this is the most important one).

4) Visit my website (www.JessEvander.com)

5) Subscribe to my newsletter. Subscribers find out release dates and news before anyone else including information about the upcoming books in this series.

6) Ask your librarian to order a copy for your library so others can read it.

7) Take a look at the book recommendations on the next few pages.

Thank you for anything and everything you do to help authors.
Without you, there would be no more books.

If you enjoyed Saving Yesterday you might also enjoy the following books:

Soar into adventure with the Dragon Eye Series

Ilsa has been afraid of dragons ever since she saw them in the sky the night she was chased from her village as a child. She's always longed for the truth, but once she learns it, can she accept it?

Is she...a dragon?

Purchase *Dragon* on Amazon:
www.amazon.com/dp/1503235017

Journey to far off lands full of magic, romance, knights and pirates in the Eyes of E'veria series

Centuries ago, an oracle foretold of the young woman who would defeat E'veria's most ancient enemy, the Cobelds. But after two centuries of relative peace, both the prophecy and the Cobelds have been relegated to lore—and only a few remain watchful for the promised Ryn.

Purchase *The Ryn* on Amazon:
www.amazon.com/dp/1493551051

Visit a future full of suspense where one wrong action can mean your life in the State v. Sefore series

Noah's mission?

Stop the resistance at any cost.

The problem?

His loyalty's never rested with the Elite.

Purchase *Haunted* on Amazon:

www.amazon.com/dp/1496028120

CPSIA information can be obtained
at www.ICGtesting.com
Printed in the USA
LVOW08s0723071216
515996LV00017B/187/P